The Qte

The Queen's Last Salute

Moupia Basu

❀ juggernaut

JUGGERNAUT BOOKS
KS House, 118 Shahpur Jat, New Delhi 110049, India

First published by Juggernaut Books 2019

10 9 8 7 6 5 4 3 2 1

This is a work of fiction. Any resemblance to persons, living or dead,
or to actual incidents is purely coincidental.

ISBN 9789353450243

Typeset in Adobe Caslon Pro by R. Ajith Kumar, Noida

Printed at Manipal Technologies Limited, Manipal

For my mentor Dr Daisaku Ikeda

For my parents, who instilled in me the love for stories; and my husband Rajib and son Pronoy, who always patiently listened to all the stories I told them

For Nandini Sengupta, who believed that this story was good enough to be told to the world

Prologue

The year is 1842. In a small principality somewhere in central India, politically christened the Bundelkhand Agency by the British East India Company, an event is unfolding at this very moment that has its entire population in the grip of frenzied excitement. Nothing like this has ever been seen before, nor heard. Tucked away in the deepest recesses of Britain's much prized jewel in the crown that is Hindustan, lies this expanse of barren and stony plain, punctuated by patches of forests which are mostly dry given the long spells of the blistering heat that scorches the ground, and leaves the rocky outcrops that arise every now and then, sizzling. Amidst this igneous sandstone landscape springs up the principality of Jhansee, flanked by the Indo-Gangetic plain to its north and the Vindhyachal mountain range to its south.

Not too many people live here. Their livelihood depends on trade, mostly weapons and warfare implements. Under the patronage of a rather hedonistic and self-indulgent ruler, the inhabitants of this sluggish kingdom are in a perpetual

state of torpor. Blame it on the weather that renders even
the sprightliest of beings lethargic and inactive. Or the
fact that this sleepy province, eclipsed by its more glorious
and mightier neighbours, Awadh and Gwalior, is yet to
be nudged by any event of purport, political or otherwise.
Rarely does the state warrant a visit even from the officials
of the East India Company, who are already troubled by the
several warring principalities of the northern and central
provinces of India. These kingdoms are often engaged in
ascension disputes or with each other. To resolve such
conflicts, the East India Company, commonly addressed
as the Company Sarkar or Company Bahadur, has to
often intervene by placing its own candidates on the
thrones. Caught in such a conflict, and not meriting any
entitlement to a dynastic lineage, Jhansee has suddenly
moved into the ecliptic orbit of the Company Sarkar who
is observing it keenly. Why? This particular event is by no
means insignificant and has raised the hackles of the East
India Company.

'So, what's brewing here in Jhansee, Colonel Sleeman?'
Lord Auckland asked. The Governor General of India drew
on his pipe as he scanned through the reams of paper that
lay strewn on the desk before him. The faint swish of the
punkahs above was the only sound that filled the sahib's
ears, and the occasional call of the cuckoo pierced the still,
hot afternoon air.

'I hear it was a close shave for you right after you arrived
here. That Afghan sepoy nearly killed you,' frowned the
Governor General. 'What a war it has been! I'm told the
Duke of Wellington is none too happy with our invasion

of Afghanistan. Were you injured in that attack, Sleeman?'

'Oh no, sir! I've seen much worse when I was in charge of the suppression of thugee and dacoity,' said Sleeman.

'You did some remarkable work there. You caught their chief, didn't you? What was his name . . .?' Auckland snapped his fingers.

'Ferringheea,' Sleeman replied.

'Ah yes!' Auckland nodded. He turned over a page of the record book kept on the table. 'So, this contains all details of the entire thugee operations?' he asked, looking up at Sleeman.

'Sir!'

Auckland went back to the register. 'It's a pity you let go of the Residency of Lucknow offered to you last year in acknowledgement of your having squashed the thugee menace! Thugee Sleeman, indeed!' Auckland laughed loudly. 'Although I'm mighty glad to have you in charge of matters here in Bundelkhand. This place needs a lot of organizing!'

Sleeman nodded. He was feeling quite despondent of late. Lord Auckland was on his way out. It had been a productive association and the Governor General's support had been crucial in crushing the ruthless thugs who had rampaged through territories of central India for several decades.

'I would have liked to have met all the kings in this region, especially the Raja of Jhansee, Gangadhar Rao,' continued the Governor General, 'but Lord Ellenborough takes over next month and I have to get back to Fort William. Moreover, this place is bloody hot, I say!'

Sleeman smiled at Lord Auckland's obvious discomfort. It was the month of March and the soil of Bundelkhand was already simmering. He sighed thinking of his current appointment. He had been called back to Bundelkhand to sort out a few administrative issues. It was an arduous task that lay ahead of him. He had a fairly large territory under his supervision and, given the endless royal intrigues that crackled in almost every court of Bundelkhand, he was sure this would not be a particularly pleasant task. Shrugging off such unsavoury thoughts, he turned his attention back to his superior who had taken out a rather large and soiled handkerchief and was wiping the sweat off his brow.

'Sir, thank you for your visit to Jhansee. It has boosted the morale of our men, especially the English troops. As for Raja Gangadhar Rao, he is now firmly ensconced on his throne!'

'But I hear he rules neither wisely nor well and spends most of his time in the pursuit of dance and drama. Fraser told me that the man even dresses up as a woman to perform in these plays he puts up.' Lord Auckland snorted. 'Does a ruler of a kingdom ever warrant such behaviour? What do you think, Sleeman?'

'He's quite a patron of art and music. But he has brought about a fair amount of law and order in the state. His people are happy.'

'I would keep a strict watch over Jhansee,' Auckland cautioned his junior. He paused to drink water and drained the glass of its contents entirely. 'I can't hold him to his trespasses, though. The man is widowed, I believe, and has no children?'

'That's right, sir! But there's been a development. The Raja is getting married again. In fact, the wedding takes place this week. He hopes his new bride will give him an heir. She's still very young, you see.'

Lord Auckland looked up sharply. 'Eh? Gangadhar Rao is remarrying?' A crease appeared on his forehead. 'Who is he marrying?'

'A fourteen-year-old girl from Benares. She grew up in the court of the exiled peshwa, Baji Rao.'

The crease on Auckland's forehead deepened. 'A Maratha again?' He didn't like the Marathas. Three wars had already been fought with them. They were a source of incessant trouble.

'I don't like this development. Not one bit. Another heir means more trouble,' Auckland said, his lips set into a thin line. But after a brief pause, he smiled. 'She's only fourteen, you say? Then that's not much cause to worry about.'

'But sir, she will grow up, won't she?' Sleeman pointed out.

Auckland frowned briefly. Then he smiled. 'But the king is old!' he said smugly. Then the frown reappeared. 'Though you never know with these kings. I admire the vitality of the Easterners!'

Sleeman was trying hard to maintain his composure. The Governor General's mood was rapidly changing. He must step out to tell the punkah-wallahs to move the punkah faster. He clicked his heels and saluted. 'I'll take your leave, sir!' As he turned to go, Auckland interjected.

'Sleeman, when is this wedding?'

'Sir, the day after tomorrow.'

Book I

Jhansee

(1842–1855)

1

'Where are we going?' Meera asked her mother who was trying hard to wrap the slippery chanderi sari around her daughter's nimble waist. It was proving to be a herculean task as her slight frame and undeveloped body were unable to hold the six yards of clothing in place.

'Stand still, Meera,' Saanvali said sternly as she slid the shorter edge of the sari from between her legs and brought it up from behind to tuck into the satin leggings that the little girl wore underneath. Saanvali then folded the longer edge neatly into pleats, gathered them at Meera's waist and stuffed them into her leggings, yet again.

'Bau, I can't breathe,' said Meera angrily as she tugged at one of the pleats. The sari came off and lay in a heap around her ankles. Meera looked up at her mother guiltily.

'Do I really have to wear this? Can't I go in my angarkha?'

'No, you can't,' Saanvali replied humourlessly.

'Why not? I'm neither the bride nor the queen. Who's going to look at me?'

'Today is a special day. The new queen will be introduced to the ladies of the harem. Do you want to meet her in your usual rags, looking like a boy?' Saanvali asked through gritted teeth as she attempted to wrap the sari around her ten-year-old daughter in vain. The heavy silver embroidery on the sari made it quite difficult to negotiate the folds of the cloth. But it was Saanvali's treasured sari that she had carefully kept away all these years. She had no use for it any more. Her beauty had faded with the passing of years, and over time, summons for her to appear before the king were becoming increasingly rare. She would be called to sing in front of the king once in a while as there was still no one in the whole of Jhansee with a voice as melodious as hers. But she was unable to do any riyaaz lately due to her failing health. As a result, her voice would often crack. The last time she sang before the Maharaja was almost a year ago. But she never wore her blue chanderi sari.

'Why don't you ever wear it?' Meera asked her mother.

Saanvali was silent, intent on the task at hand, her mouth stuffed with betel leaves, eyebrows knitted into a frown.

'Why have you kept this beautiful sari hidden from the rest of us?' Pannabai asked. The women were gathered in Saanvali's room for their usual afternoon session when the zenana women would drop in to talk animatedly about the latest developments in the palace. Right now, the only topic being dissected was the marriage of the ageing king to a girl young enough to be his daughter and with no pretensions to any royal bloodline.

Saanvali picked up the spittoon lying next to her and spat out some of the red juice into it. 'This sari was gifted to me by the king when he first saw me perform. I wore it a few times when I performed in a mehfil, but have now kept it away. Meera will wear it on her wedding day.'

'Do you really think there will ever be one, Saanvali?' her friend asked.

'Yes, there will be a wedding day for Meera. I will ensure it,' Saanvali instantly retorted. 'I will not let her grow up in these quarters. I will not let my daughter share the same fate as mine. She will have a husband, children and a home of her own,' Saanvali said emphatically.

Outside, the nagadas boomed and the tutari blared.

'Jhansee Naresh ki jai! Maharani Lakshmibai ki jai!' The walls of the palace reverberated with the cries of people who had thronged the fort, breaking through the palace security to catch a glimpse of the new queen. Never before had the town of Jhansee witnessed such excitement, nor had its populace been so eager to be a part of any royal event. But this was no ordinary event. The ageing king had brought home a wife, years after his first wife had died. And from the reports that were being circulated in the kingdom, the new queen was anything but what a queen was expected to be.

No one had seen or heard of a woman as strange as this new bride. But what really interested Meera was that the queen was very young, in fact, only a few years older than her.

'Has the queen arrived?' Saanvali asked nervously. They should have been present in the Diwan-e-Aam by now.

She looked at the other women. 'Aren't you all coming to meet the queen?'

Most of the women shook their heads. 'We've not been asked to be present,' Pannabai replied. She looked at Saanvali.

'We don't matter, Saanvali. But the king has not forgotten you, the koel of Jhansee,' Pannabai said, with a hint of envy in her voice.

Saanvali knew what Panna said was true. The lives of most women in the zenana were wasted. They waited, hopeful that one day the king would send for them. They dressed up, they laughed, they cried, and even fought with one another. They were secure within the confines of the zenana, involved in their petty squabbles and jealousies, sharing with each other their joy and grief. But to the world outside, they were nameless, faceless entities with their identities long wiped out of existence. They were just a part of what was simply known as the zenana. That was the only life known to them.

'Why did the Maharaja marry this girl? She's neither beautiful nor does she belong to a royal family,' one of the women asked. No one knew the answer to that. 'She is quite arrogant, I heard. During the wedding ceremony she told the priest to tie the knot tightly. Has any bride ever done that?'

Meera giggled. The woman turned to look at her, irritated by the interruption. 'What is so funny, Meera?' she asked.

'All weddings are so boring. The queen must have thought this was a good way to break the monotony.' Meera offered her two cents in defence of the queen.

'Your daughter will give you cause for trouble one day.' Panna clucked her tongue. 'You better rein her in,' she warned Saanvali.

Meera came and sat right in the centre of the group. 'Tell me more about the new queen,' she insisted.

'Why are you sitting here? Go away and mind your own business,' Saanvali reprimanded her daughter.

'I am minding my business. She is my queen too, isn't she? I want to know how our lives will change with the arrival of this queen,' Meera asked, wide-eyed.

The women laughed. 'How can a new queen change the lives and destinies of the people of this kingdom? It is the Maharaja who rules our lives. All that the queen will do is adorn herself with precious jewels and give birth to heirs of this kingdom. Like all other queens in the past have,' Kasturi said, bringing down the nutcracker hard on the betel nut, snapping it into two neat halves. She then placed the halves neatly on a betel leaf smeared with lime powder, added some zarda to it, and folded it into a triangle. 'In all my years here, I've seen so many queens come and go. What difference has it made to our cursed lives, haan?' said Kasturi stuffing her mouth with the freshly made paan.

'A new sari gets added to our wardrobe! And of course the kings let us lie in peace for some time,' Mumtaz said with a chuckle.

The women joked and passed around the paandaan. 'But I believe that this queen, or rather this girl, can ride horses and wield a sword as well! She has played only with boys throughout her childhood and thus dresses up like them,' Pannabai remarked as she dipped the cotton bud into a bowl of alta. 'She grew up in Peshwa Baji Rao's court and has been trained in the art of swordsmanship by Tatya Tope himself!'

'Have you ever heard of a *Brahmin*'s daughter doing such things?' Kasturi asked, her eyebrows shooting up.

Meera's ears pricked up. A woman, and a queen at that, who rode horses and flourished swords? She had never seen any woman sit on a horse, leave alone ride one. She was intrigued. She had seen only men tend to horses and brandish their swords. She had stroked the muzzles of horses a few times when no was looking and had run her hand down their manes. She liked being around them, but she knew she could never ride. Girls were not allowed to indulge in such activities. She would often loiter in the stables, and if ever found in one, she would be chased away by the courtiers and ushered back into the zenana where she would resume her dance lessons.

'There, it's done!' Saanvali gave a final tug to the pleats and stepped back to look at the young girl who stood before her, transformed. 'You look beautiful, Meera! Now let's go and meet the new queen!'

As though in agreement, the cannons boomed and a glittering spray of fireworks lit up the evening sky.

Saanvali walked out of the zenana with Meera in tow, who much to her discomfiture, was greatly hindered by the yards of silk wrapped around her. Negotiating the innumerable layers and putting on a scowl on her pretty face, Meera took each step cautiously, certain that she would step on one of the pleats of the sari, and it would come undone, much to the horror of all present. And indeed, it was quite a crowd that thronged not only the royal premises, but the streets of Jhansee, too, which were lined with hordes of people eager to catch a glimpse of their Maharani.

Meera stood squashed between her mother and another woman. 'Bau, I can't see anything,' she moaned, craning her neck. Her mother held her arm in a tight grip.

The new queen arrived astride an elephant, amidst a shower of coins, roses and lilies, glittering in gold and diamonds. She was seated in a bejewelled howdah atop the elephant, gently swaying to its motion. She looked like a jewel, radiant and dazzling. And before Meera could see her face properly, the Maharani had passed by and was headed towards the durbar hall. The crowd went berserk and broke through the security trying to gain access into the palace but was deterred by the guards with great difficulty.

Saanvali pulled Meera towards the durbar hall. The Maharani had got off the elephant and was now, flanked on both sides by courtiers, entering the hall. She walked up the few steps to the throne and took her seat beside the already seated king.

'Let the ceremonies begin!' the king exclaimed with a flourish of his hands. The new queen smiled and straightened up. A flicker of impatience flitted across her face, but she was quick to cover it up with a smile. It was going to be a long evening.

All the important women of the palace – relatives, wives of noblemen – came up to the queen, one by one, to bless her and offer her their gifts, who in turn, touched each platter and sent it away. She had a smile on her lips, but her eyes flickered nervously every now and then. She heaved a sigh of relief when the last person finally left, and the durbar hall suddenly reverberated with the beats of the dholaks. Within minutes, a troupe of Gari dancers swept in, their colourful ghagras swirling, and their ornaments jingling. The queen sat back and relaxed.

The evening sky had given way to a starry night. Strains of music and the rhythmic beats of dhols filled the air. The crowds slowly thinned out, and the last of the remaining citizens returned home after a day of uncontained excitement. The lamps had been lit and the illuminated palace atop the Bangra Hill cast a luminous glow for miles around.

After the dancers left, Saanvali walked up to the dais, bowed her head and folded her hands. The Maharaja turned to his new bride. 'This is Saanvali, the best singer in Jhansee. No one can sing the Miyan ki Malhar like her,' he said. 'So, Saanvali, what will you sing for us today?'

Saanvali kept her head bowed. 'It is my daughter who will dance for the new Maharani today,' she said. Then turning to Meera who was standing behind her, she signalled for her to come forward. Meera walked up to the dais and instead of bowing her head, looked straight into the eyes of the queen.

'Is it true that you ride horses?' she asked curiously.

The courtroom lapsed into silence. People looked at this impudent girl, aghast. Saanvali almost fainted. There was no knowing what the punishment would be for such impudence. Never before had anyone had the cheek to look straight into the queen's eyes and demand an answer. And that too, a courtesan's daughter!

'Hush, hush, you wretched girl, what have you done?' Saanvali spat through clenched teeth. Surprised, Meera looked at her mother and then turned back to the queen, waiting for an answer.

'What is your name?' the queen asked. Saanvali knew what that meant. Meera was now a marked girl, an offender who would be remembered for years. Saanvali fell down on her knees.

'Please forgive her, she's a mere girl. She is foolish and knows not what to say. Pardon her, Maharani! She will be your slave for years.'

'Why would she be my slave? I just asked her name,' the queen replied, puzzled at the woman's behaviour.

'Her name is Meera.'

The girl who stood before her reminded the queen of a peacock, her long sinewy neck rising above a slender body, draped in voluminous layers of turquoise silk, iridescent in the shower of light that fell upon her from the glass chandelier that hung directly over her head. Her tawny skin, like her sari, was luminous in the glow of the lamps. It lent softness to the otherwise stern face with a hooked nose, high cheekbones and a defiant chin. It was a face that defied servility and would have passed off as an arrogant one had it not been for Meera's large dark eyes that sparkled with innocence.

'She is Chandraki, my companion!' announced Queen Lakshmibai.

2

Chandraki, a natural dancer, was a mirror image of her mother. She was being trained in the art of music, dance and coquettishness with the sole objective to please and humour the king. But Chandraki didn't just want to be another jewel in the king's dazzling crown. She loved to dance, but only for her own pleasure and was often found missing when summons for her to entertain the king arrived. Her mother would go in search of her all over the zenana. It happened again that evening. Chandraki was supposed to accompany the lead dancer in the evening's musicale and was to play the role of Lalita, Radha's companion. But she had, as usual, gone missing.

'Chandraki!' Saanvali called. She was furious. She searched the whole room but she was nowhere to be found.

'Let me catch you, you wench, and then I'll tell you what happens when you disobey your mother,' Saanvali hissed through gritted teeth. She pulled back the curtains to see if the girl was hiding behind them. No, she wasn't. Nor was she under the bed. Huffing and puffing, Saanvali rose from the ground. 'This wretched girl will bring ruin upon all of us in the zenana.' Saanvali sighed as she slumped on the bed, exhausted with the hunt.

Of late, she found herself panting often. She tired easily and turned down invitations for festivities and celebrations in the palace. The only summons she couldn't reject were those of the king and the queen.

Though life had not been kind or fair to Saanvali, she was not too unhappy in the royal palace, and she had, like most women, accepted her lot. The life of a courtesan had been forced upon her, though she was born a Brahmin. She had quickly learnt that caste was of no use when it came to the matter of survival. And being part of the king's harem was survival for her, nothing beyond that. The king had been kind and ensured that her daughter and she were well looked after. Yet, she winced at the indignity of her life. The silks and jewels didn't matter to her, the honour of being proclaimed as the best singer of Jhansee was a mere embellishment. Of what use were the gilded ceilings or the polished floors covered with exquisite Persian carpets when it lacked the warmth of a home, the sense of belonging to a family?

But in her heart she knew what life could have been like had she not found refuge in this palace. Saanvali had been pushed into the raging pyre that slowly licked the lifeless body of her husband of one year whilst carrying Chandraki in her womb. Her uncle had pulled her away even as the flames leapt at her. Her parents threw her out of the house since she was not a sati, and her husband's family blamed her for his death. She started living in the village temple, but the priest, subject to immense pressure from the people of the village, asked her to leave the temple. So she took refuge in a mosque. Her uncle smuggled her out of the village and brought her to this kingdom. She thanked the lord every day for allowing her a roof over her head and meals each day. She needed all of that, not for herself, but for her daughter.

Saanvali didn't know when the tears had started trickling down. She wept for what she had lost. She wept for the defilement of her body. Wiping away the tears with the edge of her sari, she slowly rose. Her lips were set in a thin line, and her eyes glowed with a strange fire.

'I will not allow my daughter to share my misfortune. Her destiny will be different,' she said to herself defiantly.

Outside, the sun playfully smudged the sky with myriad colours as it began to set, like an artist at play with her palette.

A girl came charging into Saanvali's room.

'Kaki! Where is Chandraki?' she asked as she looked around the room.

'I can't find her,' said Saanvali, who by now at her wits' end, had finally given up her hunt.

Chandraki, who was not found till after the show had ended, had been hiding in the stables. Saanvali gave her daughter a piece of her mind that night.

'I will not dance in front of the king,' the girl offered by way of explanation. 'You know I love to dance, Bau, but only when no one is looking.'

Saanvali gave up. 'What will happen to this girl when I'm no longer alive?' she thought gloomily. And in that instant, she made a decision. She rose from her bed and lumbered towards the small statue of Goddess Durga placed on a narrow shelf in one corner of her room. Folding her hands in front of the warrior goddess seated on a lion, Saanvali picked up the small metal box kept next to the idol and gently took out the amulet that lay in it.

'This taweez will always protect you. It's God's word,' the imam had said while tying it on Saanvali's arm. For Saanvali, the amulet was more precious to her than all her other possessions. It represented life. She wouldn't trade it for anything nor give it to anyone for anything in the world.

'What is this for?' Chandraki asked as Saanvali tied the amulet around her arm.

'This will always protect you from harm.' Saanvali smiled. 'Remember, separating the taweez from yourself would be separating yourself from me and from God!'

The next day Motibai paid Saanvali a visit. She was the chief courtesan and was in charge of the shows to be put up for the king. 'Chandraki was missing again last evening. This is happening far too often now, Saanvali! You better clip her wings before it's too late,' she warned Saanvali sternly. 'She's now fifteen, and it's time you prepared her for the royal bed as well.'

Saanvali was quiet. Motibai looked at her hard. Then taking Saanvali's hand in hers, she said softly, 'There's no point in running away from destiny. No one knows it better than you do. Do you really think you have a choice? So, straighten out your daughter. The sooner you do it, the better!'

3

Lakshmibai stood before the mirror, adjusting the Chaumet Collier d'Esclavage necklace that her husband had especially ordered from London for his new bride. She had never seen anything like it before, and it pleased her to know that the necklace was the current rage among the aristocrats of England. Her husband had spent a tidy sum on it, and to have it further shipped to Bombay and then brought to Jhansee amidst heavy security had cost him half a year's revenue. She was, after all, his second bride, and although she was still a child, he earnestly hoped that she would, in time, provide him with an heir.

Two women arranged the pleats of her sari while another pinned a diamond-encrusted brooch on it. Her hair was yet to be tied and the dark tresses fell loosely around her shoulders, reaching her waist.

'Are we done?' Rani Lakshmibai asked the ladies surrounding her, rather impatiently.

'No, Your Majesty, not yet. We have to put on your jewellery!'

More jewellery! Lakshmibai grimaced. She resigned herself to being treated as some sort of a mannequin and gave herself up to the half a dozen women surrounding her. She had, of late, taken up the duties of a queen quite seriously and often sat beside her husband when he held court and even offered her suggestions during the proceedings. The king took her advice earnestly and found himself increasingly turning to her for guidance. It was now five years since she had arrived in Jhansee. She was beginning to enjoy her role as the queen of Jhansee and had an easy camaraderie with the people. The only thing she didn't like was having to dress up and being laden with heavy clothing and jewellery round the clock. Oh, what wouldn't she give to dress in her angarkha! But Maharani Lakshmibai knew that she had an image to maintain for the dignity of the throne occupied by her husband. So she allowed herself, albeit reluctantly, to be adorned the way a queen was expected to appear in court.

'Maharani ki jai!' a dasi announced. 'Saanvali seeks an audience with you, Your Majesty!'

Lakshmibai looked at her image in the mirror. How the years had flown! At nineteen, she was a woman, a far cry from the gawky teenager she had been when she married the king. She was well endowed and bestowed with a fine figure. Hers was not a pretty face, unlike most queens who were chosen for their beauty. Nor had she been raised as one since her family had no claims to any royal lineage. There had been a prophecy that she would one day become queen, but despite her father's best efforts, she was not trained in the etiquette of royalty. But even if she wasn't endowed with the privileges of a royal birth itself, she didn't lack the required intelligence and prudence in any way. The rest she was learning quickly. And she enjoyed every moment of it.

Pleased with what she saw in the mirror, Maharani Lakshmibai smiled. The only thing she didn't like about herself was her voice. If only it could be sweeter. Oh well, that can't be helped, she thought.

'Send her in,' she told the dasi.

Saanvali walked into the queen's room, her head lowered and hands folded.

'Maharani Lakshmibai ki jai!' she saluted.

Lakshmibai liked Saanvali. But more than Saanvali, it was her daughter who had endeared herself to the young queen right from that very first day of their meeting when Chandraki had asked in all her awe and innocence if she could ride horses.

Lakshmibai now looked at Saanvali benevolently, waiting for her to speak.

'Maharani, would it be possible to speak with you in private?'

This was a rare request. Not many asked for a completely private audience with the queen. But Lakshmibai knew that Saanvali had asked this with the utmost humility. Lakshmibai sensed Saanvali's urgency, and so she dismissed the rest of the women.

'It's about Chandraki,' Saanvali said meekly. The queen raised her eyebrows. Now what had that girl done? She loved the way Chandraki would disappear every now and then. Often when she tired of being the dutiful queen, she thought of asking Chandraki to take her along with her on her rendezvous.

'What about her?'

'Please save her, Maharani. Take her out of the harem and keep her beside you. I don't want her to be trapped in this life of indignity that I have suffered all along. She can be naive and impulsive, but she will not survive indignity. I may not live long. I entrust her in your care,' the mother entreated, falling to her knees.

Lakshmibai held Saanvali by her shoulders and pulled her up gently. Their eyes locked. The mother's gaze held the queen's stare beseechingly.

The young queen noticed the premature wrinkles on the once beautiful countenance and the helplessness that reflected in the tired amber eyes. 'It will be as you wish. If that's what you want, Saanvali, you have my word,' Maharani Lakshmibai said softly as she held Saanvali's hand. 'Send her to me tomorrow.'

Saanvali fell at the queen's feet. 'Thank you, Your Majesty! She will serve you loyally till her last breath. I give you my word. She is yours and will remain so till her dying day.'

And with that the mother took her leave. As Lakshmibai looked at the receding figure it seemed as though the woman had suddenly shrivelled up in just those few moments.

～

Four months later, Saanvali died. Chandraki, who had moved into the quarters of the queen's close aides following her mother's desperate appeal, was devastated. How would she live without her? She refused both food and water for two days and lay on her mother's bed crying copiously.

On the third day, Lakshmibai visited her. Chandraki didn't rise to greet her but lay on the bed curled up like a foetus, sobbing. The queen's heart crumpled to see the young girl in such a state.

'I have work for you, Chandraki!' Lakshmibai announced. Chandraki did not look up. The queen sat down beside her.

'I want you to distribute clothes and food to the poor in the name of your mother, who as we all know was a good woman. Wouldn't you want to honour your mother's name?'

Chandraki turned and looked at the queen through a flood of tears. Wiping her tear-stained face, Chandraki sat up with her knees drawn up to her chin and nodded her head slowly.

'Then get dressed and be at the central courtyard by eleven,' the queen said, and stroking her head, left the room.

Chandraki wore her mother's chanderi sari. She had tied her long hair into a bun just like her mother used to. She looked much older than she was. Only her large eyes, though tired, betrayed her young age. She made a pretty picture in the peacock blue sari, the silver zari shimmering under the rays of the midday sun. Yes, indeed, she stood like a peacock that would, at any moment, spread out its plume.

The people queued up before her and accepted the

alms that she gave away. The queen sat on a couch placed next to the table. Chandraki broke down once during the ceremony, but Lakshmibai squeezed her hand and urged her on. She regained her composure and handed over the bundle of coins and sweets to each person who showed up. When would this end, Chandraki wondered as she handed the bundle of coins and some clothes to the man who stood before her with outstretched arms. She glanced up at him.

He was quite tall and dressed in a white angarkha that was smeared with dirt and mud and frayed at the edges. Evidently, he had been travelling for many days. A long scar ran across one side of his face, from his left cheekbone, right up to the curl of his upper lip. As Chandraki offered the small bag of coins to him, their eyes locked briefly. A tremor coursed through her, making her hands shake a bit. The man took what she offered and, saluting her, moved on. Chandraki suddenly wanted the whole thing to end.

'Your Majesty, I'm not feeling well. Is it fine if I leave?' she asked Lakshmibai. The queen nodded. Once back in her room, Chandraki fastened the door and stood with her back against it. Her heart was beating hard and her fingers trembled. She remained standing against the door for quite some time.

4

Maharani Lakshmibai sat alone beside the empty throne. Maharaj Gangadhar Rao, it seemed, was in no mood to preside over matters of the state today. Not a bird chirped, and the sweltering heat kept everyone indoors. There was an air of indolence that hung all around.

Chandraki loved to watch the court proceedings – verdicts being passed, cases being discussed. Other girls her age would rather spend time sitting in front of polished mirrors, admiring themselves, or be busy wooing the young men with their newly mastered art of seduction. But Chandraki would be in the courtroom watching Lakshmibai, who was now a frequent participant, resolve cases and issue decrees. And today, too, Chandraki decided to be present as it would take her mind off her mother's absence.

There were just a few cases to be dispensed with, among which was one that an Anglo-Indian lady brought forth.

'Your Majesty, we have two children. While my younger son is being allowed to inherit his father's assets, my older one is being denied so. Does he have no right over his father's property?' the lady cried.

Maharani Lakshmibai pondered over the matter. 'Both your children have the right to their father's property. How can your husband's family deny one of them that right? On what premise?'

'My older son is adopted, Your Majesty. My husband's family says that he doesn't belong to their bloodline; hence, they believe he has no right over any of the family's property. My husband and I have never discriminated between our two children. I want justice for him,' the mother pleaded.

'If he is your legally adopted son, he has as much of a right over the family property as your natural heir, and I will see to it that your adopted son receives what he is entitled to.' Lakshmibai turned to the prime minister. 'Prepare the necessary documents for the adopted son to be recognized as an equal heir to his father's property.'

A tall and dishevelled man walked in next. Chandraki recognized him as the same man who had taken alms from her the day before. Beside him stood a woman whose face was covered by a veil. As he approached the queen, he glanced at Chandraki who stood beside Lakshmibai. Their eyes locked and Chandraki felt a strange sensation grip her. She quickly lowered her eyes.

'I am Riyaz Khan and I come from Gwalior. My uncle, Abdul Jabbar, is a trader in the kingdom of Jayaji Rao Scindia. He sends this letter for the king,' he said as he handed a letter to the courtier. The queen looked him over and then turned her gaze to the woman who stood beside him.

'Who is she?'

'My begum, Heerabai,' replied Riyaz Khan.

There was something about him that made Chandraki uncomfortable each time he looked at her. A vague sense of dread gripped her. She chose to ignore the strange effect the man had on her. She licked her dry lips and retrained her focus on the proceedings in court.

'Where are you from?' the queen asked.

Riyaz Khan's presence in the courtroom was overwhelming. All eyes were on him. Well over six feet tall, his rugged, almost wild appearance, made him stand out from the rest. His wife stood beside him, still and silent.

'My family lives in Calcutta. My father works for the East India Company at Fort William,' he replied matter-of-factly.

'Then why are you here in Jhansee?'

Riyaz Khan was quiet. The court waited for his answer.

'I . . . I left home,' replied the man hesitatingly, 'I want to seek my own fortune.'

'The letter speaks highly of you. You've been recommended especially for military service. Would you like to join our army?' Maharani Lakshmibai asked.

'Ji huzoor!'

5

Riyaz Khan was a sharp man. In the span of a couple of years, he rose to the post of rissaldar. His superiors as well as the king were impressed with him. Riyaz carried out his duties with the kind of expedience and agility that had been rarely seen in anyone else before. He never asked questions and was seldom seen talking to anyone. His intimidating presence kept most people out of his way, and his proximity to the king made others wary of him. The women, though, loved him. But Chandraki thought differently.

'I don't like him,' she confided in her friend, Gauri.

'Why?' Gauri asked.

'I don't know. He disturbs me.'

Chandraki often bumped into him in the palace. The effect of that encounter was always the same. Both would pause briefly and look into each other's eyes. Riyaz Khan was always the first to look away and walk off. Gauri had often noticed the exchange.

'I think he likes you,' she told Chandraki one day.

'No, I don't think so,' Chandraki replied almost instantly to cover up her embarrassment.

'I can bet on it. I've seen the way he looks at you,' Gauri insisted.

'Gauri! Can you stop speaking such nonsense? I don't like him one bit. He is too proud.'

Gauri smiled and held Chandraki's hand. 'And very good-looking!'

'Good-looking? Have you seen that scar that runs down his cheek? He looks sinister. He is not the kind of man I find attractive,' Chandraki replied firmly.

Perhaps he finds you attractive?' Gauri smiled.

Chandraki shook her head. 'He has a wife and they are very happy together,' said Chandraki as she pulled her hand away from Gauri's and walked away in anger.

Chandraki knew Gauri was wrong. He was married to a good woman, why would he even want to look at her? She knew he was an able officer and a brave soldier. She just couldn't fathom why he affected her so. 'Why do I care?' she asked herself and resorted to prepare for a session of sword fighting later in the afternoon.

6

The troops of the 68th Bengal Native Infantry reached Jhansee on a dreary April evening in the year 1850. Though the sun was well below the horizon, and the shadows of dusk coated the sky, there was no respite from the heat. The evening was as still as death itself. It had been a long and difficult march of nearly two months since the regiment had set off from Calcutta for the Mainpuri cantonment that was still over 150 miles away. By the time they hit the Jhansee cantonment, the troops were exhausted, drained of energy and resources, and, above all, severely parched. They were more than relieved to halt at the Jhansee cantonment where they could recover their strength and energy and replenish their resources.

The moment the convoy reached the cantonment that was located on the outskirts of the walled city, Jagat Singh, the local tehsildar, approached the commanding officer of the troops. Welcoming the officer with folded hands and with a tone that was at once syrupy and servile, he said, 'Salutations, sahib! Welcome to Jhansee!'

The commanding officer nodded. 'How far is our mess?'

'Just a few miles ahead, sahib!' replied Jagat Singh. 'All the arrangements have been made.'

The convoy broke up. The three officers straddled their horses and rode off in the direction of the officers' mess. The rest of the troops trundled off towards the barracks of one of the regiments. Jagat Singh followed the convoy up to the barracks, and once they reached there, he signalled his men, who had followed behind in bullock carts heaped with huge amounts of cargo, to come forward.

'Load the cargo on to those carts,' he told his men, pointing to the long line of bullock carts, ponies, and camels laden with weapons and ammunition.

~

Captain Alexander Skene, who had recently relieved Colonel William Henry Sleeman to take over his position as the superintendent of Jhansee, awaited the arrival of the 68th regiment eagerly. It was his parent unit. He had been notified of its impending arrival at the station a fortnight ago, and he now welcomed his regiment with open arms, ensuring that adequate arrangements had been made for its stay in Jhansee. Skene had been posted in Jhansee a few months ago. Jhansee could hardly be called a cantonment, with just a handful of officers and troops stationed in the town. But life was comfortable. Major Ellis and Major Malcolm kept him company, and he liked the king quite a bit, who was pleasant and eager to please.

'Excited to meet your old pals, Skene?' Malcolm asked,

amused at the younger officer's restlessness. The officers sat in the veranda of Skene's bungalow where he lived with his wife and two children.

'Yes.' Skene smiled. 'The regiment will be here for three days, and I need to meet all their requirements. They have a rather long march ahead!'

'Don't worry. The tehsildar has assured me that all their daily necessities have been arranged for.'

'Major Malcolm, please make an inventory. The accounts will be settled soon.'

'I've told my officers to make the payment. They said it's already been done.'

'Thank you, sir!' Skene smiled and saluted. 'I better get going, they will arrive any moment now.'

As he turned to leave, a chaprasi ran in, bowing nervously. He was immediately followed by the naib tehsildar, Sarmad Shah.

The two British officers turned around, surprised at this sudden intrusion.

'What's the matter, Chaman Lal?'

'Sahib, there are two men who have been waiting at the gate since sunrise. They say they have waited the whole night to seek an audience with you.'

Skene and Malcolm exchanged confused glances.

'Who are these men? And why do they want to meet me?' Skene asked.

Before Chaman Lal could reply Sarmad Shah interjected. 'It's nothing, sahib. A petty matter. I've resolved it.'

Skene looked at Sarmad Shah doubtfully. He didn't like the naib tehsildar nor his superior. The two were hard on people and several complaints against them had filtered in. Whenever questioned, they evaded answering and used some pretext or the other to put the blame on the people they were harassing.

'What is it about?' Skene asked.

'It's about the payment for their goods, sahib,' said Chaman Lal quickly before Sarmad Shah even got the chance to reply. Shah was about to open his mouth to retort when Skene raised his hand and stopped him. He stepped down from the porch, crossed the driveway, and approached the gate. Two men sat there on their haunches and rose the moment they saw him walk towards them.

'Mai baap!' the men cried and fell at his feet. 'Forgive us. We will wait till you've had your breakfast.'

'It's almost midday, I had my breakfast long ago. And what has my eating breakfast got to do with your situation?'

Chaman Lal, who had followed Skene to the gate, intervened. 'Sahib, they think you are a tiger before breakfast,' he said apologetically.

Skene turned towards him. His eyebrows shot up. 'Eh?'

'They have been told that you are in better humour once you've had your breakfast.'

'Who told them this?' Skene asked sharply.

'The tehsildar, sahib.'

Aghast, Skene looked at Malcolm who had followed him to the gate.

'What's going on, Major Malcolm, do you have any idea?'

The two officers walked back to Skene's bungalow quietly. They sat down on the chairs without a word. A servant brought out a tray of sherbet and placed it on the table.

'I think it's to do with the payment of the goods that have arrived for your regiment. I wonder if the vendors have been paid for them,' Malcolm said thoughtfully. He rang the little bell that lay on the table. An orderly appeared instantly and saluted.

'Ask Sarmad Shah to come here.'

The naib tehsildar was engaged in an animated conversation with the two men at the gate. He came running in and stood before the two officers.

'Who put in the requisition for the goods that have been offered to the regiment that arrived last night?' Skene asked sharply.

'The thanedar, sahib. And the tehsildar.'

'What all has been ordered?'

'Wood, grass, fowls, wheat grains, vegetables, and pots.'

'Have the men been paid?' Skene asked.

Sarmad Shah remained silent. He stood with his head bowed.

'I asked you a question!' Skene raised his voice.

'We'll pay them once we've got everyone together. We don't want to pay them twice,' Sarmad Shah replied shiftily.

Skene nodded. 'Ensure that it happens. I will keep a check on this!'

7

Chandraki and Gauri stood in front of the palace gates, watching the elephants laden with huge bags walk out of the fort one after another.

'What's in those bags?' Gauri enquired.

'Sugar,' Chandraki replied.

'For what?' Gauri asked, perplexed.

'To be distributed across the kingdom. The next king of Jhansee has just been born, Gauri!' Chandraki exclaimed. 'The king wants everyone to know the "meethi khabar".'

Gauri jumped with joy. 'Oh, how sweet!'

Giggling, the girls ran down the road towards the town to witness the celebrations. As they glided from shop to shop, they bumped into their friend Amba, who stopped them from crashing into her.

'Watch your step, girls!' she admonished.

Amba, who was Gauri's childhood friend, had been married off a few years ago and now lived outside the main town, along the road that led to Gwalior. Her husband was a vendor of daily commodities that included wood and grain and had a shop in the market just outside the walls of the city. His business was doing well, and the couple had managed to get a house of their own. The two friends embraced each other.

'We are so happy that the Maharaja now has an heir,' Gauri said.

'Maharani Lakshmibai has brought great fortune for Jhansee.' Amba smiled.

'You are soon to be a mother, too,' Gauri said, clasping her friend's hand. 'So, when is the baby arriving?'

'In four months,' Amba replied shyly. 'Join us for a meal and the badhaiya dance once the baby is born.'

'We'll visit you the moment we hear the good news,' Chandraki promised.

~

Jhansee celebrated the birth of its heir with great fervour. Food and clothing were distributed to the poor, and the kingdom feasted and rejoiced for weeks. Chandraki was especially happy now that her Maharani was mother to the future king of Jhansee.

'It pleases me to see the Maharani so happy,' she remarked to Gauri as the two of them made their way through the multitude of devotees who thronged the big temple situated at the far end of the town. It was the month of Ashvin and the Navratri fair was in full swing. The bazaars swelled with people and goods. Jhansee's Navratri fair was well known in Bundelkhand. Devotees and tourists came from far and across kingdoms to participate in the

ten-day-long festival. Scores of tents were pitched on the
open grounds around the temple. Colourful stalls selling
bangles, clothes, accessories, sweetmeats, and utensils had
sprung up along the streets that led to the temple dedicated
to Siva and his royal consort, Gauri.

People came with jasmine garlands, offerings of rice,
and gaudy red veils embellished with zari. The queues
were long everywhere, at the temple, at the stalls, and at
the fair. The king and queen graced the temple on Maha
Ashtami, the eighth day of Navratri. The king arrived atop
an elephant swaying to the rhythmic chants of 'Durga
mata ki jai', 'Maharaj ki jai', and 'Maharani ki jai'. The
queen followed in a palanquin, with her newborn child
in her arms. The strains of achri wafted through the thick
autumn air.

The priest blessed the royal family and offered a puja
in the name of the newborn prince, after which they
were escorted to one of the tents that was bigger than
the rest. It was decorated with garlands and festoons.
Women blew conch shells as the queen alighted from
the palanquin. An attendant raised the flap of the tent,
and Maharani Lakshmibai stepped into its cool interior.
Almost immediately, the nagada sounded, and a troupe
of badhaiya dancers converged in front of their tent.
The splash of colours was almost blinding, and with that
the bright sunshine created a psychedelic effect as the
dancers swirled and swished to the beat of the dholaks.
Hundreds of people had gathered, they pushed each other
to catch a glimpse of the king and, especially, the queen.

It wasn't every day that they witnessed such a sight. The dancers spun around like whirling dervishes, their ghagras flaring and ghungroos jangling loudly. Lakshmibai smiled radiantly through all of this and looked at her husband who seemed to be enjoying himself.

Chandraki, who had accompanied the queen, stood outside the royal tent watching the show and admired the efforts of the spirited performers to dress up in all that finery and dance so passionately in this heat. As the dancers came closer and closer to the tent, spinning and jangling, and the various drums thundered in unison, the prince suddenly let out a piercing shriek and followed it up with a loud wail. The dancers continued dancing, and the dhols blared even louder in order to be heard above the baby's shrieks. The higher the pitch of the music, the louder the prince howled. Lakshmibai tried to silence him, rocking him gently and caressing him, but his wails got shriller with every thundering beat of the nagada.

'I think we better leave, the prince is uncomfortable.' Lakshmibai nudged her husband. The king heard her silently, drumming his fingers on the couch and continued watching the performance for another five minutes, after which he rose from his seat and summoned one of the attendants.

'Get the palanquin ready for the queen. We are leaving!' He emerged from the tent followed by his queen and waving to the people who had gathered on either side of the arena, walked up to the elephant as cries of 'Maharaj ki jai' filled the air.

8

Damodar Rao, the heir to the throne of Jhansee, died after four months. Jhansee cried, and so did the king and queen. Chandraki was beside her queen always, trying to console her, but all efforts were in vain. What could she do to alleviate the queen's grief? She urged her to step out of the palace and go horse-riding with her. But the queen remained ensconced in her chamber, refusing to budge.

'I just don't know how to get the Maharani out of the palace. If she shuts herself within her room, the memories of the prince will continue to haunt her,' she confided in Gauri.

'Why don't you organize some recreation for her in the palace itself?' Gauri suggested.

Chandraki was quiet. Would the queen agree to it?

They had been invited to Amba's house for a meal. As promised, Chandraki and Gauri came over to celebrate the arrival of Amba's baby into this world. This was the first time that Chandraki had been invited for a meal to someone's house. Excited at the thought of a wholesome, joyous, cosy afternoon and some delicious food, she reached

Amba's house much before the designated time. Amba
was a great cook, and Chandraki had once sampled her
ras kheer, a pudding made from sugarcane juice and rice.
The taste lingered in her mouth for days, and her mouth
watered to this date whenever she thought about it.

Amba and her husband, Sankara, lived in a house that
stood among a cluster of four houses facing each other.
Each house had two rooms, a kitchen with an earthen
stove in one corner, and a veranda that led to the common
courtyard in the centre. A low wall encircled the four
houses. An arched doorway in the centre of the wall that
faced the road served as a common entrance to this cluster
of houses. Madhumalati vines grew abundantly around,
hugging the walls to form a canopy over the doorway, thus
offering a bowered pathway that led inside. Their lingering
fragrance enveloped the visitors in a warm embrace.

Amba greeted Chandraki at the entrance and ushered
her in. It was cooler inside, and the air smelt sweet with
the scent of the flowers mingling with the aroma of spices.
The singular window offered a view of the mango orchard
that grew behind the wall.

Two men, one of whom was Sankara, Amba's husband,
sat on the bamboo mats spread out on the floor. Chandraki
pulled her veil over her face and sat down facing the men.
She wished Gauri would come soon. Amba emerged from
the kitchen holding a tray with four brass bowls containing
maheri, a dish made from crushed sorghum and buttermilk
and flavoured with green chillies and spices. She set the
tray on the ground.

'This will work up an appetite and keep you cool,' she

said, handing the men a bowl each. And as she offered one to Chandraki, Gauri came in. Chandraki heaved a sigh of relief.

'Oh, here comes Gauri!' Amba smiled at a beaming Gauri, who plonked herself next to Chandraki. The two girls looked at the stranger from under their veils.

'You can throw back your veils. We are all friends here,' Amba reassured the girls. The girls hesitatingly removed their veils, though glad to do so in the heat that slowly took control of the room. The stranger's eyes flitted from one face to the other and came to rest on Chandraki. Those huge, dark eyes of hers were so enchanting. Amba took in the scene and cleared her throat. The girls looked up at her. She noticed Gauri's puzzled look.

'This is Jaywant, Sankara's friend. He is visiting from Orchha,' she said.

'Orchha?' Chandraki, who had been sitting quietly all this while, suddenly spoke up.

'Our neighbouring state? Isn't Orchha an enemy state?'

Jaywant smiled at her. 'The kingdoms may be enemies. But surely I can visit my friend here? He is not my enemy,' he said softly, looking straight into Chandraki's eyes. She lowered them, and her cheeks flushed with embarrassment.

'I'm . . . I'm sorry,' she stuttered. 'I didn't mean it that way.'

'It's all right. I like coming to Jhansee. And I like its people too,' he said as he leaned closer to Chandraki. Then lowering his voice, he said, 'The women, especially. They are rather beautiful!' Chandraki smiled shyly.

All was quiet as everyone drained the contents of the bowl. The drink refreshed them and the conversation picked up. Gauri let loose a volley of questions at Jaywant who answered each one rather patiently. Chandraki had slipped into the kitchen to help Amba with laying out the meal.

'This is such a lavish spread,' exclaimed Chandraki as she took in the array of dishes spread out before them. There was nighauna, bafauri, meeda, puri ke laddoo, bijora, murka, lapsi, luchai, kentha chutney and papariya.

'This is made from red pumpkin, isn't it?' Jaywant asked as he gulped down the kumhade ki kheer. Amba nodded.

'This is delicious,' Chandraki remarked as she bit into a bijora. Bijora were thick fried cakes made from sesame, white pumpkin, lentils, ginger, and green chilli. They tasted quite different from what she had tasted in the palace. She told Amba so.

'Naturally,' Amba said. 'It's prepared much more elaborately in the royal kitchen.'

'But this tastes so much better!' Chandraki smiled. 'You have taken so much trouble to put all of this together.'

'Oh Chandraki, this is such simple fare,' Amba replied, embarrassed at Chandraki's praise.

'I've prepared it with minimum ingredients. The royal chefs enhance the taste with many more spices.'

'You call this simple fare?' Jaywant exclaimed as he gestured to the numerous dishes. Amba and Sankara exchanged glances.

'This is probably the last time we can lay out a spread like this,' Amba said quietly. Her three guests looked up.

'What do you mean?' Jaywant asked, puzzled.

'We may have to move out of Jhansee for good. Sankara's business has closed down,' Amba replied.

Inside the room, the heat was oppressive. A fly buzzed around and sat on the leftovers of the meal. Amba shooed it away, but it kept returning. Other than the buzzing of the fly, the stillness of the afternoon was almost deafening. Once everyone had finished eating, Amba rose to collect the sal leaves in which the food had been served. Chandraki and Gauri picked up their own leaves and followed Amba into the kitchen and threw the leaves over the wall into the mango grove.

The three women returned to the sitting room after washing up.

'What has happened, Sankara? Why do you have to shut shop?' Jaywant asked as he wiped his mouth.

'Officials from the East India Company force us to supply passing troops and their officers with goods from my shops. Not only my shop. Vendors dealing in grains, wood and pottery all over Bundelkhand are facing a similar problem. They send requisitions on behalf of the British officers and sometimes, even the king. Of course we are never paid for our service, because we are obliged to follow the orders.'

Sankara's ancestors were Koshti weavers known for the chanderi saris they manufactured. One of the few Hindu families to be in the business, the rest of the weavers being Muslims, Sankara's family had migrated from Jhansee to Chanderi almost 500 years ago. During the reign of the Mughal kings, their business boomed, but with the advent of the British and their goods, their business dwindled, and Sankara's family opted out of it. His grandfather returned to Jhansee at the end of the last century and set up a shop selling day-to-day necessities such as wood and grain.

'Our business thrived till my father was alive. But ever since my father died eight years ago and I took over the business, everything has gone downhill.'

Chandraki was surprised. She had always thought Amba to be rich and happy. She had known them for several years, and not for a moment had Amba let it be known that they were struggling.

'Why have you not informed the king?' Chandraki asked. 'I'm sure he would speak to these officials and ask them to mend their ways.'

'Some of us tried to reach him but were denied access. Some of the courtiers are hand in glove with these officials. The moment they get to know that we have tried to speak to the king or the sahibs, they threaten us and tend to get violent. Three vendors who tried to approach the king were killed over the last two months.'

'And what about the sahibs? Do they know that goods are being requisitioned in their names?'

'These government officials act as a buffer between the firanghees and the vendors and thus they ensure that we don't meet them. Mostly, it is carried out under the protection of the British army. British officers, though they know of the corruption, turn a blind eye towards it, pocket the money themselves knowing that the intermediary officers won't pay the traders. The condition of landowners is even worse. They are obliged to supply wood, grass, and pots as part of their contract in order to retain the ownership of their land,' Sankara explained.

Amba was crying by now. Chandraki and Gauri held her hands and wiped her tears. 'Don't worry, Amba. Something will be done to stop this practice,' Chandraki assured.

'This injustice has taken over the entire region, right up to Benares where permanent landowners have it signed in their contract. How can you stop it? It has not only ruined us but is also a huge drain in the commerce of this region.' Sankara sighed.

'I'll speak with the Maharani,' Chandraki assured Sankara. She hugged Amba and then turned around and walked out of the house. Her steps had been light when she had entered Amba's house, but she left it with slow and heavy ones.

After seeing off Chandraki and Gauri, Amba went back to the room where Jaywant was now getting ready to leave. Regaining her composure, and putting on a smile, she said, 'So, you like my friend Chandraki?"

Jaywant smiled and avoided looking at Amba.

Sankara patted Jaywant on his back and said, 'I think you now have a better reason to keep coming to Jhansee, don't you?'

'You must come for Ram Navami next month when this city truly comes to life. Chandraki will be there too,' teased Amba.

Chandraki walked back to the palace, sad and forlorn. Her heart wept for Amba and Sankara. How would they manage with their newborn child? 'They would soon have nothing to eat,' she thought pensively. 'This is a case of extreme injustice. The Maharani must know about this.'

~

'Maharaj had spoken about this issue a few times, but nothing was done to stop this practice. I will have to do something soon,' said Lakshmibai upon receiving Chandraki's information.

'And, Your Highness, this isn't just restricted to Jhansee, it has taken over all of Bundelkhand and further north, right up to Benares!' Chandraki exclaimed.

'How long has this been going on?' the queen asked.

'For several years! The poor traders are being exploited in the name of the British officers, and sometimes even the king himself,' Chandraki said, fuming over the events.

'This doesn't augur well for the kingdom, especially our people,' the queen said. Then turning to Chandraki, she exclaimed, 'Good work, Chandraki! You have no idea just how important this issue is.'

She clapped her hands. An attendant appeared. 'Tell Maharaj that I need to see him immediately.'

'Thank you once again, Chandraki. You should have been a hurkurus – a part of our secret service. I'm proud of you!'

Lakshmibai smiled to herself as she watched Chandraki walk away. She knew just the right person who could put an end to this.

9

'Offload!' Riyaz Khan bellowed. The four men did not move an inch and continued to stare at him.

'Didn't you hear me? I said get those sacks off the carts!' Riyaz thundered as he slashed one of the bales with his bayonet. A drizzle of golden grains fell out.

'Huzoor, mercy!' one of the men pleaded, his fists clasped, begging for pardon.

'Wheat as well?' Riyaz enquired.

The man nodded.

Riyaz ignored him and moved to the cart behind him. He prodded the sacks roughly.

'Take the sacks back to the shop,' Riyaz ordered his men.

The four men watched terrified as Riyaz Khan and his men emptied the carts.

'Huzoor, spare us. We are only carrying out orders.'

'Whose orders?'

'The naib tehsildar's orders.' The man's voice shook as he stood with his head bowed, hands folded.

'Tell him I want to see him,' Riyaz Khan roared.

'And tell him I want a list of all the vendors you have appropriated, do you understand?'

The man nodded. Riyaz turned to face Sankara who stood in front of his shop silently.

'How long has this been going on?' Riyaz asked.

'For several years, huzoor,' Sankara replied as he helped the king's men shove the bales of grains back into his shop. 'Many shopkeepers have suffered. The landowners, even those who have permanent holdings, are in a condition worse than mine. They are forced to supply pots and grass – it's part of their contract. If they don't, their lands are confiscated.'

Riyaz was silent for a while. He turned to the group of men who stood trembling and asked, 'Who is the naib tehsildar here?'

'Sarmad Shah, huzoor. But he takes his orders from Tehsildar Jagat Singh Kachwaha.'

Riyaz beckoned one of his men. 'Send a message to Jagat Singh asking him to appear before the king. And I want that message sent today itself!'

~

'I should have looked into the matter when two men approached me a few years ago,' Captain Alexander Skene said angrily, banging his fist on the table. 'Were you aware of this, Captain Gordon?' he asked his colleague.

'Not entirely, sir, though I had heard of such practices being carried out in some places in Bundelkhand. Both Captain Brown and Captain Ternan had hinted about it.'

'This is ridiculous. I didn't have a clue that it was this bad. What a shame that this was going on right under my nose. And now Gangadhar Rao wants to know how we could have possibly let this happen. I have no answer.'

'Such a kind of purveyance system is well in place in large parts of India and all across Bundelkhand. Captain Brown says that in Jalaoun the poor vendors have been told by the tehsildar that Captain Brown requires all the wood for his regiment. How can they defy the Captain's orders?'

'And they have not yet been paid a penny?'

'Apparently not.'

'Is this happening here too?'

'Yes sir!'

'Why didn't you tell me this before? This puts me in a very precarious position,' Skene said angrily. 'Who's the tehsildar here?'

'Jagat Singh Kachwaha. But he gets all his work done by his deputy, Sarmad Shah.'

'Oh yes, I've met Shah,' said Skene. 'The rascal. He told those vendors some cock and bull story about me being a tiger before breakfast and scared the living daylights out of them. I need both Jagat Singh and Shah to meet me.'

~

Jagat Singh drew hard and long on his hookah. His eyes had narrowed and his face was flushed. 'The longer a sore is allowed to fester, the more poisonous it gets,' he said, his voice hardly audible.

Sarmad Shah looked up as he stuffed a paan into his

mouth. Picking up the silver spittoon that lay by his side, he spat out some of the juice.

'So what do you want to do? Have him killed?'

Jagat Singh shook his head. 'No, that will be too simple. He has given us a lot of trouble and has almost single-handedly taken away our major source of income. Besides, it's too risky. He is a senior officer of the imperial army. We must have him removed from Jhansee.'

'He is just a pawn, he simply carries out the king's orders,' Shah replied.

'I know, but a dangerous one. He's much too daring and much too honest. My man, Khilawan, offered him a bribe, but he took him straight to the king. He's ruthless.'

'How will removing Riyaz Khan help? The king will replace him with some other officer.'

Jagat Singh nodded. 'Yes. But that other officer could be more obliging.'

'The king has sent out his men all over the state of Jhansee to nab intermediaries like us. And how do you propose to remove Riyaz Khan from Jhansee unless he's finished off? He is one of the king's most trusted and important officers. This is his home and his family lives here. He can't be made to move.'

'Exactly.' Jagat Singh smiled. He turned to his subordinate. 'Sarmad, you once told me that you have a niece in Calcutta, whom you wanted to bring to Jhansee and get married off? You also told me that she was bad-tempered and your brother, who is ready to pay a huge dowry, has failed to secure a match for her?'

Sarmad nodded. 'Yes. She's a vixen. She had brain fever

as a child and never quite recovered from that. She can turn violent and aggressive. We are very worried. She turned eighteen last winter.'

Jagat Singh's lips curled, and his face turned sinister. 'Well, I think your niece will find her match very soon.' Sarmad's eyes widened, and he looked at Jagat Singh, confused.

'How are you so sure?'

Jagat Singh grinned, flashing his tobacco-stained teeth. 'I have a plan. Now, write a letter.' He grinned.

'To whom?'

'To your brother. Ask him to go meet Riyaz Khan's father who is posted in Fort William and offer him double the dowry for his daughter's hand in marriage.'

Sarmad was so surprised at his superior's words that he was left speechless for a while. Clearing his throat, he said, 'Who will marry her?'

'Riyaz Khan.'

'How would that help? How will that take him away from Jhansee?

'You do as you've been told. Leave the rest to his father. Riyaz Khan won't be killed, but he'll be finished. Trust me, I'm quite sure that he will not be seen in Jhansee for very long after that.' Jagat Singh smiled menacingly.

10

Chandraki had not been very far from the truth when she had said that Riyaz Khan was happily married. His house was situated far away from the palace and close to the river that flowed behind the fort. Riyaz Khan's duties kept him out at all odd hours, but once he returned home, it was only to be with his wife Heera and their two children. But on this particular evening, Riyaz came back home early. He undressed quickly and went straight to bed. Heera, who was always ready with a delicious meal just in case Riyaz arrived home suddenly, was surprised. She laid out his food, but he left it untouched.

'What is it, Riyaz?' she asked quietly as he lay in bed looking up at the ceiling vacantly, one arm thrown over his head. They never spoke much because they didn't need to. Heera always anticipated his needs and always knew what was bothering him by simply looking at him. He too, on his part, loved her with all his heart. They were wrapped up in their own little world where there was no space for anyone else.

'Is it your father?' Heera knew Riyaz wasn't ruffled easily. There was only one thing that always disturbed him and that was his family, especially his father.

Riyaz was quiet. 'What is it, please tell me!' Heera insisted. Suddenly, she was scared. His father had disowned Riyaz because of her. She perpetually lived in the fear of being separated from Riyaz by his father under some pretext or the other. She could not bear to think of a life without him.

If Riyaz Khan was capable of loving anyone, it was Heerabai, whom he had married when he was only nineteen years old. Riyaz's father lived in Calcutta and worked as a guard at Fort William, the headquarters of the East India Company. His ancestors, who had been simple peasants from Bhati, the deltaic region of Bengal, converted to Islam with the advent of the Sufi missionaries. Over time, they changed their profession from farming to craftsmanship. Riyaz's father was ambitious. He saw profit in aligning with the British and decided to take up a position at Fort William, the only one in his family to have ever done so. He had wanted his son to join the East India Company as well.

Riyaz, meanwhile, had fallen in love with Heerabai, a courtesan. He first visited her with a friend one evening and was smitten the moment he set his eyes upon her. He had gone back to her a few days later and asked her if she would marry him. She had thrown her head back and laughed, her lips smeared scarlet with the juice of betel leaves. No one in her thirty-two years of existence had ever wanted to marry her.

But his father would not hear of it. She was a courtesan, a kothewaali thirteen years older to him, and most importantly, a Hindu. When Riyaz realized that his father would not even allow Heera into their house, he decided to leave Calcutta and settle down elsewhere.

With Heerabai in tow, he reached Gwalior where he sought out his uncle Abdul Jabbar and intimated him of his predicament. Jabbar sent him off with a letter to Raja Gangadhar Rao in Jhansee where he built this little home for himself, Heera, and their children. He lived in constant dread of this world of theirs shattering. He knew his father wouldn't give up so easily. Riyaz shielded Heera from the outside world with a kind of fierceness that was dangerous. He wouldn't allow anything or anyone to destroy his home. Nobody was capable of taking Heera away from him. Not even his own father.

'Abbu is dying. He has sent for me,' he told Heera quietly.

Heera received the news with trepidation. But she couldn't allow Riyaz to see her distressed. She took his hand in her own.

'Then you must go to Calcutta.'

'How can I leave you here alone?'

'I'm not alone, the children are here with me. You must go. If Abbu dies, you'll never be able to forgive yourself. Nor will I be able to forgive myself.'

Riyaz Khan looked at Heera. How could anyone be so kind-hearted? 'Why are you so good, Heera?' he said as he took her in his arms.

'We must do what is right, Riyaz. Now, don't waste any more time and leave before it's too late.'

Riyaz hugged her tightly. 'Thank you so much, my darling.'

After taking his leave from the king, Riyaz Khan left for Calcutta with a heavy heart. He had no idea how the encounter with his father would pan out. Their last meeting had been a bitter one – on the day he had decided to leave Calcutta and walked out of his house along with Heera. His father had shut the door on Riyaz's face. Riyaz had no idea how his father came to know about his whereabouts in Jhansee. Perhaps his uncle had informed his father. Something told him that this was just the beginning of his troubles once again.

11

Chandraki was still recovering from the first flush of excitement that often precedes an imminent romance. She didn't know what to make of the emotions that rose within her. Jaywant often visited Jhansee now, and each time Chandraki met him, her heart fluttered, and each time he left, she yearned for him. He showered her with compliments and made her feel rather special. She felt at ease with him and slowly started opening up about her life – how her mother had died, how Maharani Lakshmibai had helped her overcome her grief and had supported her while she was mourning her mother's death.

'Maharani Lakshmibai is everything for me,' said Chandraki. They were sitting outside the Mahalakshmi temple near the palace. The air pulsated with the shrill sounds of the huge brass bells ringing as devotees poured in and out of the temple.

'Don't you ever wish for a home of your own? Or your own family?' asked Jaywant.

Chandraki was quiet. A home of her own? A family?

For her the palace was her home and the people she lived with were her family.

'Come away with me,' said Jaywant, suddenly. Chandraki, who was lost in her thoughts, looked at him startled.

'Where?'

'To Orchha.'

Chandraki shook her head. 'I can't leave Maharani Lakshmibai. She's all I have. This is my home!' she said emphatically.

'Will you then serve her for the rest of your life? Would you want to be her slave all your life?' Jaywant asked angrily. 'Every woman has to leave her home one day. Didn't your Maharani leave her father to come to Jhansee?'

'I need to go,' cried Chandraki, upset at being asked to leave Jhansee. Jaywant held her hand.

'I'm sorry, I didn't mean to hurt you. I really love you and want to be with you always,' he said, his tone turning gentler.

Later that day, and for many days thereafter, Jaywant's words kept playing over and over in Chandraki's mind. He had said he loved her. It was a heady feeling. Jaywant's visits to Jhansee increased. They met at Amba's house, or they would sit hand in hand on the green patch that surrounded the Lakshmi Tal or go walk in the bazaars. Jaywant pursued her relentlessly and she felt happy and comfortable with him. Jaywant was her window to the outside world and he made her believe she had the right to make her own choices. Wasn't that what her mother had wanted? That Chandraki should have her own home? Her own family?

The festival of Holi arrived in all its multihued splendour, spraying rich colours amidst the fragrance of spring. The evening before Holi, Chandraki, along with Gauri and Amba, gathered in the courtyard of Amba's house. Sankara and Jaywant were there too. Everyone waited for the sun to set after which a bonfire would be lit to destroy the female demon, Holika, a symbolic depiction of the victory of good over evil. It was a warm evening, and there was a whole lot of cheer and joy in the air as everyone chatted and relaxed over bel sherbet.

Suddenly Sankara rose to his feet. 'I forgot the firewood in the shed behind my shop. I'll go fetch it,' he said. The shop was a few miles away and it was nearly dark.

'I'll go get it. I have my horse with me,' Jaywant offered.

'I'll come with you,' said Chandraki, all of a sudden.

Jaywant hesitated and then nodded.

The two got on to Jaywant's horse and within minutes, were sprinting ahead, raising huge clouds of dust behind them. Chandraki sat behind Jaywant, her arms tightly clasped around his waist. It was the first time she had held him so close, and she shut her eyes as she rested her head against his broad back. She felt happy and didn't want this ride to end. Lost in her dreams, she didn't notice the sky darkening in the distant horizon or the wind slowly gather force. Within minutes, the dark clouds that had seemed far away against the evening sky now hovered above them menacingly. Chandraki opened her eyes when the strong winds whipped her face. She squinted as grains of dust blew into her eyes. A strong gust of wind blew her veil away. There was a flash of lightning in the distant horizon and the wind howled as it swept across the dusty countryside.

'My veil,' Chandraki screamed as she slid off the horse and fell over before getting up to run after it.

'Chandraki! What are you doing?' Jaywant shouted over the rumble of thunder, but before Chandraki could respond, his horse galloped away leaving her behind. At that moment the skies burst and within minutes the land was soaked. There was no one in sight for miles around the drenched countryside. The curtains of darkness fell over the city. Chandraki looked around for some shelter and spotted an empty cowshed at some distance. She ran into it and sat down on the mud floor, praying for Jaywant to return soon. She was completely lost and had no idea how to get back to Amba's house.

It was quite some time before she heard the sound of hoofs approaching the cowshed. Chandraki stiffened. It was pitch dark outside.

'Chandraki, where are you?' the voice rang out loud and clear over the rain. Without a second's hesitation Chandraki rushed out of the cowshed.

'Oh Jaywant, I've been so scared! I thought you'd left me here all alone!' she cried as she hugged him tightly.

'How could I?' he said as he led her into the cowshed. 'Let's wait inside until the rain stops.'

It was pitch dark inside and the two of them sat pressed to one another. Jaywant could feel Chandraki shivering and as he hugged her tighter, she suddenly threw her arms around him. Taken aback, Jaywant was motionless for a few moments and then slowly put his arms around her and drew her closer to himself. Chandraki allowed herself to be enveloped in his warm embrace. She felt secure with him, and before she could stop herself, she had surrendered to this man who now meant the world to her. She could not resist him when he reached out for her. He slowly unlaced her choli and slid it off her moist shoulders. She closed her eyes and let the tide of emotions engulf her.

Later, as they lay in each other's arms, spent and content, their hair dishevelled, clothes lying in a heap around them, Jaywant whispered, 'You are mine, Chandraki. We are now man and wife. You will never belong to another man.'

'But we are not married yet,' said Chandraki softly.

'Of course we are! Marriage is a union of two bodies, two hearts and two souls. We have accepted each other in our primeval forms. Just like the gandharvas did when they chose one another and consummated their union without any rituals or witnesses. We don't need a banquet, horses, elephants or even a priest to validate our marriage. The sky and the earth have been witness to our union and they have blessed us in the form of this storm.'

Chandraki smiled. 'Just like how they blessed Shakuntala and Dushyant?'

Jaywant nodded. 'Perhaps!'

'But he left her and went away. Will you do the same to me too?'

'Never! I love you more than life itself!' Jaywant replied and kissed her tenderly. Chandraki was quiet. She felt a sense of calm that she had never experienced before. She belonged to him. Chandraki, who had fiercely guarded her pride all these years, had now given herself up to Jaywant. It felt strange to belong to someone. She looked down at the amulet that her mother had tied on her arm. She took it off and tied it on Jaywant's arm.

'What is this?' Jaywant asked, bemused.

'My most precious possession. My mother, the only family I've ever had until this very moment, had made me promise to never part with this amulet. She said it would protect me for life. But now that you and I are one, I want you to have this amulet. A piece of my soul resides in this stone. I promise you that I will never again belong to another man.'

~

Chandraki considered Gauri's suggestion to organize some recreation to help the queen overcome her grief. Ever since the heir to the throne of Jhansee had died, there had been no revelries in the palace. So Chandraki got a few women from the zenana together and decided to put up a show for the royal couple in the privacy of their boudoir. For this purpose she visited the florists in the town market where she bumped into Heerabai. Chandraki had seen her a few times when she had been strolling around the fort and Heera would be cleaning her courtyard or playing with her children.

'Aren't you Heerabai? Riyaz Khan's wife?' Chandraki asked.

Heera nodded. 'How is Her Majesty?' she asked. For some strange reason Chandraki felt drawn towards this quiet woman.

'Not too good, I'm afraid.'

'Would it be possible for me to meet her?'

'She rarely meets anyone these days,' said Chandraki.

'I understand. But still, could you ask her?'

Chandraki nodded and the two women parted.

Maharani Lakshmibai granted Heerabai an audience when Chandraki told her she was Riyaz Khan's wife. The queen had never met her before and having heard the king's endless praise for Riyaz, she was curious to know more about him, his life and his family.

The two women met in the queen's chamber.

'I have come to offer you my deepest condolences, Your Majesty. Your grief is immeasurable. Is there any way I can help?'

The queen shook her head. 'Thank you, Heerabai. I really appreciate the fact that you came to see me. It means a lot to me. I haven't seen Riyaz around in a long time. Where has he gone?' Lakshmibai only knew that he had left in a hurry. The Maharaja had been quite concerned about him.

'Abbujaan is unwell. This may be the last time my husband would see his father.'

'That is really unfortunate, Heerabai,' said Maharani Lakshmibai. The two women were quiet for a while and then Lakshmibai broke the silence by asking her, 'Is there anything I can do for you?'

'Thank you very much, Your Majesty. It is magnanimous of you to even say so. I don't need anything. My husband provides me with all that I need. There's just one thing, Your Majesty.'

'And what would that be?'

'As long as I'm around I promise you that Riyaz will never fail in his duties towards the king,' said Heerabai humbly.' But if he ever commits an offence, I ask you to spare his life, Maharani.'

The queen nodded. 'I don't think I will ever have to punish Riyaz. Your husband is a good man,' she said reassuringly. Heerabai left the chamber, her restless mind finally at peace.

Chandraki, who was present during the meeting, turned to the queen.

'How can someone like Riyaz Khan get such a good wife?' she wondered aloud. Lakshmibai frowned.

'Why? What is wrong with him? Has he said something to you?'

Chandraki shook her head. 'No, Your Majesty. However, there is something about him that makes me uncomfortable. I can't lay a finger on it.'

12

Chandraki had a hard time keeping her marriage a secret from the queen. She felt guilty and scared at the same time. If her mother had been alive, she would have surely known by now. But, in her absence, it was only Lakshmibai who filled up that space in Chandraki's life. 'She's still distraught over the prince's death, and with the Maharaja not keeping well nor taking an active part in the affairs of the kingdom, the Maharani has enough troubles hounding her from all sides. I'll wait for a while before I tell her about Jaywant,' Chandraki thought to herself. Ever since that fateful day when she gave herself up to Jaywant, Chandraki had been moving around in a trance. Nothing seemed the same. It was as though everything – the palace, the people in it, the gardens, the flowers, the sky, the birds, animals – had taken on a different hue. She felt that everyone was smiling at her knowingly and that they were all privy to the intimate moments she had shared with Jaywant. She feared that someone would tell the Maharani about her secret marriage. She knew she had to take the queen into confidence. But every time an opportunity presented itself to her, Chandraki hesitated. First weeks and then months passed, but she could not muster the courage to confess to the queen.

Jaywant was getting impatient. 'Have you told the queen about us?'

'The queen is still in mourning,' Chandraki replied.

Jaywant shrugged. 'It's time you introduced me to the Maharani, isn't it? We are man and wife and I want to be allowed inside the palace. It feels extremely odd meeting you on the sly,' he said, agitated by Chandraki's refusal to inform the maharaj about their marriage.

'How does it matter if you don't enter the palace? It's me you come to visit in Jhansee, isn't it?'

'Yes of course. But I want to know more about your life here. I want to know where you live, how you live, and what your queen is like. I want to see the palace, the fort and the throne. After all, this is my sasural.' Jaywant smiled.

But it was a long time before Chandraki could break the news of her marriage to Lakshmibai. And by then everything had changed.

13

Riyaz Khan had been gone for more than four months and when he returned, he wasn't alone. Heera was surprised to see her husband with a young girl in tow, but she didn't ask Riyaz anything about her. She waited for him to tell her the truth instead.

'How is Abbujaan?'

'He's no more, Heera,' Riyaz replied as he washed his hands.

'I'm so sorry to hear that,' said Heera as she embraced Riyaz. She then laid out the food she had cooked for him. She had been laying out meals for him every night hoping that he'd return soon. She had been overjoyed to hear the familiar footsteps in the courtyard. However, she had expected him to be alone.

Mustering up courage and bracing herself for an answer that she already knew, Heera finally asked her husband the inevitable question: 'Who is she?'

'My new begum,' replied Riyaz without meeting her eyes.

Although Heera had known the answer all along, her heart sank when Riyaz uttered those dreaded words. She knew his religion allowed him to keep more than one wife, yet Heera was unable to accept the fact that Riyaz would actually do so. She knew Riyaz loved her more than anyone else in the world. This was their home, their haven, the world that they had built together. How could she allow someone else to enter that world? How could he bring home another wife? A stranger?

Riyaz knew what Heera was thinking. 'I don't love her, Heera. I feel nothing for her. Abbu forced me to marry her. She's his choice, not mine. He wanted me to leave you and marry this wretched girl and stay back in Calcutta. But I refused. When he realized that I will never leave you, he forced me to marry her as he had made a promise to the girl's father. He further convinced me that if I made him break the promise on his deathbed, Allah's wrath will be unleashed upon my entire family. I feared losing you. I feared losing our children. I was scared. Abbu died a day after I married this wretched woman.'

Heera was quiet. Riyaz sensed the agony that was wreaking absolute havoc within her.

'She can never replace you, Heera. As far as I'm concerned, you are my only wife. I can never love anyone else,' he said taking her in his arms and kissing her on her forehead.

'But this other woman is your wife too and she has as much of a right over you as I do, Riyaz. Bring her inside.'

'No, I won't. Let her stay outside. I have nothing to do with her.'

Heera rose and went outside into the courtyard. The girl sat hunched in one corner.

'What is your name?' asked Heera gently. The girl was quiet. Heera repeated her question.

'Noor,' she whispered without looking at Heera.

'Come inside. This is now your home too,' Heera said as she led Noor inside their home that she had so lovingly built for her family over the years. Noor removed Heera's hand from her arm almost immediately and gave her a look that clearly asked her to stay away. Heera was startled at this unexpected behaviour.

'Where is your luggage?' asked Heera. Noor did not reply.

Heera was at a loss. Noor simply refused to respond to anything she said. This was not a good sign. They would be living together and it was necessary to communicate with one another.

Heera was in a dilemma. She was Riyaz's begum, after all. It was her duty as the senior wife to prepare the new bride for the marital bed. It was time Riyaz stepped in. She walked up to the bed and nudged him gently. When he didn't respond, she shook him.

'What is it, Heera?' Riyaz asked indifferently.

'Noor is waiting!'

'For what?' Riyaz turned his back to Heera, a hint of irritation in his voice.

'For you,' Heera offered by way of explanation.

Riyaz opened his eyes wide and sat up on the bed.

'What am I supposed to do with her?' he asked angrily.

'Fulfil your duty as a husband!' said Heera.

Riyaz looked at her, his face hardening. 'Are you a normal woman? You are sending your own husband into the arms of another woman?' Riyaz had raised his voice for the first time in all the years that Heera had known him. 'I'm only *your* husband, Heera,' he said in a tone of finality and rose from the bed in a huff. 'I'm going to meet the king!' He pulled on his angarkha, picked up his sword and strode out of the room.

'Riyaz, stop!' Heera called out to him. 'You can't leave like this. What am I supposed to do?' Riyaz stopped and cast a scornful glance at his new bride who stood by the door. She looked straight into his eyes. He turned away from her in disgust.

'Let her stay in the other room. The one outside the house. I have nothing to do with her.'

As Heera picked up Noor's belongings to keep them in the room outside the house, she felt her arm being twisted from behind. She let out a cry and turned around to find it in Noor's tight grasp.

'Please let go of my arm. What do you want?' Heera pleaded.

'Leave my belongings alone. I'm not going anywhere. You will be the one to stay outside. Do you understand me, you bitch?'

Heera was so shocked that she didn't realize it when Noor kicked her in the stomach and she slumped to the floor.

As the days went by, Heera, who now lived in the room outside her house with her two children, became more and more reticent with Riyaz. And try as he might, Riyaz couldn't bring Heera back into their bedroom. The very sight of Noor would send him into a frenzy. Each time he saw her, he would fly into a fit of rage and lash out at her. The girl would cower under his assault, and the moment Riyaz left the house, Noor would beat Heera. Though heavier than Noor, Heera was no match for the girl's hardened limbs. When Riyaz returned and saw Heera in this condition, he would go back to assaulting Noor. Then one day, Riyaz picked up his sword.

'Stop, Riyaz! You'll kill her!' screamed Heera as she flung herself between them and caught the sword before it could come crashing down on Noor's neck. In the process, the blade of the sword dug deeply into her palm, slashing it and leaving a pool of blood on the floor. Riyaz simply couldn't bear this sight. He threw his sword aside and cried aloud, 'Ya, Allah, have mercy!' He fell to his knees with his hands clenched and turned to Noor.

'What is it that you want, you wretched woman? Why do you hate my Heera so?'

'She can't live in this house. I'll kill myself if you don't throw her out this very second!' Noor shrieked.

'Go ahead, then. Kill yourself. Who cares? But Heera isn't going anywhere. Isn't it enough that she doesn't live here in this room any more?'

'No, it isn't. She has to leave this house along with your children who are absolute pests. Because as long as she is here, you will not consummate our marriage!' screamed Noor, her face red with anger and hatred.

'I don't care what becomes of our marriage. Heera and my children are going nowhere,' Riyaz said firmly. 'You do what you want.'

Things got so bad in Riyaz's house that news of it reached the king, who was quite distressed to receive this information. Riyaz Khan was one of his favourite officers, and his domestic battles could hamper his performance at work. Gangadhar Rao didn't want that. He wanted all of Riyaz's troubles to end at the earliest. He asked the queen to meet Heerabai.

Lakshmibai couldn't get much out of Heera, who was unwilling to speak about her domestic issues. She was shocked at Heerabai's appearance which had deteriorated drastically from what she had seen a few months ago. Lakshmibai prodded, but to no avail. After a while, the queen sent her away and called for Chandraki.

'Do you have any idea what is going on with Heerabai, Chandraki?'

Chandraki nodded and provided the queen with all the details. News of what was happening in Riyaz's life circulated all around the palace and was the source of much gossip and scandal. Disappointed with the events that had taken place in Riyaz Khan's home in the last few months, the queen was upset that she had let such a situation prevail in her kingdom. She had been too wrapped up in her own grief and her husband's deteriorating health.

Lakshmibai summoned Noor who appeared before her, irreverent and haughty.

'Don't you know you can't throw Heerabai, your husband's first wife, out of your house?' Noor kept quiet. Her face was marked with bruises.

'Answer me!' Lakshmibai thundered.

'My husband has not consummated the marriage because of her, Your Majesty. I want a child!' cried Noor.

'It will all happen in good time. You must have patience,' said the queen, her voice turning gentler. 'I'll speak to your husband. But I don't want you to misbehave with Heerabai, do you understand?'

The girl nodded. Lakshmibai then sent for Riyaz.

'Riyaz, you are His Majesty's most trusted and efficient officer. He is already unwell. Please do not trouble him any further. Consummate your marriage with Noor. She wants a child from you!' ordered Maharani Lakshmibai.

Things were quiet for a while before they erupted yet again. Riyaz, by now, was well into his twenties and his marriage to Noor had changed him. He hated her and she hated him. He drank excessively and beat her up regularly. Noor wanted Heera out of his life and Riyaz wouldn't hear of it. One day, Noor consumed a few thorn apple seeds and feigned to die. Heera could not bear this barrage of threats, screams, abuses and Riyaz's drunkenness. She could no longer continue to witness so much violence.

Finally the lava that erupted from the volcano that was Riyaz's marriage to Noor consumed Heerabai's home, her family and Riyaz Khan himself. Heera entered their room to make some food for her children. Noor caught her unawares and kicked her in the stomach. It wasn't long before Heera fell unconscious, her body

unable to bear the trauma. When Riyaz returned soon
after, he found his children crying and Heera lying on the
floor. Noor was sitting on the bed when Riyaz walked in.

'What did you do to her?' he growled. Noor looked up
at him and shrugged.

He dragged her out of the bed, pinned her to the wall
and drew his sword.'

'Today I will kill you. No one can save you.'

Heera opened her eyes when she heard Riyaz's voice
and found that he was about to slash Noor's throat.

'Riyaz, I beg you. Show some mercy. Don't kill her. For
Allah's sake, for my sake, leave her.'

Riyaz turned around to find Heera slowly rising from
the ground with great effort. Something withered inside
him and the naked sword fell from his hands. He strode
out of the room just as he had walked in a few moments
ago. Heera looked at his receding figure wistfully. She
picked up her son. Her daughter sat hunched outside in
the courtyard. Heera signalled to her.

~

Riyaz returned late that night. When he entered the house
he found that peace had been restored. The floor had been
swept and all stains of food had been removed. It was neat
and tidy. Noor sat in front of the mirror, tying her hair.
His heart revolted at the sight of her. He looked around.
There was no sign of Heera or the children.

'Where is Heera? Where are my children?' he bellowed,
seizing Noor roughly by the arm.

'How do I know? I'm not their keeper,' she replied casually as she continued to tend to her hair. Riyaz knew there was no point in asking her any further questions. He pushed her away and went looking for Heera. He soon realized it was futile. She was gone.

Heera never returned. Riyaz found out she was living on the outskirts of Jhansee with their children. He began visiting her regularly. Heera protested and told him not to come.

'Leave us alone, Riyaz!' pleaded Heera.

'How can I? You are my family. How can you possibly think I'll survive without you?'

Noor found out that her husband regularly went to meet his first wife, so she went to Heera and insisted that she leave Jhansee at once.

'If you don't leave Jhansee by dawn, I'll poison the love of your life. If I can't have him neither can you!'

Fed up, Heera left Jhansee and returned to Calcutta with her children. Riyaz never saw her again.

He took out his anger on Noor and one night, nearly beat her to death after which Riyaz left the house only to return much later in an inebriated state. On entering his house, he saw Noor sitting by the window, mumbling to herself, oblivious to his arrival. He was about to undress when he saw a young girl standing in one corner of the room, holding a grindstone. He was taken aback, not expecting to find a stranger in his house at this hour.

'Who are you?' he asked angrily.

'Mohsina,' the woman murmured.

'What are you doing in my house?'

'I have come to see my sister.'

The real reason was, of course, quite different. Noor's father had sent his younger daughter, Mohsina, to Jhansee assuming that his son-in-law had considerable influence in the court and that he would be able to find a suitable groom for her.

Riyaz was speechless. He walked up to Mohsina and hissed, 'Get out!'

But the girl refused to move. Riyaz walked up to Noor and pulled her off the bed.

'If you and your sister don't leave now, I will kill both of you,' he hollered. Noor did not respond. She stared at him blankly and continued mumbling to herself. Riyaz was beside himself with rage. He pulled Noor by her hair and dragged her across the room.

'Was one of you not enough that another member from your family has been shoved into my life? You bashed up my Heera, nearly killed my children, and threw them out of the house. I will never be able to see the one person I love more than life itself. And now you expect me to harbour your filthy brood in my house?' He punched Noor hard on the nose. She started bleeding.

'Don't hit her, you scoundrel!' Mohsina came charging at him with the grindstone. Riyaz caught her hand in time and trapped her in his tight grip. She struggled frantically. He overpowered Mohsina with ease and managed to grab the stone from her. The moment he let go of her hand Mohsina clawed at his face. Riyaz was momentarily stunned.

Then he stepped forward. 'If you try that again with me, I'll shred you to pieces,' he growled and squeezed her hand tightly. She tried to break free from his iron grip but couldn't. She struggled like a trapped animal, and in the scuffle, his hand swept over her young body. Riyaz couldn't hold himself back. Before he knew it, he had thrown her on the ground and raped her. He then stormed out of the house leaving an unconscious Mohsina lying on the floor.

~

'Maharaj ki jai ho,' the guard called out. 'Riyaz Khan wants an audience, Your Majesty!'

The king who, following the death of his son, was no longer interested in the matters of his kingdom, sat up the moment he heard Riyaz's name. He was extremely fond of Riyaz. He was one of his best men. It was true that of late the man had been a shadow of his former self, yet he still possessed the drive and efficiency required of an able soldier. The king knew all about the trouble brewing in his life. He also knew that Riyaz's beloved wife, Heerabai, had left him a while ago, taking with her their children. His family. Yet the man never failed in his duties and never gave the king any cause for complaint.

'Send him in!'

Riyaz Khan entered the chamber slowly, his head hanging low.

'Maharaj ka iqbal buland ho!' he said as he offered his salaam.

'What brings you here, Riyaz?' The king instantly knew that all was not well. Riyaz Khan, in the six years that he had been here, had rarely ever taken the liberty of meeting the king in his chamber.

'I have committed a crime, Your Majesty!'

Riyaz narrated all that had happened.

Maharaj Gangadhar Rao was shocked. He gave Riyaz a stern warning. He also told him that he would be imprisoned for any further violence. Riyaz begged for mercy. He pleaded that he was ready to atone for it. The king decided to give him one last chance. He ordered Riyaz to marry Mohsina as well and look after both sisters for the rest of his life.

Riyaz was left with no choice. He married Mohsina. It was just as well, as he had impregnated her, and in time she gave birth to a daughter. Noor never really recovered from the trauma of the marriage, and over a period of time, lost her sanity.

Frustrated with his life, Riyaz was pushed more and more into that world of abysmal darkness from which he never returned. One offence led to another and he began treating women as objects to satiate his lust for revenge. He had never once looked at another woman while he was with Heera. But she was taken away from him, for no fault of hers, or his. He swore he wouldn't forgive Allah for as long as he lived. Occasionally he would remember Heera and his children, and his heart would grow tender. But upon realizing he would never again see them (Heera had made him promise never to seek her out as long as she was alive), his heart would harden once again.

While Noor remained oblivious to their present condition, accepting Riyaz's violence as a daily occurrence,

Mohsina lived in constant terror. She knew Riyaz hated her and her child. She would try her best to keep herself and her daughter out of his way. But one day, when she couldn't bear his blows any more, she sought an audience with Maharani Lakshmibai and informed her about her situation.

'He is inhuman and cruel. He has ruined our lives. Please help us, Maharani, or he'll kill us!' cried Mohsina, cradling her daughter in her arms.

Lakshmibai was furious. She was well aware of all that had happened in his life, and there had been a time when she actually sympathized with him. But rumours about how he behaved, not just with his own wives, but other women in the zenana, had begun to disturb her. She would have women, from within the palace and outside, come to her every now and then with complaints against him.

'Riyaz Khan called me to his room and then beat me up, Maharani!'

'He came to our kotha to watch a mujra. In the middle of it, he got up and started brandishing his sword. He hurled abuses at us and said we were terrible dancers. He was drunk. When our madam objected, he threw the contents of his glass at her face and stormed out.'

It was not just the women who were fed up with him. Shopkeepers and people on the streets also put forth their grievances.

'He came to my shop to buy a khet and began to haggle about the price. He started abusing me and then tore up the piece of clothing and refused to compensate for it,' groaned a cloth merchant.

Even the mullah was not spared. 'I saw Riyaz Khan pass by the mosque yesterday. When I asked him why he had stopped coming to the mosque to offer namaz, he told me to mind my own business. He even said there is no Allah, and even if there was one, he didn't believe in him. That's outright blasphemous, Your Majesty!'

'You insulted the mullah?' Maharani Lakshmibai asked Riyaz.

'Your Majesty, my religious practices are my business. Who is he to question me about my faith?'

'Since you have been a devout Muslim throughout your life, it's only natural that the mullah wanted to know why you're not offering prayers any more.'

'Pardon me, but that's my business, Your Majesty!'

The queen sighed. There was no point aruging any further.

As days passed, complaints continued to pour in. Lakshmibai was fed up with the daily torrent of accusations heaped on Riyaz Khan. She summoned Riyaz once again and warned him that any more transgressions against his wives or other women of the zenana would warrant disastrous consequences for him.

Riyaz, who had never liked the queen as she frequently pointed out his offences to the king, writhed in anger. He resented her growing power. But there was nothing he could do. He took out his frustrations on Mohsina, as Noor no longer offered any resistance. His entire being was filled with so much hatred against the two sisters that their very presence would drive him into fits of uncontrolled rage. He could never forgive them for what they had done to

Heera, the only woman he had ever loved. But she was no longer with him. A world without Heera was abysmal. It was a world without love. There was no reason for him to be good any more.

So, despite the queen's warnings, nothing changed in his house, and Riyaz's savagery continued, unabated and undisputed.

Lakshmibai summoned Riyaz to court one day. When Riyaz walked into the hall, he found Lakshmibai on the throne instead of the king. He knew instantly that things would be unpleasant.

'Riyaz Khan! You are much loved by my husband, and you've been an exemplary officer. You can handle any military offensive with the utmost precision and can carry out your duties quite efficiently. We are indeed proud to have you as one of the top officers of our army. The queen paused briefly and then continued, 'However, your domestic matters are a mess and it is evident to all that you are incapable of taking care of your own family and cannot be trusted to look after it. You have failed as a man whose primary duty is to be a responsible husband and father. A man who cannot love and respect his own women cannot be expected to defend the honour of others.'

Riyaz Khan stood listening to the queen pass her judgement on his life.

'I, therefore, order you to send your wives and daughter back to their parental home. You cannot be trusted with their well-being.' She turned to one of her ministers and said, 'Please ensure that Riyaz Khan's family is sent back safely to Calcutta.'

The moment Riyaz walked out of the durbar, he was accosted by two of his fellow comrades.

'Riyaz miyan, is this really true? You, who are in charge of 200 men, cannot handle two women? Come on! You shame us, you bring shame to our entire lot!' The men who had by now been joined by several others guffawed and jeered at him. The news had spread like wildfire. Many who had envied Riyaz's swift rise up the ranks and his considerable influence over the king were delighted to see him fall from grace. This was the moment they had been looking for and they tore his character and dignity to shreds with great fervour. Riyaz didn't say a word and walked off towards his house.

The next few days were quite terrifying for Riyaz. Wherever he went, men laughed at him and mocked him. Even the women didn't spare him. The humiliation in the open durbar followed by the sneers and jibes seared through his chest. And what hurt Riyaz more than anything was the fact that the king didn't say a single word in his defence. All those years of loyalty and sincerity with which he had served the king, the royal family and the kingdom were simply washed away in one stroke by the merciless words of Maharani Lakshmibai.

Riyaz, though relieved with the departure of Noor, Mohsina and her daughter, could not forget how the Maharani had rebuked him in front of everyone and then sent his wives back to Calcutta. His friends had jeered at him, taunting him with remarks that questioned his very manhood and made him believe that he was incapable of looking after his family. This humiliation proved to be the ultimate blow. The queen had taken away the one thing he had cherished the most and guarded with his life – his honour.

'I will never forgive you, Maharani Lakshmibai! Never!' he cursed. Nothing else mattered. 'I will show everyone just how much of a man I am,' he thought bitterly. His misadventures with the women in the zenana increased. It was true that he was terribly attractive and the women fought for his attention. But his behaviour towards them sent many crying to Maharani Lakshmibai over and over again.

One day, Lakshmibai asked to meet with Riyaz Khan.

'Riyaz Khan, leave the women of the palace alone,' she commanded.

'But they throw themselves at me, Your Majesty. What can I do?' replied Riyaz, smirking ever so slightly.

'Will you marry these women?'

'How many women will I marry, Maharani Sahiba?' Riyaz asked, feigning innocence. 'I can't possibly marry all of them.'

'He has changed so much,' thought the queen to herself. 'He used to be such a fine man – a loving husband, a doting father, a devout Muslim. Oh, Heerabai, I wish I could bring you back,' thought Lakshmibai.

But her words betrayed no emotion when she turned to Riyaz and said, 'That is up to you, Riyaz. What you want doesn't count when you ravage the modesty of young women,' said the queen, her voice raised and trembling with anger.

Riyaz Khan paid no heed to the queen's warnings. This infuriated Chandraki, but she could do nothing about it.

She knew that rest assured, she would never let Riyaz get his hands on her. She was no stranger to the ways of Riyaz Khan. Many of her friends had come crying to her when spurned or abused by him.

'He satiates his lust and then dumps them,' she complained to Lakshmibai on several occasions. 'Please do something about him, Maharani.'

Lakshmibai looked at Chandraki enquiringly. 'Has he ever misbehaved with you, Chandraki?'

Startled, Chandraki looked up at the queen. She bowed her head. 'No,' she said, 'never,' she added in a whisper.

14

While Riyaz Khan's violations increased by the day, Maharani Lakshmibai gradually started taking over the reins of the kingdom from her husband, Maharaja Gangadhar Rao. With each passing day, the king's health deteriorated and it was no secret that he didn't have much time left on earth. He spent most of his time resting in his chamber while Lakshmibai tended to matters of the state. She never tired of listening to people even if it demanded endless patience from her. There were times when the rest of the people in the courtroom would begin to get fidgety, but not a single crease could be seen on Lakshmibai's forehead, who sat erect and bright-eyed. She was well aware that her troubles were just beginning but she braced herself for whatever lay ahead, her demeanour stoic and resolute. There was a niggling fear though and she spoke to her husband about it.

'The Company Bahadur has sent two new officers, Maharaj. Why are they increasing their strength? I hear

Lord Dalhousie is eyeing all the kingdoms without an heir,'
said Lakshmibai, her voice laced with concern.

The king was quiet. He knew what that meant. He had
been thinking about it. It was time he took a decision. He
was exhausted. But he reassured his wife, nonetheless.

'Don't worry, Lakshmi. I have thought of something.
You will soon know.'

~

The rumble of British intrusions into the kingdom of
Jhansee became louder with every passing day. More and
more firanghees could now be seen in the streets of Jhansee.
There was a kind of tautness in the air that everyone felt.
The lazy indolence of a sleepy kingdom was slowly being
replaced by a nervous energy that often rises from an
unknown fear. There were chilling rumours that Lord
Dalhousie, the Governor General of India, was annexing
various kingdoms under the Doctrine of Lapse. Satara,
Jaitpur and Sambalpur had been already annexed three
years ago. Every king of every principality in the country
was now living under the shadow of uncertainty. Who
would be next?

Maharani Lakshmibai refused to let her apprehensions
hinder the execution of her royal duties or create obsctacles
in the daily lives of her subjects. In a bid to reinforce the
appearance of normalcy within the kingdom, she ensured
that everything functioned the way it had been functioning
all along.

It was the year 1853. It was also more than a year since

the heir to the throne of Jhansee had died. Lakshmibai knew that with the king bedridden, she could not afford to grieve for much longer. She began to take renewed interest in all events. Each festival was celebrated with much gusto. The Dussehra festivities had just ended. Preparations for Deepavali had now commenced. The queen decided to visit the Mahalakshmi temple in the town to check if all was well. She sent for Chandraki.

'Get the palanquin ready. And send word to the zenana that we are going to the temple.'

It was a hot day and the small procession set out for the temple that stood outside the fort. As the entourage proceeded towards it, Chandraki broke away from the group and headed towards the small market along the border of the temple premises. The market was lined with shops selling flowers, incense and various commodities required for performing the puja. Chandraki bought flowers and garlands, and as she was walking away from the shop, she overheard a male voice that stopped her in her tracks. She turned around to catch a flash of red disappear behind a shop. Chandraki pulled her veil over her face and withdrew into an empty, dilapidated shed beside her. She stood waiting but couldn't see anything.

'Has anyone seen you come here?' a firanghee's voice rang out. Chandraki flattened herself against the wall of the shed.

'No, sahib, I'm too clever for that.'

'Okay, okay, don't try to be smart with me,' the firanghee replied gruffly. 'Now tell me, why did you call me here?'

'I have news to give, big news,' the Indian replied in

Hindi. 'Bada khabar, sahib!' That voice. It was very familiar. Chandraki was sure she had heard it before.

'Kya khabar? What news? Jaldi bolo, quick!'

'The Maharaj is dying. But before that happens, he plans to adopt a son who will be the heir to the throne.'

Chandraki heard a sharp intake of breath.

'Pukka khabar? Are you sure?'

'Ji sahib, bilkul. He is going to adopt Anand Rao, a distant relative of his.'

'When?'

'Pata nahin. But it will be soon. You will have to act fast.'

Chandraki didn't wait to hear anything else. She tiptoed to the edge of the wall and peeped just in time to see the firanghee hand over a small purse to the other man who wasn't as visible. The Indian declined to take it.

'I will convey the news to Major Malcolm. We meet again next week, same time, same place. If there is any new development, let me know,' Chandraki heard the firanghee say.

'Ji sahib. I must go now.'

Chandraki froze. That voice! 'Oh my God! It is Riyaz Khan!'

Her heart was beating so loudly that she was sure everyone around could hear it. Her lips were set into a thin line and her eyes flashed with anger. 'I should have known it. The brute has the gall to sell Jhansee to these firanghees! 'Riyaz Khan, I will make sure you're punished for this, you traitor,' she growled.

Chandraki joined the queen's retinue after a quick darshan of the goddess at the temple. Her mind was in a state of chaos, her heart was a flood of swirling emotions. She felt shocked, confused, horrified and helpless. But above all she was angry. How could someone betray the very person who had offered him refuge?

'How could you do this to our Jhansee, Riyaz Khan?' she cried as she ran all the way back to the palace, ahead of the small procession, and didn't stop till she reached. *'You will have to act fast.'* Isn't that what Riyaz Khan had told the firanghee?

What were the firanghees planning? Why did Riyaz ask the sahib to act fast? Once she reached the palace, Chandraki waited at the entrance of the queen's quarters. The small procession had not yet reached the palace. She could hardly control herself. 'Should I inform the Maharaja straight away?' she wondered but eventually decided against it. It was better to inform the Maharani who would know what measures to take. Chandraki rubbed her palms and stomped her feet impatiently. How long would it be before the queen reached?

After what seemed an interminable wait the queen finally arrived. As she entered her chamber Chandraki followed. The queen stopped and looked at her.

'I would like to be left alone for a while, Chandraki. Don't come in now. Ekaant!' she said and attempted to draw the curtains. Chandraki was silent but did not move. Lakshmibai frowned, annoyed at her stubbornness.

'Is there anything you want, Chandraki?' the queen asked somewhat brusquely, her voice spiked with irritation. Ever since she had lost her baby, Lakshmibai, otherwise of a most cheerful disposition, had been short of patience and almost always wanted to be left alone.

'Yes, Your Majesty! I want a word with you. It's very, very important.' The queen resigned and allow her into the room. She knew that Chandraki wasn't an obtrusive person, so this had to be something really serious.

'Fine! Tell me. But make it brief as I want to rest,' she said impatiently.

Chandraki nodded. 'Your Majesty, pardon me for this intrusion, but what I have to tell you is of utmost importance for Jhansee! While you were at the temple, I had gone to a shop to pick up flowers. I overheard Riyaz Khan talking to a firanghee. He informed the English sahib that the Maharaja is planning to adopt Anand Rao and urged him to act fast.' Chandraki narrated the whole conversation without pausing for breath. The queen's expression changed from one of irritation to shock and then to fear in a matter of seconds. She slumped on to the bed, her head in her palms.

'I know what they are talking about, Chandraki. Major Ellis had given the Maharaja hints about such a situation arising. That's when Maharaja took the decision to adopt Anand.'

'Hints about what?' Chandraki asked.

The queen did not reply. Instead, she said to Chandraki, 'Send the Maharaja a message that I want to meet him immediately.'

Chandraki knew the information she had provided required urgent addressal. She ran out of the room, but suddenly stopped and returned to the queen's bedchamber. 'Maharani!'

The queen looked up. Her face was drained of colour. 'Yes?'

'So what will you do with Riyaz Khan?'

For a moment, the queen didn't know what to say. Then in a tired voice, she replied, 'I don't know about Riyaz Khan. In fact, right now, I can't think of anything else. I just want to see the Maharaja.' She paused briefly and then said, 'Chandraki.'

Chandraki stopped at the door and turned around to face the queen.

'Thank you! Once again!' Lakshmibai smiled, but her eyes were sad.

15

There had been hushed whispers since the little prince's death that the king of Jhansee had lived his last summer. Doctors and vaids had been summoned from neighbouring kingdoms, and even the British physician who had come all the way from Cawnpore saw no hope of his recovery. It was a matter of days, perhaps weeks, before the king would breathe his last, doctors told the family.

Gangadhar Rao knew it himself. His heart was heavy, his mind was murky. The events of the past few months had taken a toll on him.

'Maharaj ki jai! Your Majesty, the queen requests an audience with you,' the dasi announced.

Lying on his bed, the ailing king nodded weakly and then with great effort, sat up as Lakshmibai walked in.

'Why is the room so dark? I can't see anything,' the queen said, signalling a dasi to draw back the curtains. Two women rushed to pull back the heavy brocade drapes that had enveloped the king's chamber in a shroud of gloom and despair. Sunlight streamed into the unwelcoming room, dispelling the shadows of impending sorrow. Gangadhar Rao shielded his eyes from the sudden brilliance of light that dazzled him.

Lakshmibai looked at her husband's gaunt frame and his tired eyes. She sat down on the bed beside him. Everything that she loved and cherished was being taken away from her – her son, her husband and now her Jhansee. She wondered how to break the news to her husband.

'Maharaj, I have something to tell you,' she mumbled.

Gangadhar Rao did not look at her. After what seemed to be an endless pause, he whispered. 'Is it good news or bad?' He was having difficulty speaking of late.

Lakshmibai was quiet. She took his withered hands in her own. Tears welled up in her otherwise fierce eyes.

'Bad news, I'm afraid.' She choked on her words.

'It's only bad news these days, isn't it?' said Gangadhar Rao matter-of-factly. 'Tell me. I'm ready for anything. What could be worse than losing my little prince.'

'The Company Sarkar is planning to take over Jhansee,' the queen replied quietly.

A shudder coursed through the wasted body of the once robust and powerful king, and his clasp around his wife's hands stiffened. Lakshmibai covered his hands with hers.

'I think it's time, Maharaj!' she whispered.

Gangadhar Rao didn't reply immediately. He stared vacantly at the walls of the room, inlaid with bold and bright images of various gods slaying the asuras. He turned his head slowly and was greeted by dancing peacocks and elaborate floral motifs. No matter where he looked, these figures leapt at him from all around and were slowly closing in and seemed to be mocking him. They seemed to laugh at him, ridicule him, even threaten him. He could not bear the assault and shut his eyes.

Tears rolled down Lakshmibai's cheeks as she looked at her husband's crumpled visage. He was just a shadow of the man he had been in the past. She squeezed his hand.

'Your Majesty, I think we need to act fast,' she said. She needed to steer his thoughts away from the despair that had engulfed him. 'Should I send out the message?'

Gangadhar Rao, though frail, stood up from his bed with considerable effort and called for his attendant.

'Send a message to both Major Ellis and his subordinate Captain Martin to present themselves before me tomorrow morning. I have some announcements to make,' he said firmly and dismissed the attendant with a wave of his hand. He was still in command, weak, broken, but still the reigning king of Jhansee. And he would make sure the British knew that and acknowledged it. Lakshmibai smiled. Things will change, she told herself.

With the arrival of a fresh dawn, the king and queen of Jhansee dressed up for a very important announcement that was bound to change their lives. Although weak, the king still made it to the durbar.

'Good morning, Your Highness!' Major Ellis greeted the king of Jhansee, raising his hand in a salute. 'We are sorry to hear of your ill health. Is there anything we could do, perhaps?'

'In fact, you can,' replied Gangadhar Rao in a raspy tone.

The two British officers stood with their heads bowed, waiting for the king to drop the bombshell.

Turning to his minister, the Maharaja said, 'Bring the boy in.'

Maharani Lakshmibai smiled from behind the purdah. There was a pregnant silence in the durbar.

The five-year-old boy walked into the lavish durbar, escorted by two men. A few days ago he had been whisked away from his home and brought to Jhansee. They woke him up today, even before the sun rose, bathed him in the cold, dressed him up, and brought him before the king. He was missing his mother and about to burst into tears when the king's voice rang out, piercing the stillness of the room. The little boy trembled as he was suddenly lifted and placed on Maharaj Gangadhar Rao's lap.

'Major Ellis and Captain Martin, let me introduce my son, Anand Rao, to you,' the king said. And then, addressing the rest of the people, Gangadhar Rao Newalkar, the king of Jhansee, said in a clear, firm voice, 'My wife Maharani Lakshmibai and I have adopted my relative's son, Anand Rao, as our son. I, therefore, officially declare him my legal heir with immediate effect. He will henceforth carry the name Damodar Rao, the same as our own son. He will be acknowledged as next in line for the throne of Jhansee and lay claim to all that belongs to me. Recognize your future king, the future king of Jhansee.' He paused. Talking was straining him and he was almost panting by now.

He took a deep breath and continued. 'In the event

of my death, and until the time my son grows up, the government of Jhansee will be passed on to my wife and the queen, Maharani Lakshmibai, and all imperial matters will be conducted and dispensed by her until her death. In effect, she will be your ruler.' Then turning to the two British officers, Gangadhar Rao said, 'You will convey this to the Company Sarkar.'

He signalled to one of his ministers who handed the officers the letter that bore the contents of the announcement, secured with the royal seal.

And with that the king of Jhansee dismissed the court and stepped down from the throne. As he slowly walked out of the durbar hall, everyone rose to the cries of 'Jhansee naresh ki jai! Maharani Lakshmibai ki jai! Yuvraj Damodar Rao ki jai!'

The king knew that things were about to change, but unlike his queen, he was not too optimistic.

'I think you should rest now, Your Majesty!' Lakshmibai said, pulling the covers over her husband as he settled back in his bed. The events of the morning had been too much for him to bear and he was exhausted with the effort.

'Lakshmi, take care of my Jhansee and of Damodar Rao. Don't trust the firanghees,' Gangadhar Rao mumbled.

'Don't worry, Maharaj! I will protect both till my last breath – our son and the kingdom. I will never give up my Jhansee! Main apni Jhansee nahi doongi!'

The king smiled weakly as his wife took his leave. He knew he had entrusted his kingdom in the right hands. In the eleven years that they had been married, he had watched his bride transform from an impulsive and brash teenager to a strong and brave woman who loved Jhansee and its people as much as he did. 'Perhaps, even more than I do,' the king thought to himself as he looked on his wife with immense affection.

Lakshmibai retired to her room for the day and dismissed her attendants. She wanted to be alone. There was much agony in her heart regarding the condition of her husband. But mingled with it was also a strange kind of joy that she couldn't identify. Was it because she was once again a mother? It was true that the newly anointed prince wasn't her biological son, but she would experience the joys of motherhood in raising him. She suddenly desired to see her son and clapped her hands but then remembered that she had dismissed all attendants.

'Maharani ki jai!' Chandraki stood before the queen with folded hands.

Surprised, Lakshmibai stammered. 'Wh–what are you doing here? I thought I asked everyone to go away!'

'I decided to wait as I thought you may need something, Maharani! Is there anything you want?'

Lakshmibai smiled. How did this girl always anticipate her needs? 'Where is my son?'

'I'll send him to you, Your Majesty!'

Lakshmibai retired to her room and had barely sat down when Chandraki was back with the prince in tow. Damodar Rao folded his little hands before his new mother in a gesture of salutation.

'Come here, my son!' Lakshmibai signalled to him to come and sit on her lap.

The prince hesitated. Although he was too small to

acknowledge the change in his fortune, he was aware that this lady who was calling him her son was an important person. Simply because she wore lots of jewellery, had a lot of servants and lived in a palace. She was much more important than his own mother. He was scared to disobey her, so he walked up to her slowly. Lakshmibai lifted him on to her lap.

'I'm your mother, you need not be afraid of me,' she said as she caressed his little head.

Chandraki stood in the far corner of the room watching the mother and son. Her eyes were moist. She knew just how much the queen had suffered when her own son had died a year ago. Moreover, the firanghees planned to take over the kingdom. What if the Maharani was asked to leave the palace? She shuddered at the thought. She was relieved that the king had decided to adopt this boy. The queen could be a mother again. And the throne of Jhansee was secured with a male heir. She was happy for the queen. With that thought, she quietly left the room, unnoticed by Lakshmibai.

But there was one niggling thought that kept creeping in – what would happen to Riyaz Khan? She was desperate to ask the queen, but decided against it. This wasn't the right time, she thought. It was an important day in the queen's life, a moment of joy, and she didn't want to spoil it by talk of Riyaz Khan. She was sure he would be punished. The penalty for treachery was always severe. If not killed, he would certainly be thrown out of Jhansee, Chandraki hoped. She could almost see him being dragged across the streets of Jhansee, bound in chains, begging for mercy. It was a scene that Chandraki fantasized about almost every day. Yet, as the scene played out in her mind's eye, she was momentarily shaken. It was not easy to imagine Riyaz Khan in such a state, a man as powerful as him. What a shame it would be, what a pity that Jhansee would lose one of its bravest soldiers in such a manner.

Chandraki tossed and turned through the night and eventually drifted into uneasy sleep. But Riyaz Khan haunted her even in her dreams. She dreamt that he was riding away on a horse, throwing up a cloud of dust as it sped past the rocky terrain and she was with him, bound in chains. She woke up with a start, and despite the chill of the November night, beads of perspiration had collected on her forehead and upper lip. Sitting up, she looked around nervously. Her eyes took some time to adjust to the darkness, and slowly, in the faint light of the dawn, she could make out the silhouettes of the objects in the room. There was no one else around her.

The temple bells pierced the morning stillness and the crisp air carried the strains of a bhajan into her room. Wiping the perspiration off her forehead and wrapping her stole around her, she looked out of the window. Across the courtyard, soldiers were marching a man towards the prison cells. She soon realized it was Riyaz Khan being taken away. Chandraki ran out of her room and down the narrow flight of stairs that led to the central courtyard. A group of people was slowly gathering to witness the spectacle of a senior army officer being taken away as a prisoner.

'What has happened?' Chandraki asked one of the men.

'Maharaj has given orders to imprison Riyaz Khan.
Gaddar nikla!'

Chandraki couldn't believe her ears. This was the news
she had been waiting for. She almost jumped with joy and
clapped her hands but refrained from doing so when she
realized people were staring at her. She slid past them to
confront Riyaz Khan just as they reached the flight of stairs
that ran down to the prison cells located underground.
Pushing her way through the guards, she came face to
face with Riyaz.

'So?' she asked, trying to catch her breath. 'What
will you do now? Join the East India Company?' She
sniggered.

Riyaz looked at her. As usual, he felt uncomfortable.
They had never exchanged a word, yet he felt she could see
right through him. It was as though he stood naked before
her. He knew she was somehow responsible for this state
of his. He averted his gaze and tried to walk past her, but
she blocked his way.

'Move,' one of the guards guffawed. Reluctantly,
Chandraki stepped aside and watched him being led away.
She felt a strange sense of foreboding. Something told her
this wasn't the last time she would see him.

But she had no time to brood over her gloomy thoughts.
A loud wail went up, and within minutes the palace had
erupted into a scene of bedlam and mayhem. There
was complete pandemonium all over. People rushed out
from their quarters, screaming and wailing. Cries of 'The
king is dead! Maharaj nahin rahe!' rang out. Chandraki

stopped in her tracks, caught in the centre of all the commotion.

'The Maharani! I need to be with her,' thought Chandraki and rushed towards the queen's chamber. But there was no one there and the curtains were drawn. Only one attendant waited outside.

'Is the queen inside?' Chandraki asked.

The girl shook her head. 'Maharani is with Maharaj in his room,' she replied.

Chandraki rushed to the king's chamber. This was a place she rarely visited and she hesitated before entering.

'Can I go in?' she asked one of the guards posted outside.

'The Maharani has ordered that no one should be allowed to enter the room.'

'When did Maharaj die?'

'About half an hour ago,' the guard replied.

Chandraki stood outside the room not knowing what to do. It would not be appropriate to disturb the queen in her moment of grief. But what if she needed something?

'Is anyone else in the room?'

'Only the prince,' the man replied. Chandraki knew that it would not be long before the rest of the Newalkar clan would arrive to offer false sympathy to the queen. There would be an ugly scramble among these relatives to prove their loyalty to the crown, eager to seek favour with the queen. There would now be a sudden rise in the number of claimants to the throne. Each would swear that he was the direct descendant of the king and had the right to succession more than the next. Poor Maharani, Chandraki thought. How would she be able to ward off

such people? But she knew that Lakshmibai was no fool
and was extremely brave. But she was also extremely alone.

It was a while before the queen emerged from the
chamber. She signalled to the guards.

'Call the durbar! I have to announce His Majesty's
death. Also, start making preparations for Maharaj's
funeral.' She pulled her veil across her face and walked
towards her own chamber on the first floor. There was
nothing in her gait that showed she had just turned a
widow at twenty-five, and that her whole world had
collapsed. She not only had a five-year-old son to raise
but also an entire kingdom to take care of and thousands
of lives for whose welfare she alone was responsible. Or,
that the Company Sarkar was already knocking at her door
and that she was completely alone.

Maharani Lakshmibai appeared in court a few hours
later to officially announce the death of the king of Jhansee.

'From this moment onwards, I am your queen, your
ruler, and all decisions regarding the administration of
the kingdom will be taken by me with immediate effect.'
Instantly, shouts arose across the durbar hall that echoed
with cries of 'Maharani Lakshmibai ki jai! Maharani
Lakshmibai ki jai! Yuvraj Damodar Rao ki jai!'

The assembly of people gathered outside the durbar hall
went berserk. Word had spread that Maharani Lakshmibai
was now the new ruler of Jhansee. People thronged the
palace gates, and it became a huge task to hold back the
jubilant crowd from breaking into the palace. The shadow
of gloom that had been cast over the kingdom following the

king's death was suddenly dispelled with the heartwarming news that it was their own Queen Lakshmibai who would now rule the kingdom. Joyous cries filled the air. Trumpets blew and dhols thundered as emissaries set out with news of the turn of events.

Chandraki too rejoiced. She stood beside the queen holding the prince's hand. She had been unable to meet the queen after the king's death. And now, here she was, standing beside the throne, watching her queen address the sabha. What a momentous occasion to be a part of! Yes, things had changed in a matter of hours, but with the Maharani on the throne, everything would soon be all right, and things would go back to normal. What Chandraki didn't know was that things had changed indeed, but nothing would ever be normal again.

Maharaj Gangadhar Rao was cremated later in the day and with that the fate of Jhansee was sealed. The queen observed the mandatory rituals, all but one.

'I will not shave my head,' she told Chandraki.

16

The king's death left Lakshmibai devastated. She wasn't prepared for such a tragedy right after having lost her child. But not one to sit and mourn while her kingdom passed into the hands of the firanghees, Lakshmibai spurred into action. Among the first few things that she did on taking over as the ruler of Jhansee was complete one task that the king had left unfinished. She banished Riyaz Khan from Jhansee without further ado.

Chandraki was surprised. 'Why this sudden decision, Your Majesty?' she asked the queen. 'He's already behind bars, isn't he?'

'Yes, he is. That was an interim measure that His Majesty took in a hurry. Riyaz Khan is a dangerous man. He will not sit still for long. He will definitely look for ways to get out of prison, and if he succeeds, he can do anything. And now that Maharaj is no longer alive, we are even more vulnerable. I don't want a man like him to be on the loose. He has already betrayed us, and he will not shy away from inflicting further damage.'

'Isn't he aware that the punishment for betrayal is death?'

'You know Maharaj has banned capital punishment except in extreme cases, and though his offence *is* the ultimate one, I had given my word to Heerabai that I will spare his life.'

'But he has to fear the consequences of betrayal.'

'Riyaz Khan has no fear of consequences because he has nothing left to lose. And when a man has nothing left to lose, he can be very dangerous,' Lakshmibai said quietly.

Stripped of his uniform, weapons and all his belongings, Riyaz Mohammad Bashir Khan was left outside the Jhansee border to fend for himself. With his horse gone, he had no choice but to walk. He hung around the border for half a day, wondering where to go, and despite having three wives and three children, Riyaz Khan had no one to turn to when he was banished from Jhansee. He had never bargained for the king to die so soon and for the queen to take over the reins of the kingdom. That was the last thing he had wanted, but since he had no choice, he resigned himself to his fate. Yet, deep within, he nursed a hatred for the queen so severe that he began looking for ways to get her overthrown. But right now, no such opportunity presented itself. For the time being, he decided to go back to his uncle Jabbar in Gwalior.

17

The people of Jhansee loved Maharani Lakshmibai and the few liberties she took even as a widow were either ignored or forgiven by everyone. She would walk into the durbar brisk and confident, flashing her sunny smile. She was neither shy nor diffident. In her bid to take on the guardianship of the state of Jhansee, she had cast away the stereotypical notions of her gender.

But Chandraki was not too happy about it. She was now a familiar figure beside the queen. The queen often shared her worries and problems with her. Chandraki was always around if Lakshmibai needed something to be done, be it running errands, carrying messages, or looking after the prince while the queen addressed matters of the court. She often helped the queen dress up for special events, and on those occasions, Chandraki would insist that Lakshmibai dress more as a queen and less as a widow.

'You have not worn this for a long time, Your Majesty! Wear it today. Let your firanghee guest know how beautiful you are,' Chandraki said as she handed the queen a nose ring studded with pearls and rubies and a singular emerald that hung like a teardrop.

'I can't wear this, Chandraki! Only women whose husbands are alive can wear it.'

Chandraki frowned as she kept the ring back in its box. 'Why not? Is it your fault that the Maharaj died? If you died before him, would he have stopped wearing colourful clothes or jewellery?'

Lakshmibai smiled. 'I haven't invented these customs. Who am I to question them? But I didn't shave my head, did I? Nor do I wear white clothes all the time,' she pointed out to Chandraki.

'Your clothes are hardly colourful. You dress like a man and when you dress like a queen, you wear only white saris. Here is your white sari,' Chandraki said angrily as she shoved a white piece of clothing made from very fine muslin into the queen's hands. Lakshmibai took it from her and kept it away.

'Won't you wear your favourite white sari?' Chandraki mocked.

'Not now,' the queen replied, ignoring the sarcasm. 'There are some military matters that need immediate attention. I will change into the sari when I meet Major Malcolm in the afternoon.'

Lakshmibai strode into the courtroom purposefully, sporting pyjamas, a jacket, her long hair gathered up and covered by a turban, her bejewelled sword dangling by her side. She did not wear any jewels other than a pearl necklace, a diamond ring and diamond bangles around her wrists.

'Kaale Khan, I would like to inspect the armoury tomorrow. Have you drawn up the list for the new rifles that we require?' she asked her commander-in-chief as she sat on the throne.

'Yes, Your Highness. Also, the new consignment for the Beaumont Adams Revolver arrived last evening.'

'Good! I will also visit the stables tomorrow. Nana Sahib has sent two thoroughbreds. I want to take a look at them,' the queen announced. Then turning to Chandraki, she asked, 'What news of the traders, Chandraki? Any more requisitions being made in the name of the firanghee officers?'

'Your Majesty, Lallan Powar, who owns a shop on the eastern side of the city was approached by the thanedar to supply wood to the two regiments that passed through Jhansee in the last few days. The neighbouring shop has been asked to supply weapons to the British troops.' Chandraki drew in her breath sharply.

'Your Highness, the firanghees are fully aware that these vendors are not being paid. Even if some senior officers do pass orders for the payment to be made, the underlings don't hand over the money and pocket it themselves. I spoke to the vendors myself. In disguise, of course.' She smiled, eyes sparkling.

'Good girl, but be careful,' Maharani Lakshmibai warned. 'Send a note to Lieutenant Governor Colvin that I want to meet him at the earliest,' the queen said.

~

Major Colvin hated these meetings with the queen. She always made him feel that he was inefficient and incompetent even if the matter at hand wasn't his fault. He squirmed under the fiery gaze of Maharani Lakshmibai.

'Why are your officers paid so little? The tehsildar gets just 250 rupees a month, but he's expected to maintain a lavish lifestyle as per his position. And the thanedar gets only fifteen to twenty rupees as salary? No wonder they resort to these practices,' Lakshmibai said.

'That's not in my jurisdiction, Your Majesty,' Major Colvin replied somewhat brusquely. 'All this is decided by those sitting in Fort William!'

'But it's my people who are suffering,' she said. There was silence for some time. Major Colvin shifted nervously. He could feel Lakshmibai's piercing gaze on him.

'Since you have been most inefficient in resolving this problem either on purpose or because you've been incompetent, I'm forced to write Lord Hamilton a letter to acquaint him with the situation and the financial losses being faced by my subjects.'

Colvin sighed. He knew the letter would further reinforce Hamilton's belief in his incompetence as an officer, and his days here were numbered. But there was little he could do. In any case, the earlier he left this place, the better it would be for him.

With Riyaz Khan gone, Lakshmibai knew Jhansee had lost one of its best officers. He was capable of executing any task with a force of intent that was most extraordinary. Following Chandraki's tip-off the year before, Riyaz Khan on the king's orders had successfully and ruthlessly put an end to the exploitation of Jhansee's small-time traders and vendors at the hands of the officers of the Company. Most of the officers had been severely reprimanded while Jagat Singh and Sarmad Shah had been removed from office. Even the British officers who had supervised this process had not been spared.

Lakshmibai felt Riyaz Khan's absence all the time. Sadly, there was no one to fill his place. But, not one to sit and cry over her loss, she took over the governance of the state with much gusto. It was evident that the British officers who were directly associated with her were impressed by her confidence as well as her diplomatic skills. Major D.A. Malcolm, the political agent in Gwalior for Rewah and Bundelkhand, forwarded her case to Fort William, the headquarters of the East India Company.

'Maharani Lakshmibai is highly respected and is fully capable of assuming the reins of Jhansee. She has single-handedly stemmed the wave of corruption that had swept across the kingdom and restored to her people what was their right,' he wrote in his letter to Lord Dalhousie. But Malcolm's pleas fell on deaf ears. It seemed that Fort William had made up its mind.

Lakshmibai would attend to the matters of the court regularly and stay up late in the night working out various arguments to support her pleas.

'According to Dalhousie sahib, since Jhansee was once a peshwa stronghold, with the British having taken over the Maratha empire, the Company Sarkar holds supremacy over it,' she said as she held up a letter in her hand in front of her council of ministers. Suddenly she rose from her seat and started pacing up and down the room. Her ministers looked at each other.

'On one hand, Major Malcolm says he thinks I'm capable of ruling the state and has spoken to the Company Sarkar in Calcutta. But he is insisting that we keep a regiment of the Native Infantry and Irregular Cavalry stationed here. He's scared that the zamindars may take advantage of a king's absence,' she said, addressing her council.

'Why? Damodar Rao is the king of Jhansee, isn't he?' quipped one of her ministers. 'Agreed, he is a minor, but you are the ruler until he grows up. Maharaj Gangadhar made that very clear.'

Lakshmibai shook her head. 'That argument is not being accepted by Fort William. Dalhousie says that Damodar Rao is not the biological son of Maharaj!' She clapped her hands. A dasi walked in. Lakshmibai turned to her and said, 'I want to see Mr Lang immediately!' her face set in a firm expression.

'Who is Mr Lang?' one of her ministers asked.

'He's my solicitor.' She grinned.

Lord Dalhousie's reply arrived a few weeks later, turning down Lakshmibai's appeal. He argued that Jhansee was a British creation and could be disposed of by British authority.

'He has cited Sir Charles Metcalfe's ruling in 1837 which says that adoptions are recognized as "regular" if made by ancient hereditary kingdoms of India, but they will be considered "irregular" if the state exists under a paramount power, which in this case, he says, is the

East India Company!' the queen said, her eyes flashing with fury.

'So what do you propose to do now, Your Majesty?'

'The firanghees think they will quote some obscure ruling made decades ago and use it against me? I will quote several more such obscure rulings and treaties and throw it at them. I'm not going to give in,' she said emphatically.

The missives went to and fro between Maharani Lakshmibai and Lord Dalhousie for several months. During this time, the queen continued to sit on the throne with aplomb even as she pushed her appeal with a continuous volley of arguments through a string of letters to Fort William.

~

One morning, in early February 1854, Chandraki went looking for Rani Lakshmibai when she failed to appear in court. Chandraki had decided that it was now time that she told Queen Lakshmibai about Jaywant, who was pushing her to take him to the palace and make him meet the queen. Though she did not want to leave Jhansee, Chandraki could no longer bear to be away from him. She was willing to follow him wherever he went.

But the moment she entered the queen's chamber, she gave up the idea of talking about Jaywant. She found the queen in a rage, pacing back and forth in her room frantically, holding yet another letter in her hand.

'Look at this! Just look at what Dalhousie is saying. He quotes his predecessors, Lord Auckland and Lord

Ellenborough, saying that Maharaj Gangadhar Rao, when entrusted with the kingdom by the British, "ruled it for eleven years, neither very wisely nor very well"! Can you imagine? He is saying that under the Maharaj's rule, Jhansee had been misgoverned, revenues had declined and order was not being maintained. Can you believe this?' She thrust the letter into Chandraki's hands.

'It's a pity you can't read what is in that letter. I'll tell you,' she said, raising her voice and flailing her arms. 'He further says that Jhansee's incorporation within the British territory would greatly benefit the people of the state as it had in the past. And . . . that the construction of roads and railroads in India was was one proof of the benefits of civilization,' she stammered, voice trembling with anger. 'Does he mean we were uncivilized before these firanghees came? Were we savages?'

She banged her fists in anger on the various pieces of furniture she passed as she marched up and down her room.

'I know what the problem is. Dalhousie doesn't like female rulers. Ellis told me that he's old-fashioned and a woman sitting on the throne doesn't agree with his notions of how a woman is supposed to live her life. I'm going to change his way of thinking, just you wait!'

She sat down to draft a letter to Dalhousie, citing examples of how loyal the kings of Jhansee had been to the Company Sarkar, and how equally loyal their representatives had been. She described Jhansee as 'a powerless native state', dependent on the protection of the British.

My late husband devoted his attention to the arts of

peace, not to keeping up even the semblance of a warlike state,' she wrote.

Lakshmibai stopped and thought for some time. Then she picked up her quill once more and wrote deliberately and carefully. Once she finished, she summoned an attendant. 'I want this to be sent to Lord Dalhousie immediately!'

Dalhousie read the letter he had just received and laughed loudly once he finished reading it.

'Queen Lakshmibai is one smart woman. Look what she writes,' he said to the men who were sitting around him in his office in the East India Company headquarters in Fort William. 'Can you believe it? She says, 'Helpless and prostrate, I once more entreat Your Lordship to grant me a hearing ...' Dalhousie read her words aloud. 'Helpless and prostrate? Maharani Lakshmibai? Now that her arguments hold no steam with me, she is using the tool of the helpless widow! This is not going to work, my dear queen,' snorted Dalhousie.

His rejection of her plea came as a slap to Lakshmibai. Chandraki watched her day and night as she engaged in these exchanges with Fort William.

'Why don't you let them know how much the people of Jhansee loved the Maharaj? Let Mr Dalhousie know, Maharani, how much your subjects love *you*. If they want you as their ruler, how can he deny them their wish?'

Lakshmibai thought over this. In her next letter she wrote, 'The people of Jhansee were content under the rule of the late Raja as well as of their queen who writes to you. They are doing as well as those under British rule. Good roads, tanks and bridges had been constructed and spacious bungalows were erected for the accommodation and comfort of travellers passing through the territory. Moreover, a large mansion had been provided rent-free to officials of the Governor General and Jhansee maintained an efficient police force. Under this good government, the people had no complaints nor did they wish to be transferred to the East India Company.'

The British officers were impressed with the way Lakshmibai carefully drafted each letter.

'I must grant it to her that she has all the makings of a lawyer. Such clear and precise arguments!' Malcolm told Lord Robert Hamilton.

Hamilton, the Governor General's agent for central India, had a soft corner for this young queen who looked up to him as a father figure. He admired the way Lakshmibai's tone changed with each letter – argumentative, angry, pensive, meditative, logical, precise, methodical, unambiguous and even pleading at times.

'She's hell-bent on getting her Jhansee back. She loves her people, and she knows they will be the happiest under her rule. For that, whether she has to stoop or raise the sword, she will not dither,' he remarked.

'Her people adore her. I'm always scared she may take some step that will trigger resentment in her subjects towards us,' Ellis observed.

Lakshmibai wrote her next letter in consultation with Barrister Lang. 'I want all the following treaties to be documented. Don't miss a single one – 1804, 1817 and 1832,' she instructed her solicitor. 'I want them to see that they are dishonouring their own decrees.'

'If the government wanted to bring the state of Jhansee under its rule, it should have followed the course of negotiation and agreement rather than the exercise of the power, without the right, of the great and strong against the weak and small. The gross violation and negation of the Treaties of the Government of India … if persisted in they must involve gross violation and negation of British faith and honour,' she wrote.

Finally, she alluded to her own distress at the deprivation of her 'authority, rank and affluence' and how she had been reduced to a state of 'subjection, dishonour and poverty'. Lakshmibai pointed out that for four months she had ably conducted the affairs of state in Jhansee.

She told Lang that the government order came to resume the state and seize the property and treasury of Jhansee.

'Though I have already demonstrated my capacity to continue being in charge of state affairs, the government has ignored my competence to rule,' she stated in her letter.

Maharani Lakshmibai's tone by now was insistent and assertive, but Dalhousie did not budge from his decision.

'I will fight this lapse. I will fight it tooth and nail. I will not hand over my Jhansee to the firanghees. It is a matter that concerns the well-being of my subjects. Please send out the message that I want to address my people,' Lakshmibai told her ministers resolutely.

Within the next hour Rani Lakshmibai appeared before her subjects.

'The Company Sarkar says that Jhansee belongs to the British.' Her high-pitched voice sliced through the evening air as she spoke to her people from the ramparts of the fort. 'They have even refused me His Majesty's inheritance. In its place, they have offered me a pension of Rs 5,000 per month from which the state debts will be deducted. But I promise you, my people, you who were much beloved of my late husband, that I will continue to be your queen and fight for our kingdom till my last breath. Main apni Jhansee nahi doongi,' she bellowed.

Cries of 'Maharani Lakshmibai ki jai' erupted in chorus through the multitudes of people who had gathered to listen to their queen.

18

The stillness of the hot afternoons stretched well into the evenings. Even the crows had disappeared.

Chandraki came into Lakshmibai's chamber looking for Damodar. He was playing truant. The moment she walked in, she knew something was wrong. Chandraki found the queen standing in front of the jharokha.

'Maharani ki jai ho!' Chandraki saluted.

Lakshmibai spun around instantly. Chandraki was shocked to see her face. It had taken on a deep hue. Her eyes were red and her nostrils flared. She stood with her arms flailing as she clutched a letter.

'They've done it, Chandraki, they have done it. They have taken my Jhansee.'

'When . . . when did this happen?' Chandraki asked, stunned.

'Major Ellis informed me a few hours ago. I have been asked to vacate the fort,' she said, holding back tears. 'But I will not give up. I will get my Jhansee back,' she said resolutely.

Fort William was worried. Hamilton was asked to visit her and convince her to accept the pension of Rs 5,000 a month as well as the new terms that the Company had decided upon.

Although Rani Lakshmibai received Hamilton, along with Superintendent Skene and Captain Gordon, with grace, she refused to accept the pension. If she accepted the pension, it would mean that she had acquiesced to the Company's terms and conditions.

'If you insist that I accept your terms and conditions, Mr Hamilton, I will move to Benares!' she threatened.

Hamilton duly conveyed this to Lord Dalhousie. 'She is unrelenting, though I must admit she is most civil and polite and quite the lady. It is a pleasure to talk to her!'

'You seem to have quite a soft corner for her, eh Hamilton?' Dalhousie laughed.

Despite the easy banter, Hamilton knew his task was tough. 'Neither is Lakshmibai relenting nor is Dalhousie. I don't know what to do, Skene!'

'Leave it to me, sir! Sooner or later, Queen Lakshmibai will have to give in,' Skene reassured the rather harried Hamilton.

'Be careful in your dealings with her, Skene. She is a rather strong-minded woman who talks cleverly and clearly!'

But no matter what Lakshmibai did or said, Dalhousie was firm and resolute in his decision to annex Jhansee. The queen had to leave the fort, her home for the last eleven years, and move into the Rani Mahal, a modest two-storeyed building with six rooms and an open courtyard.

Chandraki went with her, and slowly they built a life outside the ancestral home of the Newalkars. Lakshmibai may have been ousted from what she perceived was her rightful place, but her lifestyle as the queen of Jhansee was de rigueur, and her people continued to perceive her as their ruler. In the year that followed Jhansee's lapse to the East India Company, she appeared in court regularly and settled matters that her subjects brought in, who still preferred to approach her rather than the British officers who now occupied the erstwhile throne of Jhansee. She met her subjects, settled cases, personally trained the soldiers of her all-women regiment of which Chandraki was an integral part, indulged in swordsmanship and went riding. And she kept up her correspondence with Fort William, appealing against the annexation of Jhansee with a persistence that was rare.

~

There was one more thing that worried the queen of Jhansee. She had heard lately that the neighbouring state of Orchha was gathering its forces. She knew that the General of the Orchha army was an ambitious man and he had his sights set upon Jhansee. In order to curry favour with Orchha's ruler, the General was itching to win Jhansee back for Orchha that was once a mighty kingdom, the capital of Bundelkhand. And now with the fort taken over by the British, and the kingdom almost lost to them, Orchha would surely exploit the opportunity and try winning back its lost territory. 'How do I get to know about Orchha's intentions, what do I do? I wish there was someone who could get me some information from Orchha.'

Lakshmibai pursed her lips and drummed her fingers on the buffet table kept by the side of her bed.

Chandraki was wary of the queen when she appeared in one of these moods – angry and restless. And those moods were pretty frequent nowadays. Chandraki knew that the only way to pacify her was to go riding out of the palace together or engage in a session of sword fighting. She managed to persuade Lakshmibai to do so often and the two would ride for miles together.

'You're a much better rider than a dancer,' Lakshmibai once remarked when the two of them were riding down the Bangra Hill, towards the stark rocky plains spread out below.

At twenty-one, Chandraki still looked more like a girl than a young woman, especially when she dressed in one of her military outfits. The queen often teased her, 'If you continue dressing up as a soldier, you will never find a man to marry you, Chandraki.'

Chandraki blushed at the thought of marriage. Should she tell the Maharani that she was already married? She had kept it a secret for a whole year. That was bad enough. And when she knew that her husband was Jaywant, the queen would be livid. Chandraki shuddered. No, she told herself, not now. She would rather wait for some more time before she told the queen about Jaywant.

But her heart pined for Jaywant, whose visits to Jhansee had reduced considerably. It had now been several months since Chandraki had met him. The Shivratri festival, which witnessed one of the biggest fairs in Jhansee, was over but there was no news from Jaywant. It was imperative that she meet him soon. But how could she leave the queen at this time when everything was in turmoil in Jhansee?

She was restless. He was her husband and her rightful place was beside him, wherever he was. What if he married someone else? Chandraki would never be able to recover from that. She had offered him everything – the amulet, her heart, herself – everything she had ever believed in.

She took out the chanderi sari that her mother had kept away for her wedding and draped it around herself to see how she would look dressed as a bride.

'Not bad, though I do wish I was a shade fairer.' She scowled as she observed her reflection in the mirror. She was wearing her mother's jewellery. She had looked like this the day she had met Lakshmibai for the first time. Only now, her face was more angular, her skin more taut and her figure more curvaceous. She imagined Jaywant looking at her with admiration and could almost hear him whisper how beautiful she looked.

Why did she have to fall in love with a man from Orchha of all places? He could have been from anywhere else. She resigned herself to her belief that God's ways are indeed inexplicable and made up her mind.

'I think it's time I told the queen,' she decided.

19

It was one of those mellow afternoons when the countryside was bathed in the warm glow of a late winter sun – the perfect weather for a gallop across the rocky plains. And like on all the other afternoons, the two women were seen exiting the fort, astride their horses, Badal and Bijli. Badal, loyal and obedient, was always eager to please Her Majesty. But Bijli was her favourite. Like her mistress, the mare was daring and tempestuous, often crossing boundaries and venturing into the unknown. Lakshmibai was mostly seen astride Bijli, but today when she noticed Chandraki's wistful eyes look longingly at the sturdy chestnut mare, Lakshmibai handed the reins to her.

'She's yours for the day.' The queen smiled as Chandraki took the reins, her hands quivering.

'Thank you, Your Majesty,' she stammered, overwhelmed at the queen's magnanimity. The queen had never allowed anyone to ride the mare. Bijli was the king's gift to her two years ago when he first learnt of her pregnancy. Lakshmibai was so possessive of her that she did not allow the grooms to attend to her except when the stables needed to be cleaned. She even fed the mare herself. But lately she could not allow herself that luxury. Ever since the king had died, Lakshmibai would hardly get the time to indulge in any of her favourite pastimes. State matters kept her busy and officials from the East India Company would constantly be at her door with 'extremely urgent' matters. In less than three years, she had lost almost everything that had once belonged to her.

'I cannot allow them to take over Jhansee. There must be something that can be done,' she said aloud as she mounted Badal. Chandraki got on to Bijli.

'You are trying your best, Your Majesty!' Chandraki reassured her.

The two women were now riding their respective horses and raising a cloud of dust behind them. They rode on in comfortable silence for some time, heading towards the road that led to Dutya. The dry terrain of Jhansee spread out before them, punctuated by rocks and boulders. Chandraki cleared her throat.

'Your Majesty, I wish to tell you something,' she said softly.

The queen, who was wrapped up in her own unpleasant thoughts, started at the sound of Chandraki's voice, which, though soft, broke through the stillness of the afternoon.

'Yes?'

'I've got married.' Chandraki came straight to the point, like always.

Maharani Lakshmibai pulled Badal's reins sharply.

The horse came to a halt. Chandraki drew up beside her. Lakshmibai turned towards Chandraki.

'Wh . . . what?'

'I'm married,' Chandraki replied softly.

'Chandraki . . . married? No, it can't be,' Lakshmibai told herself. She looked at her young companion. Did she hear her right? How was this possible? She mulled over this piece of news. But then, why was she so disturbed by it? Chandraki was, after all, a young, beautiful girl who had several admirers in the court. The queen knew about them. It was natural that she would want to have her own home, her own family. Why should she expect that Chandraki would never marry? She was not her slave. She knew that as much as she wanted to, she could not stop Chandraki from charting her own course in life. It would not be fair. Her loyalty could never be questioned, and her companionship was most cherished. Yet, she would have to let her go at some point. Lakshmibai sighed. 'Everyone is leaving me one by one,' she thought. 'Am I destined to lead this long life completely alone?'

She turned towards Chandraki, who was waiting right beside her.

'Who is he? What does he do?' she asked.

This was the moment that Chandraki had dreaded all along. She knew the Maharani would ask the inevitable question and the answer was not one she would like. But it had to be done. The sooner she got over with it, the better.

'His name is Jaywant. And he is . . . he is a courtier in the royal palace.'

Lakshmibai smiled. So this meant Chandraki would go nowhere, but remain in the palace.

'A courtier! Well! That's wonderful. What are his duties?' the queen asked. 'How long have you known him?'

The questions came in quick succession. And then there was a pause. It reminded Chandraki of rapid gunfire followed by a brief silence after which came the big blast. She prepared herself for its impact.

'Actually, he doesn't work in the court of Jhansee.'

Lakshmibai's face fell. 'Not in the court of Jhansee?'

'He's from Orchha.' It was done. She had said it.

The two women had come quite far away from the fort. The sun was dipping and the shadows were getting longer. It was time to turn back.

'I do hope you know, Chandraki, what that means, don't you?' The queen's voice was firm, her face grim as she reeled from the force of Chandraki's words.

Chandraki sat silent, her head bowed. She fidgeted with the reins that were now beginning to bruise her palms.

'Chandraki, I'm talking to you.' The queen raised her voice.

'Yes, Your Majesty, I do,' replied Chandraki.

'And you still want to go ahead with this . . .. this dalliance of yours?'

The queen received no reply to her question. After a few minutes, she kicked Badal on his flanks and started back towards the palace. Chandraki followed quietly. Once back in the palace, the queen headed straight for her chamber with Chandraki close on her heels. On reaching her room, Lakshmibai dismissed her with a wave of her hand without a word.

Chandraki, who usually followed the queen into her room and helped her undress, was taken aback at her brusqueness. But she knew it was a command and she had no choice but to obey it. She quietly turned away from the door and, wiping the lone tear which threatened to run down her cheek any moment, ran along the entire length of the corridor and did not stop until she reached her own quarters and shut the door behind her. The queen had never been so angry with her before. What should she do? She slumped on the bed, her face buried in her palms.

Outside, the birds had embarked upon their orchestra as day gave way to night. The lamps came on, and people thronged the evening bazaars. Bells clanged as the evening pujas commenced in the temples spread across the town. For the next one hour, the city would come alive before the darkness of the early spring night would wrap itself around the plains of Bundelkhand.

It was time for the puja in the temple in the palace as well. Chandraki would reach the temple before dusk and prepare for the aarti along with the priest. But today, she did not attend the puja and instead lay on her bed, watching the blue sky turn red and then grey as the night crept in stealthily, casting a black cover across the sky. She was devastated by Maharani Lakshmibai's dismissal of her. It pained her to think that the queen had actually turned her away – she, who was Her Majesty's comrade-in-arms, her confidante, her dearest companion. 'She has turned her back on me,' Chandraki cried. How could she keep living if the queen abandoned her?

'She's all I've got,' thought Chandraki to herself.

Chandraki wept as she recounted all that the queen had done for her. She was the envy of all the women in the palace because she was the queen's favourite. The Maharani had taught her to read, ride and hold her head high. 'She allowed me the respect that my mother had been denied all her life.' What would she do that she'd fallen from grace?

It was completely dark outside. The ebbing of the noises outside told her that the palace had gone to sleep. The queen had not called for her. Perhaps, she shouldn't have told her after all. What if she was asked to leave the palace? 'But why should I be subjected to such treatment? What is my fault? I've fallen in love. Will she punish me for that?' She thought of Jaywant. She saw him smile at her with eyes filled with love. His words were a caress to her willing ears, his love brushed across her like a cool breeze on a hot summer night.

She looked out of the small window above her bed. The hours had flown by, silently. The sky had turned lighter with the first light of dawn. The birds had resumed their chatter and the first stirrings of life ushered in the new day.

~

Lakshmibai tossed and turned in her bed. 'How can she even think of leaving me at such a tumultuous time? A time when I'm all alone and have no one beside me?' There was a sharp pain in her heart. 'Everyone is leaving me. She's all I've got.' Chandraki was her only true friend, her companion. They had grown up together in Jhansee. Chandraki was a soldier, and she needed her right now.

Lakshmibai thought of all kinds of reasons to keep her back in Jhansee. Her mind was in turmoil.

It was a restless night for Lakshmibai. Officials of the East India Company had given her a bad time the previous evening. She humoured them as inviting their displeasure would further stoke the already smouldering embers of a dying kingdom. She had consulted Lang on the same.

'I've sent a representation to Lord Dalhousie again,' she told Lang. 'I'm meeting Hamilton next week.'

'But Hamilton has no power over Jhansee,' Lang said.

'Yes, Jhansee doesn't fall under his jurisdiction, and he's only a political agent after all but he is a dear friend and he understands us. He can plead our case with Mr Dalhousie. He's almost like a father to me. Do you know, both of us were born in Benares?'

Lang had offered no assurance and seemed equally helpless. 'I think I can argue my own case better,' Lakshmibai reasoned.

She spent most of the night drafting her next letter to Fort William after which she tried to get some sleep. But thoughts of Chandraki kept her awake. Her words hit her again and again. She rose from her bed and paced up and down. 'Orchha! The stupid girl has no idea what that means,' Lakshmibai fumed. 'Oh Chandraki, how can you be so foolish as to marry a man from Orchha?' Orchha. A name she dreaded. Didn't Chandraki know that it was dangerous to have anything to do with that kingdom?

20

Chandraki fell asleep in the early hours of the morning. She woke up with a start as the sounds of the bells ringing from the palace temple pierced the morning air. Her thoughts returned to her exchange with the queen the previous afternoon. The queen had been furious when she had spoken about Jaywant. Lakshmibai's grim face loomed before her, and her heart softened. 'I must see Her Majesty and ask for forgiveness. I will tell her I won't meet him ever again,' Chandraki decided.

Although it was March, there was a chill in the morning air. She rose from her bed, her tear-stained face reflecting the agony that had kept her up all night. As she opened the wooden chest to pull out a fresh veil, her eyes fell on the shawl that Jaywant had once gifted her. It was a pashmina jamawar shawl from Kashmir, and Chandraki knew it was expensive. Even though Jaywant was not a rich man, he had thought of her and how beautiful she would look in it. Chandraki took it out from the chest and ran her slender fingers across it. It was very soft. She hugged it to her bosom. Tears welled up in her eyes, and she wanted to cry at the thought of never seeing Jaywant again. Would she really never see him again, nor hear his voice? Slowly her pain gave way to anger. She was angry, angry with the queen.

'How can she stop me from meeting him? He's my husband and I love him. I can't help it if he's from Orchha. I have to see the queen.' Chandraki walked out of her room in a fit of anger and made her way towards Lakshmibai's chambers. The morning sun had enveloped the world below in its warm embrace. It would be a clear day. The queen would have finished her toilette and was perhaps already at the temple. Chandraki decided to wait for Lakshmibai to finish her puja.

~

Vascillating between thoughts of Jhansee's annexation, and Chandraki's love affair through the night, the queen was in a pretty bad mood by next morning. She wondered what Chandraki's plans were. Did she intend going to Orchha? If so, how could she prevent that from happening? Orchha was not a safe place for anyone from Jhansee. But who was she to prevent Chandraki in her quest for happiness? Hadn't she taken such risks herself so many times? Moreover, she had promised Chandraki's mother that she would help her lead a life away from the world of mujras and courtesans. But why did Chandraki have to choose someone from Orchha? She knew that Orchha was festering its wounds, and she lived in constant dread that it would strike any time. Lakshmibai was aware that her position was vulnerable, and this could well be the opportunity that the enemy was waiting for. And what could be better for them than to have one of her trusted aides fall right into their lap?

Suddenly she had an idea. As the night wore on, Lakshmibai became more and more convinced of how great the idea was, and by morning she was ready to put it into action. A slow smile crept up on her lips and her eyes took on a sinister hue.

21

Bracing herself for the inevitable confrontation, Chandraki walked into the queen's chamber. It wasn't going to be easy, she knew. Lakshmibai was reading a scroll. The queen's face seemed drawn and tired. Chandraki felt a twinge of guilt. 'I have been the cause for her strain. She has enough problems of her own, and I have only given her more trouble,' she thought. 'Why can't life be simpler, God? Why do I need to hurt the one I love in order to be happy?'

Damodar was playing on the carpeted floor. Both mother and son looked up the moment she walked in. Damodar ran to Chandraki and hugged her. She was his best friend. It was a close-knit group, almost like a family. They found solace in each other's loneliness. But right now, the air in the room was heavy with the brewing tension between the queen and her protégée.

Lakshmibai came straight to the point. 'Look at me, Chandraki,' Lakshmibai commanded. Chandraki raised her head and faced her. The queen looked straight into Chandraki's eyes. 'So what do you want to do?'

The younger girl stood before Maharani Lakshmibai, her head bowed and hands folded. There was a volcano that had erupted within her which was searing through her insides and was nearly consuming her. Her eyes were clouded with tears and the intricate patterns on the Persian carpet appeared blurred. Chandraki's head throbbed. Before her stood a mighty ruler, who was not just her queen, but the charter of her destiny, her mentor, her mother, her father, her sister, her friend – a woman who had altered the course of her destiny, her very life, who had given her a new name, and a new identity. If it hadn't been for her, Chandraki would be languishing in some corner of the zenana, spending her days chewing betel leaves and stringing ghungroos around her ankles. She knew how to read. She knew how to write. She knew how to wield a sword. She knew how to ride a horse. She knew the meaning of dignity. Besides, the Maharani and Jhansee were in trouble. How could she think of only herself at this time?

'Can I go to Orchha, Your Majesty?'

Damodar Rao was swaying noisily on his rocking horse, and each time he rocked, the wooden horse would creak. Maharani Lakshmibai looked at the little boy. 'Damodar! Could you please stop making that noise?' The boy stopped instantly and the horse came to a halt. Lakshmibai turned towards Chandraki. 'So you have made up your mind to give in to this . . . er . . . your amorous affliction?'

Chandraki nodded. Now that the worst was over, she was prepared for the consequences of her decision.

'But why do you want to go to Orchha, Chandraki? Won't your husband come to Jhansee? I would like to meet him before you take any further decision,' Lakshmibai said, employing every argument she could think of to make Chandraki change her mind. 'Make her see some sense, Durga Ma, stop her from going away from Jhansee, from me. I need her here beside me. She's the only person I share everything with, the only person in the whole world I can trust blindly. She's my friend, my soldier, my family. I have no one else,' Lakshmibai prayed.

'He has not visited Jhansee for some time now. Perhaps some work has come up. Or all this talk of the Company Sarkar taking over Jhansee has kept him away. I want to go to Orchha and find out for myself,' Chandraki mumbled vaguely.

Maharani Lakshmibai shook her head in resignation. 'So you want to step into the territory of our enemies in pursuit of a man who you say you are married to? Someone who hasn't contacted you for several months now. Have you completely lost your mind?' The queen was fuming, her voice was shrill and the attendants could hear it outside. 'You want to leave me and go? Leave your Jhansee?' Lakshmibai persisted. And then she played the final card. 'And Damodar, your prince, your ward, who considers you his best friend in the whole wide world? How can you leave him alone knowing I can't be with him all the time?'

Unable to hold herself back any longer, Chandraki rushed towards the queen and fell at her feet, sobbing piteously.

'Forgive me, Your Majesty, I didn't mean to hurt you. I'll be back. Soon. We will come to seek your blessings,' she cried.

Lakshmibai sighed. Then, wiping her tears away, she asked, 'Very well, then. Is there anything you require for your journey?' She had no idea how long Chandraki would be away. Still, she would see to it that Chandraki was well provided for till the time she met Jaywant.

'I don't think I will need anything as I will reach Orchha well within a day,' said Chandraki, cheering up ever so slightly.

'Within a day? That is not possible. It's quite a long journey, Chandraki. It will take take you three days to reach,' said Lakshmibai.

'Not if you are willing . . .' Chandraki said softly, her head lowered.

'If I am willing? What does that mean?' asked the Maharani curiously.

'To give me a horse,' Chandraki replied hesitatingly.

Lakshmibai smiled for the first time since Chandraki had broken the news. She could sense the same force of intent, the same passion in this younger girl. Chandraki had the same fire within her as she did. She thought how lucky Jaywant was to have someone like Chandraki in his life, a woman willing to leave behind her beloved Jhansee and her queen, all for him.

'I'll tell Kaale Khan to give you Bijli. She's my favourite, you know that.'

Chandraki smiled and thanked the queen as graciously as she could, even as her heart did a somersault. She would be riding Bijli! The queen was trying very hard to conceal her misgivings. Something told her that it would be a long while before they saw each other again.

'Chandraki!'

'Yes, Your Majesty?'

'While at Orchha, I want you to do something for me. Let's say, it's a condition I'm imposing upon you for allowing you to go to Orchha.'

Chandraki waited patiently. Everything had worked out fine and she was leaving on a pleasant note. The queen didn't seem angry or displeased any more. She would soon return to Jhansee with Jaywant, and over a period of time, she would convince him to stay back in Jhansee. She faced Lakshmibai nervously.

'While in Orchha, you will be my eyes and ears. You will report to me all developments taking place in the kingdom. Endear yourself to everyone, especially the queen there. But don't let anyone know your purpose. Let everyone know that you are in Orchha to meet your husband,' said Maharani Lakshmibai firmly.

Chandraki was stupefied. 'You mean . . . a . . . a guptachar, a hurkurus? But, Maharani, I have no idea how to go about it.' She gulped nervously.

'Of course you do. Haven't you spied on the British on so many occasions? Haven't you hung around their camps dressed as a gypsy or as a flower girl and eavesdropped as the firanghees talked among themselves while buying flowers from you? Did I send you there to humour them? Wasn't it you who first told us about the condition of the traders? And wasn't it you who revealed to us Riyaz Khan's betrayal?'

Chandraki's heart beat faster as the queen's words fell upon her ears. Was she being trained as a spy all these years? She had not the faintest idea why the Maharani sent her off here and there under some pretext or the other. She thought she was running errands. But, oh Durga Ma, she was a guptachar after all!

'It was I who sent you out to gather information, but now, you will do it on your own. You are well equipped to carry out your duties. Your training as a soldier in my army will now be put to test. Don't fail me, your queen. Don't fail Jhansee.'

After Chandraki left, Lakshmibai sat before her dressing table and looked at her own reflection. But her mind was elsewhere. A small frown laced her brows; her lips were set in a thin line. She was broken-hearted to let Chandraki go and at the same time feared for her safety. This was the best way to send her off. Chandraki would have to remain alert, and moreover, she would be in touch with her. With that thought, her frown disappeared, and her face broke into a smile, that delightful smile that charmed even the British officers. 'I'll let her go. We'll see what happens,' Lakshmibai told herself.

22

Chandraki was ready to leave for Orchha with the first rays of the sun the next day. She didn't need to prepare much for the journey. She opened the chest kept in her room which contained her few belongings – some clothes and jewellery, most of which had belonged to her mother, and the few saris that the Maharani had given her. Among these was her mother's chanderi sari that she took out to carry with her. Also, among the clothes she was carrying was the shawl that Jaywant had bought for her. She looked around her modest quarters one last time before stepping out. She would miss it. But it was only for a short while, she would be back soon, she told herself.

Yet, she was apprehensive. She had intended to go to Orchha to find out about Jaywant. But the Maharani had now entrusted her with a task that was far more risky. 'Will I be able to carry it out?' Chandraki asked herself again and again. But she knew she had to follow the queen's orders. 'I can't fail the Maharani, I can't break her trust.' Once, she even thought of abandoning the idea of going to Orchha altogether. She approached the queen who knew instantly why she had come.

'You don't want to go to Orchha any more, do you?' Chandraki nodded.

'There's no backing out now, my dear. It's no longer your personal agenda, but a state mission. You are now going to Orchha not just to look for Jaywant but also for the sake of Jhansee. It's an order.' Chandraki left, her heart beating rapidly, her lips dry.

Outside her room, a dasi waited for her. 'The Maharani has sent these for you,' she said, handing her a small bundle and something wrapped in a silk cloth. Chandraki took them and unfolded the piece of cloth curiously. A dagger lay in it, its blade gleaming in the light of the sun. Chandraki's eyes filled with tears. The queen had thought of everything. She knew the little bundle contained money. 'I hope I can fulfil the Maharani's mission and return home soon,' she said, swallowing back her tears.

She spotted Kaale Khan waiting for her near the main gate of the palace. He was holding on to Bijli. Chandraki walked up to him and folded her hands.

'As-Salaam-Alaikum, Chandraki,' Kaale Khan greeted as he handed over Bijli's reins to her. 'Look after her well. You do know how much the queen loves her,' he said softly.

Chandraki nodded and took the reins from his hands. She stroked Bijli's muzzle and ran her hand across her mane.

'I'll guard her with my life, Kaale Khan! Don't worry!'

'And take good care of yourself too. The Maharani loves you even more! Khuda Hafiz!' His voice rang out behind her. Chandraki smiled. She would miss him.

Suddenly, a thought crossed her mind. It was ironical that both she and Riyaz Khan had left Jhansee. With his departure, she felt that her responsibility and self-imposed guardianship towards Jhansee, the queen and the other women of the palace was now lifted. He had left Jhansee for reasons entirely different – his reasons were governed by hate, treachery and betrayal, and hers by love and loyalty. Chandraki hoped their paths would never cross again.

As the sun went up in the sky, Chandraki was astride Lakshmibai's Bijli, mapping her way to Orchha, to Jaywant, and to a future ridden with uncertainties.

23

Chandraki and Bijli got along pretty well. Bijli was not unfamiliar with Chandraki as she had often had the pleasure of her company when Chandraki was out with Lakshmibai. Chandraki had made it clear to Bijli that she was one of the queen's favourite companions.

Little had she known at the time that within a few years she would be riding Bijli, but on a mission far more dangerous. She sat quite comfortably on Bijli, her sari draped in the Kashta style and her head wrapped in a turban, in the way Lakshmibai wrapped hers. Bijli trotted at a steady pace, happy to have Chandraki stroking her mane every now and then. The two went along the narrow, dusty road that led them to Orchha, fringed by scrubby undergrowth on either side. The dusty ochre terrain was spattered with huge sandstone rocks, and the path was strewn with boulders, smouldering in the April heat of central India. She hoped to reach Orchha within the next two hours. It was just twelve miles away.

By midday, Chandraki's throat was parched and her

leather flask was empty. There was no one in sight. The rocky terrain stretched for miles ahead and around her. She had been riding for almost three hours at a stretch, yet there was no sign of any habitation in sight. By now she should have reached the outskirts of Orchha. She realized she had lost her way.

'We have lost our way, Bijli, and there's no one around to guide me to the right path,' she said as she looked at the hand-drawn route map that Kaale Khan had given her. You must be tired. Would you want to rest for a while?' She caressed the horse as she pulled to a halt. Bijli stamped her feet and flicked her tail to get rid of the flies. Chandraki let her nibble the grass by the roadside. She got off Bijli and sat down on a nearby rock and hoped that someone would pass by to direct her to Orchha. Where was she? Where was this road headed? Shielding her eyes from the fierce sun, she removed her veil.

Suddenly, she heard the bushes behind her rustle. Startled, she looked around sharply, every sense of hers alert. She stood up and reached for her dagger, pulling it out from her cummerbund. She wondered what had made the sound. It could be a wild animal or a rodent, scurrying around the bushes, or it could be a human being. She quickly covered the lower part of her face with her veil and turned around to brace herself for whatever danger lurked in the bushes. From the corner of her eye, she could see Bijli chew on the grass a little distance away. She wished she had kept Bijli's reins in her hands so that in case of any immediate danger she could ride away.

She waited for the next sound. There it was. The sound

came from the clump of bushes to her right. Her grip around the handle of the dagger tightened. She took a step forward and stopped. The bushes next to her parted, and a man emerged. He was tall, but his face was almost completely covered with a piece of cloth. Only his eyes remained uncovered. His clothes were frayed, and he was barefoot as well. As he stepped out from behind the bushes, he saw Chandraki, and instinctively his hand reached for his dagger that Chandraki now saw peeping from under his waistband. Something about that sharp movement unnerved her. The man had the confidence and alertness of a warrior which was evident in the way he reached for his dagger. They looked at each other briefly and when the man realized that it was a woman in front of him, he drew away his hand from the dagger and sat down heavily on a rock close by.

Chandraki regained her composure, though her hand lingered on her cummerbund, ready to seize the dagger at any provocation from the man. She cleared her throat.

'Can you help me?' she asked. 'I've lost my way.'

The man's eyes was piercing and she felt a current shoot through her body. She quickly averted her gaze.

The man shrugged. Then suddenly he rose and walked up to the horse. Chandraki stiffened.

'Is this your horse?' he asked weakly, his voice barely audible. His throat was obviously parched.

'Yes, it is mine. Why?'

'Can I get a ride till Orchha? It is not very far from here,' he asked stroking Bijli's mane, his voice feeble.

Chandraki mulled over his suggestion. He could take

her to Orchha. She knew the man wanted to use the horse because in all likelihood he wouldn't be able to walk on his own. But who was he? What was he doing here in the middle of this desolate road all alone? He had a dagger, but no horse. Was he a thug? Why on earth should she allow him on her horse? She knew he was in a pitiable condition. But who knew what he was capable of.

'I will take you to Orchha, but you'll have to show me the way. And I will ride the horse. You will sit behind me,' Chandraki offered, monitoring the man's reaction. The man nodded and mounted Bijli. He stretched out his hand to Chandraki. She hesitated briefly and then clasped his outstretched palm. He closed his grip around it and with one sharp tug, pulled her over to him. She shuddered as her body fell across his. She straightened herself and sat upright, seizing the reins of Bijli from him. Then with one gentle kick she urged the mare to get moving and within minutes, the two were riding away, obliterating the path behind them, towards a destiny unknown and unexpected.

24

By dusk they had entered the first gate of Orchha and hit a fork on the road. One way led towards some magnificent stone structures, the other towards what looked like a fort. Beyond that, they could see a river beckon them enticingly.

'Water!' Chandraki exclaimed. 'Bijli, hurry up!' she urged the mare, who by now equally thirsty, galloped faster, and soon they hit the road that led down to the river. Chandraki pulled at her reins, but before Bijli could come to a full halt, the man jumped off and went sprinting towards the river.

'Hey, hey you,' Chandraki yelled, but she knew she had lost him. He had disappeared.

She shrugged and got off Bijli. To her left was the fort and in front of her was the river. Taking Bijli's reins in her hand, she started walking down the narrow, dusty road that led up to the boundary wall of the fort. Her throat was parched, her lips cracked. She wanted to head to the river, but right now it was more important to enquire about Jaywant. They crossed over the narrow bridge and reached the huge iron gate in the outer wall of the fort. The sun had set completely when Chandraki spoke to the guard outside.

'Bhau, do you know Jaywant Singh?'

The guard looked askance at the slender young girl draped in a dusty sari, holding the reins of an equally dusty horse, all alone, so late in the evening.

'Who are you?' he asked, eyeing her suspiciously. It was obvious that the girl had been travelling, but on a horse? Or was someone else with her? And why was she here at this odd hour? 'Who is Jaywant?' he asked, eyes sweeping all over her.

Chandraki didn't know anything about Jaywant except for the fact that he was employed in the palace. She recounted all the conversations she had had with him and realized he had hardly talked about himself or his job. She knew that at every step she would be asked about him and that she had no information to offer.

'He works in the palace,' she replied, doubtful if her answer would help.

'Arre bhai, does anyone know Jaywant Singh?' the guard turned around and asked his fellow guards. They consulted each other and then shook their heads.

'I'll wait till you find out. I have come from very far. It will soon be dark and I can't go back,' Chandraki pleaded.

'It is not possible to find out tonight. We'll see tomorrow morning.'

'But where do I go now?' Chandraki asked. 'I don't know anyone here.'

The man shrugged. 'You can't get inside the palace without permission,' he said and turned away.

25

A little while after she had been refused entry into the palace, Chandraki's afternoon companion was found lying senseless by a group of women who were frolicking in the river. They now came out one by one. Meher, a fetching sixteen-year-old, was the first to emerge. Her dupatta clung to her as she stepped out of the water, her wet hair strewn across her pretty face. She looked up at the night sky, which was illuminated by a waxing moon. The Betwa river tripped playfully over the boulders that dotted its course. It was a warm evening, but the cool breeze from the river brushed her ivory skin. She shivered just a little. Hugging her arms across her bosom, she hurried towards the palace when her eyes fell on something that lay a little distance away. She walked towards it.

'Oh my God, it's a man!' she exclaimed, looking at the inert body that lay in front of her.

She reached for his pulse and found it throbbing weakly. 'He's still alive,' Meher cried, relieved. She turned to her companion. 'Rukmini, see what I have found!'

'It's a man. Is he dead?'

'No, he's still alive. But he will die soon if we don't hurry up and take him inside,' Meher said, looking intently at the man lying at her feet.

'He's too heavy for us, we can't carry him. And what if he is an enemy or a spy?'

Meher ran to the river to get some water that she sprinkled on him. He opened his eyes slowly.

'Let's fetch the guards,' she said, and they ran towards the palace leaving the man behind.

'There is a man lying near the river. He is unconscious,' she informed at the gate. The guard looked at her suspiciously.

'Who is he?'

'How would I know?' Meher replied sharply. 'If he's not attended to he'll die.'

'I'll have to inform the diwan. We can't be picking up strangers this way,' the guard replied.

Meher shrugged. 'That's up to you. But whatever you do, be quick.'

26

Chandraki, meanwhile, had decided to wait out the night. In any case, she had no choice. She walked towards the river after having been turned away from the palace, dejected and forlorn.

'Well, it looks like we'll have to spend the night under the open sky.' She sighed. Tugging at Bijli's reins gently, she started walking down the bridge that led up to the fort.

On reaching the end of the bridge, she halted. To her right lay the road that had led her to Orchha, the road that would lead her back t to Jhansee. Her heart skipped a beat. She looked to her left. Where did the road on her left lead to? She thought of asking someone. She noticed a few shops in the faint flickering glow of their lanterns. The owners were removing the goods stocked outside and bringing down the flaps of their shops. It was time to close. She hurried towards them.

'Bhau, can I get some water to drink?' The men looked at each other. They had never seen such a sight before – a young girl, worn out and dishevelled, stood before them at this hour, holding on to a horse.

Reluctantly, one of them lifted an earthen pitcher and poured water from it into Chandraki's cupped palms which she brought up to her lips. After finishing most of the water in the pitcher, she wiped her mouth and turned to the men.

'Where does this road lead?' she asked, pointing to the far end of it. It was pitch dark, and nothing could be seen.

'It goes down to the river,' one of them answered nervously and then quickly turned around and went into his shop. The others followed him and before she could ask any further questions, they had disappeared in the dark interiors of their shacks.

Chandraki shrugged. 'Should we go down to the river, Bijli? You are thirsty, aren't you?' The mare stamped around restlessly and swished her tail to get rid of the flies and insects that buzzed around in the light of the lanterns.

Chandraki led Bijli by her reins once again and walked down the narrow dusty road that wound its way down. Soon she could hear the gurgle of water and within minutes she spotted the river.

On reaching the riverbank, Chandraki let Bijli loose and sat down on the grass that was moist with the evening dew. The Betwa never ran dry, but the water level had fallen and would remain so until the monsoon arrived. She bent and scooped out handfuls of the clear, cool water from the river, enjoying how it felt on her skin. She rinsed her face and dipped her feet, splashing water as she looked around her. Behind her, the silhouettes of huge stone structures loomed up against the darkening sky. She also noticed a few temple spires. Across the river, the outline of the fort stood up majestically, sentinel to the little kingdom as it rested.

It was a clear night. The land was bathed in the silver glow of the moon and the river tripped over the rocks and pebbles, shimmering in the moonlight. There was something strange about the night, something magical, almost sacred. Suddenly, her spirits soared. She was sure she would find Jaywant the next day. She smiled as she remembered his gentle face, so full of love. She threw her arms up towards the sky as her feet surrendered to the music of her heart. In that moment, Chandraki looked hauntingly beautiful, her face reflecting the luminous splendour of the moon.

She heard Bijli close by. She knew it was pretty late in the night as the moon was waning and the stars could be seen twinkling. She moved closer to the river and sat down on one of the many rocks that lined its banks and eyed the water longingly. Should she take a dip in it? Chandraki looked around. There was no one as far as she could see. A young girl would be scared to be out at this time of the night, alone under the open sky. But years of training with Lakshmibai had hardened her. She had often been out on nights, keeping vigil or carrying out some secret errand. Fear was not a word in her vocabulary.

Suddenly her thoughts turned to Riyaz Khan. Where could he be? She wondered why she thought of him. Why would thoughts of him still disturb her and make her shudder? Her hatred of the man had consumed her for years and she had spent the better part of her life in

Jhansee, thinking of ways to get him out of the palace. But with him gone, she suddenly felt empty.

Even though Riyaz Khan had left Jhansee, she felt his presence all around her. Even in this moment, she felt he was close by. Instinctively, she looked around, as though expecting him to appear before her, his sword drawn, his lips stretched into a thin line, his dark eyes gleaming, their gaze piercing her very soul. It was a countenance that often haunted her. She shuddered involuntarily. But there was no one besides Bijli, who nibbled at the grass a little further away.

Dispelling all thoughts of Riyaz Khan, Chandraki rose from her perch and stretched. How long had she been sitting on the rock, lost in her thoughts of Jhansee, of Lakshmibai, of Riyaz Khan? Her stomach rumbled suddenly, a reminder that she had not eaten since noon. Who knew what the next morning held for her.

Chandraki pulled out her dagger and lay it down beside her. She slowly untied her sari and flung it on the grass. It fluttered in the night breeze. She stepped into the water gently. The course of the Betwa was pretty narrow here and was strewn with rocks. She made her way to the middle of the river and placed herself on a flat-topped rock, which was partially submerged under the water. The water of the river refreshed her almost instantly. She lapped the water on her body, stroking her soft skin with it. If an artist would have cared to paint a portrait of hers, half submerged in the river, under the twinkling lights of the stars, her choli transparent with the wetness, revealing her full bosom, his work would have been nothing short of a divine creation;

was he a witness to a celestial scene in which a nymph had descended to test a man's reserves? But there was no one who saw her in that delightful state as she caressed her arms, her neck, her breasts and her belly with the water. Her olive skin glistened in the light of the stars. She untied her hair and ran her wet fingers through her dark tresses.

Chandraki unlaced her choli, working her way through the knots artfully as though performing a nritya mudra. For Chandraki, her body had been made for just one purpose . . . to dance. She may have been tutored by Lakshmibai to wield a sword and ride a horse, but even in those strokes, she found movements and traces of dance, the reason why she excelled in them. Even now, as she untied the strings of her choli, she did it in no hurry. As her fingers wove through the strands, it was as though they were intertwined in a gesture of dance.

Finally, after what seemed a long time, Chandraki offered herself to the river in all her pristine beauty, the water enveloping her slippery skin as she went under. She stayed under the surface for a while and finally emerged with water streaming down her hair, finding its own way as it trickled down from between her breasts, sliding down the flat of her stomach, encircling her belly button, and then losing its way down her womanhood to once again flow back into the river. And it was at this precise moment, enveloped in the night's blackness, with only the fort and the surrounding darkness watching over her undefiled nudity, that Chandraki became a marked woman. But unaware of it, she rejoiced in her deliverance. She knew that at this moment she had made a union with all that was meant to be, with the Almighty designing it for her. She felt fulfilled in a way not known to mortals. At the moment, under the shadow of the rocky sentinels, Chandraki had realized herself. It was her moment of liberation. She felt strange and new. The entire firmament had been witness to her union, and she rejoiced at the thought. But no mortal would ever know what she had experienced moments ago. It was her secret. Only hers. Or so she thought.

27

While Meher argued with the guard at the gate, the man slowly sat up and looked around. To his right, he saw the ramparts of the fort, towering majestically over the vast expanse of land. He tried to recollect the events of the day, but his mind was not clear. He slowly got to his feet and started walking towards the river. Stumbling once or twice, he quickly regained his step and continued walking. He faintly remembered what had happened before he lost consciousness. He had been riding on a horse with a woman. Who was she? And who were these women? He shook his head and pulled his hair. 'I have to be back on my feet,' he told himself. As he walked towards the river, in the shadows of the ruins, his strides became firmer and bolder. He intended to wash himself of all the dirt, tiredness and the past.

And then he saw her. Was she a nymph, a houri? Was she an apsara or a vision? For, no mortal could possess a body like that, and no mortal would dare to expose herself like this in the middle of the night under the open sky.

He stood spellbound as he watched her dance in the dark, caressing her body with the water, as though in the throes of ecstatic lovemaking. He squinted his eyes as he tried to focus better. He could not see her well, just her silhouette in the bright moonlight, the curves visible, deliciously sloping. He checked himself, as he felt uncontrollably drawn towards the figure. Was it an apparition? He must have stood there for quite a while, watching. When Meher returned with the men, he was still standing at the same spot.

'Oh, you are up. Did we take that long?' she said excitedly, as she saw him clearly now. He was very tall. And so handsome!

The man started at Meher's voice. He turned around to see half a dozen men with the two women.

'Who are you?' one of the men asked.

'I come from Gwalior. And you?'

'We are the palace security guards. The diwan has asked us to take you inside the fort,' one of the guards said.

The man absently followed the guard, but his mind was elsewhere. He turned to look back at the spot where he had seen the woman. There was no one there. She had simply melted away in the darkness. It had to be an apparition. It was a spirit. For only a spirit can dwell within your heart forever. He never forgot the vision he saw that night, a vision that continued to haunt him for as long as he lived. It seemed as though he had known the woman forever, and that she was an undefined part of him, of his life. In the years to come, the vision became stronger and stronger, and when he died, the last image he saw before his eyes closed forever, was of the same woman, but this time, he did see her face.

His moment of death became his moment of realization when a teardrop slid down from the corner of his eyes as they closed, his lips forming the words that he had never spoken out loud. But the words remained unheard.

~

The stranger accompanied the men towards the palace reluctantly, looking back at the river every once in a while. As they approached the palace gates, Nathay Khan spotted them. He had decided to look into the matter himself. Any outsider was suspect, even if he was nearly dying. One of the men handed him the letter that was found on the stranger when Meher had searched him. It was addressed to him.

Nathay Khan read the letter and then turned to the man. 'Abdul Jabbar is your uncle?' he asked. The man nodded weakly.

'Bring him in,' he told the guards. 'He will be of great value to us.'

But before turning back towards the palace gates, Nathay Khan looked across at the river. The woman he had seen moments ago as he waited for his men to bring this stranger back was no longer there. 'Strange! Where did she go?' he wondered.

28

As Chandraki emerged from the river, dripping rivulets of water, she heard voices that drifted through the silent night air. She looked around wondering, trying to find the source of these voices. But she couldn't see anyone. She quickly tied her choli that lay spread on a rock close by. It was so wet that she shivered. Her sari lay on the grass next to the river. She waded across to the bank and made a dash for it. Had anyone seen her, she wondered. There had been no one around when she had gone into the water. She had been alone, completely alone.

But unbeknownst to her, there had been two other witnesses to the scene that had played out minutes ago. For Nathay Khan, it was just a naked woman bathing. But, for the other man, it was a vision that he just couldn't comprehend.

~

The kingdom of Orchha lay in silent repose. Chandraki took Bijli's reins and started walking back towards the road that led into town. She remembered the temple that stood facing the fort and decided to spend the night there.

On reaching it she tied Bijli outside at the gate and walked down the passage that opened up into a courtyard lined with shops that were all closed now. A little further away was a group of Basor workers, some of whom lay awake, weaving. She had seen these people often in Jhansee. They were nomadic bamboo weavers who also went from village to village as musicians during marriages and festivals.

In front of her was the sanctum sanctorum, the door of which was shut. She sat down on a stone platform and leaning her head against one of the pillars, fell asleep instantly, only to wake up the next morning to the sounds of bells ringing. As her mind cleared up, she remembered where she was. The temple was filling with people who were gathering for the morning aarti. The bamboo weavers were still around. They had seen her arrive the night before and smiled at her. She smiled back.

Chandraki yawned and rose. It was time to set off again, and she went towards the gate where she had left Bijli the night before. But before she could reach it, two men accosted her. They were in uniform. One of them seized her arm roughly.

Chandraki wrested her arm from him and pushed him away.

'How dare you touch me? Who are you?'

'We are the queen's soldiers,' one of them replied gruffly. 'We have orders to take you to her,' he said.

'Why? What have I done?' Chandraki asked nervously.

'We don't know. We are just following orders. You come with us, or we will have to use force,' he said roughly.

Chandraki had no choice but to follow them. People started gathering around. She looked over her shoulder at the Basors, who looked completely stunned at this sudden onslaught.

'My horse,' she exclaimed, pulling back. 'She was tied here.'

'Don't worry about your horse, we'll take care of it.' The men sniggered and pulled her away.

Chandraki was brought to the palace gates. A group of armed men stood there. One of them came forward. He was of medium height and broad-shouldered and sported a short beard. He looked older than the rest and was evidently senior in rank.

'Why does a young and beautiful girl like you have to sleep in a temple all night?' he asked softly, threateningly.

Chandraki trembled. No words came out.

'Answer me, woman! Who are you?' he thundered.

Chandraki gulped. 'Don't panic,' she told herself. She had to get into the palace somehow. Composing her rattled nerves, she said, 'Huzoor! I have come to look for Jaywant Singh. He works in the palace here.'

The men looked at each other. The man who had questioned her took a step closer and bent down to bring his face at level with hers. With a menacing glint in his eyes, he whispered, 'You came looking for . . . Jaywant Singh? On a horse? All alone? At night? You think I'm a fool to believe that?'

'But that's the truth,' Chandraki replied. 'I approached the guards first, but they wouldn't let me enter the palace. I had no choice but to spend the night in the temple.'

The man looked at her intently. His gaze lingered briefly on her face and travelled down the entire length of her body. Chandraki squirmed under his scrutiny. She avoided looking at him. Suddenly he grinned.

'Get her into the palace. We'll see what can be done.' He snapped his fingers and then turned to Chandraki. His lips curled into a smile. 'I am Nathay Khan, Diwan of Orchha and General of the Orchha army. And I do hope you are not lying. For, if you are, then only God can save you.'

He turned around and walked back to the fort.

'I am Meher,' said the woman who had been entrusted with the responsibility of Chandraki by Nathay Khan. 'What is your name?' she asked as they walked into the palace.

'Chandraki!'

'Welcome to Orchha.' Meher giggled as she took Chandraki's hand and pulled her along with her into the fort.

The room into which Meher shoved Chandraki was damp and dingy. It had a musty smell and the walls were cold.

'This is only for now. Until you meet the queen,' she

said and left Chandraki cold and nervous, all by herself to spend her first night in the palace of Orchha.

As she sat crouched on her haunches, trembling more out of cold and fatigue than out of fear, her mind wandered. And much to her irritation, she could not help but think about Riyaz Khan.

'I must look for Jaywant. Why on earth am I thinking of Riyaz Khan? Why do I keep thinking about him?' Did she feel a twinge of guilt? If it hadn't been for her, Riyaz would probably still be in Jhansee. She deliberately distracted herself. She had reached Orchha as desired, and now her primary objective was to find out what was brewing here and to contact Jaywant. Shivering, she drew up her knees to her chin and rested her back against the cold wall. What would the day bring? Would she find Jaywant or be thrown out of Orchha? Her mind swirled with all kinds of thoughts, and she didn't know when she passed into a state of slumber.

Book II

Orchha

(1855–1857)

29

'Wake up.' Chandraki heard the voice drift into her ears through her sleep. Someone was shaking her violently. She opened her eyes and blinked. The room in which she was lying had allowed the day's warmth and light to seep in. A face hovered above hers.

'You are to be presented before the queen. Do you have anything decent to wear?'

Chandraki shook her head sleepily. Where was she and who was this girl? She looked around the room. Was this a dungeon? She suddenly felt cold. She wrapped her crumpled sari tightly around herself.

'Do you have anything good to wear?' the girl asked again. 'Never mind. I'll get you something.'

Chandraki felt terrible. 'I think I have a fever,' she mumbled and felt her forehead. It was hot. Suddenly, everything came back in a flash – the night before, the journey, the river, the midnight bath. She realized that she had left her dagger behind on the banks of the river. Suddenly she felt defenceless. She shivered.

The girl soon returned with some clothes. 'Wear these, okay?' Before Chandraki could reply, she had turned away.

'Where do I go for a bath?' Chandraki cried out feebly.

'The zenana hamam is close by. You can ask anyone to guide you. I'll be back in half an hour to take you to the durbar,' the girl said and sprinted away.

Chandraki did not feel like bathing. She did not feel like getting up. She lay in the same position for quite some time. She thought of Jaywant. If she did not meet the queen, her admission to the palace would be delayed, and so would her return to Jhansee. She had no desire to stay here for any longer than necessary.

Reluctantly she got to her feet. Picking up the sari that the girl had left behind, she slowly walked out of the room. Her head was heavy and her entire body ached. Her legs refused to carry her. But every step forward meant a step closer to Jaywant. Not a nice way to start a new mission, Chandraki thought as she plunged into the bath.

The girl returned after a while with an older woman who smiled at Chandraki.

'I am Taravati and I look after the zenana,' she said, flicking a stubborn strand of hair from Chandraki's face. She ran her eyes over Chandraki who presented a pretty picture in the orange kosa silk sari. Her face blushed a deep red, reflecting the colour of her sari and from the heat and the fever. Her dusky skin was set off against her black waist-long hair, reminiscent of a night sky overpowering the mellowness of dusk.

'You look lovely,' Taravati exclaimed. 'All you need is this,' the older woman said as she removed a pair of thin gold bangles from her own wrists and slipped them on to Chandraki's wrists. 'You are now ready to meet Her Majesty!'

Chandraki looked at the bangles. 'Thank you,' she said to Taravati softly. The three women left the room and arrived in the durbar hall. Her entry was announced and she soon found herself in front of Rani Ladein Dulaiya, better known as Rani Larai, the ruler of Orchha.

But before the queen could say anything, there was a stir in the courtroom. All eyes turned towards the entrance as a tall man, led by two guards, was brought into the room. He entered through the archway, erect and confident, his long strides covering the length of the durbar hall in a few paces.

'As-Salaam-Alaikum, Rani Sahiba!'

The voice resounded deeply in the room, slicing through the silence.

A tremor ran through Chandraki. That voice! She jerked up her head and turned around to look straight into his eyes. Almost instinctively, as if on cue, the man too looked at her. Their eyes met briefly. It can't be, it just can't be, she told herself.

'Who are you?' Rani Larai asked the man.

'My name is Riyaz Khan,' he answered without looking into her eyes.

'Where are you from?' asked the Rani.

Taken aback by the opulence that spread out before his eyes, Riyaz Khan staggered. Though he had heard tales of

the Bundela rulers' might and glory, he was not prepared
for what he saw. He had spent the better part of his thirty
years fighting and brandishing a sword. He had never paid
much attention to the wealth and riches he had often seen
in kingdoms. He had never been greedy for money. He had
loved once, only once, and that too was wrenched away
from him. He translated his bitterness into a language of
hatred towards the world. There was no space for anything
else in his life, not love, not wealth. No amount of affluence
could impress him. However, despite such a predisposition,
he was stunned by the magnificence of the kingdom.

He looked at the queen seated before him. Why
were there so many women on the throne? He had been
banished by one such queen, a woman of formidable
strength and power who controlled the state affairs better
than any man. And now once again, he stood before a
woman, who dressed in her shimmering white and gold
sari, seemed to be equally authoritative and formidable
despite her diminutive stature. She was seated on a throne
as imposing as that of her neighbour a few miles away.

Rani Larai repeated her question. Riyaz Khan shook
himself out of his reverie.

'She wouldn't trust me if I were to tell her that I am from
the neighbouring enemy state. And if I were to lie, sooner
or later, the truth would be out,' Riyaz thought to himself.

'I'm from Jhansee,' he replied, his lips drawn into a
thin line.

The Rani fleetingly looked at her council of ministers
seated in a row in front of her. But her face did not betray
any emotion.

'Why are you here?'

Did he detect a sudden sharpness in the Rani's voice? What should he tell her? That he was here to seek her help to destroy the Maharani of Jhansee? He hesitated for a second, and before he knew it, the answer was on his lips. He turned to the courtier who stood beside him and whispered in his ear.

'Tell the queen that I can help her get Jhansee back from Maharani Lakshmibai.'

When the guard relayed to the queen what Riyaz Khan had said, her eyes flickered just a little. She was quiet. And after what seemed an eternity to Riyaz, she turned to Nathay Khan.

'Nathay Khan! See to it that he is properly lodged within the palace.' Then, without further delay, she dismissed Riyaz with a flourish of her hand. As he was led out of the courtroom, he could hear the next person present her case before the queen. Riyaz Khan smiled just a little.

'Where are you from?' the queen asked, finally turning her attention to Chandraki.

Chandraki was too stunned to respond. The queen's words were lost on her. Her eyes followed the man who was walking out of the hall. Riyaz Khan's sudden appearance had shaken her up. He was the last person she had expected to meet here. Her antenna was up. What was he doing here? What message did he convey to the queen?

She heard the queen repeat her question. Chandraki snapped out of her thoughts and looked at the queen. This was not the way she had expected to meet the ruler of Orchha.

'I'm from Jhansee,' she replied nervously.

'So! Both of our guests are from Jhansee,' The queen frowned. 'Our enemies seem to be very fond of our kingdom. Very well. What is your name?'

'Chandraki.'

30

'This Riyaz Khan . . . why is he here?' Rani Larai asked Nathay Khan. It had been a week since Chandraki and Riyaz Khan had been presented before her. The queen had been told how they had entered the kingdom.

'What does he want? I think you better keep an eye on him.'

'If you ask me, it's not Riyaz Khan I'm worried about. I'm not too sure about the girl,' Nathay Khan said.

'Why are you suspicious of her? She looked pretty harmless to me.'

Nathay Khan smiled. 'Rani Sahiba, she says she's here to meet Jaywant, her husband. There is no Jaywant here. You are aware that I know the details of each man who works in the palace?'

Larai Rani nodded. 'Still, I think you should look for him once again. He may be a new recruit. She says she has come all the way to look for him. Anyone from Jhansee is not good news.'

Nathay Khan shook his head. 'All new recruits pass

through me. I know she is lying. She's up to some funny business. She had a horse with her when she arrived at our gate. What kind of a woman rides a horse unless she's a warrior?'

'So what do you propose? Should she be sent right back to Jhansee?' the queen asked.

Nathay Khan was quiet. He thought of the girl. It was true that there was no Jaywant Singh, at least not in the palace. Then what was she doing here? 'I'm not sure, but I think I know what this is about,' thought Nathay Khan. The only way to find out was to keep her in the palace. Moreover, she was just too beautiful. Nathay Khan smirked. 'I'm going to relish this,' he thought.

'Your Highness, she can be of use to us. We can get some information about Jhansee,' he said aloud.

'And will she provide us with that information?' Rani Larai asked doubtfully.

'That is my task.' Nathay Khan smiled slyly. 'As for Riyaz Khan, I'll handle him as well.'

The queen nodded. 'You better be sure of what you are doing, Nathay. Lakshmibai is nursing her wounds. She will not rest till she wrests full control of Jhansee once again. It's been a year since she's been thrown out of the palace. For all practical purposes, it's the firanghees who rule Jhansee. And she knows that the firanghees are not our enemies. I'm not at all comfortable to have two people from Jhansee in our palace. Besides, Lord Hamilton will be here next week. He won't be too pleased to see anyone from Jhansee in our kingdom.'

'Your Highness, Lakshmibai is not interested in

Orchha. She wants her Jhansee back. And she doesn't need to use us to get access to the firanghees. We know that she's quite capable of dealing with them on her own. I do not think Riyaz Khan and this girl have been sent here by Lakshmibai.'

'I hope not,' the queen replied, her brows knitted in a frown.

'As for Hamilton, he needn't know about either of them,' Nathay Khan assured.

'But why should we allow them refuge here?'

Nathay Khan smiled wickedly. 'Simply because they are our tools to get Jhansee!'

Rani Larai raised her eyebrows. 'What are you talking about, Nathay?'

'Yes, Your Majesty! Didn't Riyaz Khan tell you so yesterday? He hates Lakshmibai. I found out that she's thrown him out of Jhansee.'

This time, the Rani smiled. 'You are a sly man, Nathay. Now tell me, what about the girl?'

'Oh, she's just a dancer. But we need to be careful. We can get Meher to extract information about Lakshmibai from her. Apparently, Chandraki lives in the palace there.'

'But does Lakshmibai know that these two are here?'

Nathay Khan shrugged. 'I doubt it. Lakshmibai is too distraught herself to fret about two of her subjects landing up in Orchha, one of whom she has banished herself. These days, she's trying her best to appease the firanghees. It's said that Major Ellis, her solicitor John Lang, and even Robert Hamilton are backing her claim to get the legal rights of an heir apparent for her adopted son.'

'Yes, I know. The queen of Dutya sent me a message a few days ago wondering why I'm not taking advantage of the situation.'

'I wanted to tell you so, Your Highness. This is just the time to take back what Orchha lost to the Peshwas, last century. Lakshmibai, for all her bravado, is currently defenceless. Even if her son Damodar were to be recognized as the heir, he's way too young to offer any resistance, isn't he?' Nathay Khan grinned. 'The poor boy is just six years old, Your Highness. And don't we all know what intrigues are being hatched by the queen's own family members? Moreover, Lakshmibai has lost most of her advisers except a few. Her army too is now disbanded. She has no power or funds to offer any resistance. She's on tenterhooks about the firanghees, she thinks they will take away whatever little she has left, most importantly, her honour. What better time, Rani Sahiba, than now to attack?'

'No, Nathay Khan. This is not the right time. We signed a treaty together to help each other out if the firanghees attack us. She can use that to defend her position.'

'What treaty?' Nathay Khan grinned again.

Rani Larai looked perplexed. 'We signed a treaty last year, didn't we, Nathay? Have you forgotten?'

'What treaty, Your Highness? It's of no consequence. Jhansee is not even an independent Rajput state. But we are and since we have a treaty signed with the British, they will not touch us. On the other hand, Jhansee has no ruler sitting on the throne and the kingdom is in a state of chaos. It's vulnerable.'

'The Jhansee rulers too had signed a treaty with the British. Maharaj Gangadhar's uncle had joined hands with the East India Company, giving them the authority to station their commissionary in the state,' Rani Larai said.

'Joined hands? Do you think that means anything to the firanghees?' Nathay Khan's laughter echoed in the room. 'Rani Sahiba, we have Dalhousie sitting in Fort William. For us, there could be nothing better. He wants Jhansee at all costs.'

'So? Where do we stand? What would we gain by attacking Jhansee? The firanghees would take it from us.'

'Not if *we* take over Jhansee first. They won't touch Jhansee since it will be a part of Orchha then.'

Rani Larai shook her head. 'No, not now. Wrong time, I'm warning you, Nathay. It's not fair.'

'Everything is fair in love and war, Your Highness! These are not normal times. The firanghees are unscrupulous and untrustworthy. The Company Sarkar is employing every conceivable tool to expand the East India Company's territories. I hate them as much as you do or Lakshmibai does. But we can use them to our advantage. We haven't touched Jhansee so far, have we? Lakshmibai's current state of affairs hasn't been caused by us. We are just exploiting the situation to get back what is rightfully ours.'

However, Rani Larai was not convinced. 'Don't underestimate Lakshmibai. She's cleverer than you think. She will not give up so easily. She will do everything she can to keep Jhansee under her rule. For all you know, she's probably planning some strategy or the other as we speak. Moreover, the people of Jhansee worship her.'

'But she has no troops with her. She cannot repulse an attack at the moment,' Nathay Khan reminded the queen.

Rani Larai once again shook her head. 'Not the right time. Something tells me that Lakshmibai's situation will deteriorate further. We'll wait and watch. Meanwhile, keep an eye on those two. Especially the girl.'

Nathay Khan bowed and took his leave. 'The Rani is a fool,' he thought as he walked out. 'She's just too scared of Lakshmibai. But Nathay Khan is not. Jhansee will be *my* victory – with or without the Rani's help.'

31

Chandraki's first week in Orchha was a troubled one. Lord Hamilton was expected to arrive the following week, and the queen was sparing no effort to ensure that he went back pleased. The kings of Orchha were known to greet the British agents with much fanfare and extend a lavish welcome to them. Rani Larai did not want to be found lacking in her hospitality and was determined to carry forward the tradition of her predecessors.

Chandraki, who was totally forgotten, or so she thought, in the ensuing brouhaha over the sahib's arrival in the kingdom, had still no place to stay. It had been a week since she arrived in Orchha. Her mind went back to the day she had first met the queen, and much to her annoyance, Riyaz Khan as well. She had not seen him since the day he had appeared in the durbar. Why was she thinking of him? Instead, she needed to find a place for herself. She decided to put forth her plea to the queen in court that afternoon.

As she approached the courtroom, the courtiers blocked her way with their spears.

'I want to meet the queen,' she insisted.

'The queen is not here,' said one of the courtiers.

Chandraki didn't know what to do or whom to go to. The moment she approached anyone, the person would quickly hurry away. 'I'm a suspect here, through and through. No one trusts me,' she thought. But she also knew that this was the truth. 'This will not help my cause,' she mused. 'I must make an effort to get to know the people here.'

She decided to ask the one person who seemed to be favourably disposed towards her – Taravati.

'The queen has gone to Tikamgarh,' the ageing courtesan said. 'That's our capital city.'

'Then what is this place, this fort, where we are staying?' Chandraki asked. The two women were on their way to Lala Hardaul's palace.

'This fort used to be our capital earlier, the capital of Bundelkhand. But now the queen mostly lives in Tikamgarh, though she visits this place often, especially if she has to receive some guest of honour. Lord Hamilton is visiting next week. The queen will return two days before that to receive him at Palki Mahal where we are headed right now.'

'I need a place to stay. The room I'm living in is terrible. And Nathay Khan has passed orders that I cannot step out of the fort,' she said gloomily. 'Who can I approach?'

'The queen is preoccupied right now,' Taravati said.

'Once the sahib leaves, she will leave for Ladhaura. I will be accompanying her this time,' she said. Then as an afterthought, she added, 'Why don't you come with us? You may get an opportunity to speak to her.'

Chandraki was quiet. Taravati smiled. 'Have you ever seen a shrub married to a stone?'

Chandraki thought for a while. 'No, I haven't heard of a stone being married to a shrub, I've seen trees married to trees. I have witnessed one such marriage. My mother and I had been invited to a similar one long ago,' she said.

'I've heard of such marriages taking place but have never seen one. What's it like? Which trees get married?'

'Mango trees. These mango groves are grown in such a way that the trees of one man's grove would not touch a tree of another man's grove. Sometimes, they have as many as twenty-five trees in an acre. It is believed that the more the number of Brahmins fed at such a marriage, the greater will be the fortunes of the owner of the grove.'

Taravati smiled. She looked at the young girl who stood before her. In a short span of time she had grown quite fond of her.

'My friend Gauri's uncle owned these mango orchards, somewhere on the way to Jubbalpur,' Chandraki continued. 'Her uncle had forgotten to marry his mango trees, and one day they bore fruit. But he couldn't taste the fruit from his own trees until one of the trees was married. When everything was finalized, they still had to deal with one huge problem,' Chandraki paused for breath.

'What?' Taravati asked eagerly.

'You are supposed to marry the mango tree to a tamarind tree. The only tamarind tree he had died so there was no bride!' Chandraki laughed.

'And then?'

'He was forced to marry the poor mango tree to a jasmine creeper. The jasmine creeper is allowed to be the bride only if there's no tamarind tree. But even the poor jasmine tree died after marriage as the gardener had forgotten to water her!'

The two women laughed heartily.

'And there were exactly a hundred Brahmins who feasted, but Gauri's uncle was disappointed as it was too small a number,' Chandraki said.

They had by now reached Phool Bagh, the gardens around Palki Mahal. The moment she stepped on the grass there, a draught of cool air caressed her cheeks.

'It is so pleasant here,' she remarked.

'Yes, it is. That is why Her Majesty is receiving the sahib here and not in the palace. The sahibs cannot tolerate our summer. Their skins turn a beetroot red and they break into rashes,' said Taravati.

~

'I say, Colvin, would you rather not go to Orchha in my place?' Lord Hamilton asked as he paced up and down, letting out puffs of smoke from his pipe. His office was sweltering and the punkahs were of no use. 'I have to go to Jhansee to meet Queen Lakshmibai.'

The younger man was seated on the couch that was

placed at the far end of the room. Unlike his senior, he seemed more relaxed. Taking a sip of the cool sherbet that the orderly had just brought in, he looked up at Hamilton.

'But sir, Orchha does not come under my purview,' he said matter-of-factly.

'I know, I know. Though I do not understand the head or tail of such an administrative set-up. You sit here in Agra as the Lieutenant Governor for the north-west province, and for some strange reason, have Jhansee under your jurisdiction, which falls in central India and should arguably be under my purview. But it isn't so, while all its neighbouring states do,' he said resignedly. He stopped to take a sip of the sherbet. 'Ah, this is quite refreshing,' he said. But moments later, he frowned. 'I hate these state visits. They make such a spectacle of it with all those elephants and camels and the paraphernalia that comes with it. And to think I have to undergo those hours of torture in this blistering heat.' Hamilton sighed as he sat down heavily beside Colvin. 'Tell me, isn't there any place in India that is cold?'

'There is, sir!'

'Where? I will beg Lord Dalhousie to have me transferred there.'

'The Himalayas, sir!'

Enraged, Hamilton looked at the young man. 'This is no matter of mirth, Colvin.'

'I'm not joking, sir. The upper reaches have cooler climes. I'm glad I get to experience the winters.'

'Well, there's hardly any winter here. You are lucky, I say.'

'Not really, sir, look at my job alone!'

'What do you mean?'

'I have Delhi under me. Would you really want to engage with the eighty-year-old Mughal emperor who sits there? Would you envy me then? Also, I believe Oudh would be annexed next year and will fall under my jurisdiction. You've read General Sleeman's report on Wajid Ali Shah, the ruling Nawab there, haven't you, sir?'

Hamilton nodded. 'Yes, Sleeman has accused him of maladministration.'

'But his subjects seem to be happy. And when that is the case, it does not bode well for the Company. I can see trouble. And that's why Jhansee worries me. Hence, sir, my task at hand is not enviable.'

Hamilton nodded as he rose. 'None of our tasks are enviable, my dear fellow! I don't quite fancy the idea of the Company spreading its tentacles far and wide across this country. And I definitely don't fancy the idea of making that trip to Orchha next week.' The older man sighed as Colvin rose to leave.

'So long, Colvin. Hope to see you in Jhansee in a few days when I get there to meet Lakshmibai who's still hoping that we will return her kingdom to her. It breaks my heart to see that girl so desperate and yet so hopeful.'

The two men shook hands and parted. John Russel Colvin knew that he would not meet Hamilton in Jhansee. He had no desire to visit the state right now. He liked neither Jhansee nor Hamilton for that matter, who he knew thought him to be completely incompetent. Nor did he relish the idea of meeting Queen Lakshmibai one bit. She intimidated him, and he was always at a loss for words when he was in her presence.

'No, I will definitely not be there,' Colvin muttered. 'Let Lord Hamilton deal with her. If I had my way, I will stop her pension and force her to pay off all her husband's debts. That lady needs to be taught a lesson for even trying to resist the Company's decisions!'

32

Lord Hamilton's welcome in Orchha was as grand as he had feared it would be. This was his first visit to the kingdom, and the queen was most eager to please him.

She met him just outside the entrance to the city. The queen had requested Hamilton to let her know when he set off for the visit as she wanted to be ready to receive him. She put forth her request through a khureeta that had left Hamilton much impressed. The letter was enclosed in a brocade bag that was inside another one made of fine muslin, the mouth of which was tied with a string of silk. From this hung the royal seal – a flat, round mass of sealing wax with the seal impressed on both sides of it. Hamilton turned it around several times, inspected it, admired it, and finally opened it.

'Trust the Indian royals to send such fancy letters!' he exclaimed to his office bearer.

Not wanting to come across as lacking in aesthetics himself, Lord Hamilton too got the camels to carry across a khureeta to the queen, intimating her of his arrival. Now, four days later, he waited inside his tent that had been put up especially for him. On hearing the royal band, the sounds of which could be heard from a great distance, he came out of his tent and squinted. The procession was slowly advancing towards him. Rani Larai, true to tradition, arrived with her magnificent entourage of caparisoned elephants, camels, horses, and the royal band whose sounds were now defeaning. Her cortege comprised at least fifty men and women. She got off her elephant when she was around twenty paces away from Hamilton's tent, and without setting foot on the ground, entered her litter.

'Isn't it difficult to step into that litter straight from the back of an elephant?' Chandraki whispered to Taravati who had brought her along to witness the grand arrival of Lord James Hamilton in Orchha.

'The queen is a symbol of divinity. Her feet are not supposed to touch the ground, nor is the sun supposed to shine on her person. Hence, she's covered by an umbrella,' Taravati replied in a hushed whisper. 'Now, don't talk, just watch,' she cautioned Chandraki who stood with her mouth open. Chandraki had never witnessed such a ceremonious welcome of guests in Jhansee.

'This is so splendid!' she exclaimed pointing at the litter the queen had stepped into moments ago.

'You mean the nalkee?' Taravati asked, pointing to the vehicle that carried the queen up to Hamilton's tent. Chandraki nodded.

'Why shouldn't it be? It was conferred on our last king by the Mughal emperor himself. It is one of the three royal insignia that the Mughal kings bestow upon independent kings they consider to be among the finest rulers. The other two are the Order of the Fish and the Fan of the Peacock's feathers.'

'Is the ruler of Orchha so important?' Chandraki asked. She had not seen any such insignia accompany Jhansee's royal cortege at any point in time.

'That depends on the discretion of the Mughal emperor,' Taravati explained. 'It is believed that the Mughals, who are descendants of the house of Taimur, have assumed this right to confer these symbols on those they choose as the privileged rulers. It is the Farsi Order of Knighthood,' Taravati explained. 'The insignia of the Fish, known as the Mahi Maratib, was first instituted by Khusru Parviz, the king of Persia.'

The litter was then carried to the sahib's tent and placed in front of it. Rani Larai alighted from it and greeted Lord Hamilton with folded hands. Hamilton accepted her greeting, and the two walked into the tent.

'Thank you for visiting us, Lord Hamilton. I hope your journey was comfortable. We have made splendid arrangements for your stay in our kingdom. I'm sure they will agree with your esteemed self,' the queen said, taking her seat on the other side of the fine muslin purdah that had been drawn between them.

Outside, Chandraki stared at the nalkee, wide-eyed. After the queen got off, the men carrying the nalkee put it down on the ground heavily. Her Highness would be inside for some time, so they decided to take a break. Chandraki meanwhile, terribly curious about the nalkee, stepped away from the group of people she stood with and sneaked behind the tents. Nobody noticed her slip away. She spotted the nalkee placed a little distance away from the two tents. She went up to it to inspect it. Beside the nalkee were placed two long poles on which were mounted two kaukabas, balls of polished steel, representing the planets. The poles were resting against a babul tree. She stared at them wide-eyed and open-mouthed before moving away when suddenly, she heard the clear voice of Rani Larai. Chandraki caught the words Tatya Tope and Jhansee. She stepped closer to the tents.

'Deshpat and Tatya Tope have joined hands, I believe,' Chandraki heard Rani Larai say.

'Deshpat has always given us trouble. For several years now he has been refusing to pay any revenue for his jagir in Nowgong. When pressed further, he killed seven of our men,' Hamilton said.

'He's shielded by the Rani of Chhatarpur,' Chandraki heard Rani Larai say.

'But I thought the Rani of Chhatarpur supports us.'

'That's just an eyewash,' Rani Larai snapped. 'She has been supporting Deshpat by providing him with money and troops. Lakshmibai defies the Company Sarkar openly, while these regents do it on the sly. There are a few kings, though, who are loyal to you. Of them, Ratan Singh, the Raja of Charkhari, and the Raja of Bijawar, Lugasi and Gaurihar swear allegiance to you as does the queen of Dutya,' she informed the sahib.

'So does the ruler of Samthar. He has signed a treaty with us. Nripat Singh too is with us,' Lord Hamilton shared.

Rani Larai nodded. 'Ah yes, the Raja of Panna. Look Mr Hamilton, the rulers may support you, but you have to be wary of the individual jagirdars in those kingdoms.'

'Who are you alluding to, Your Highness?'

'Jawahar Singh Pawar, the Diwan of Katera, which as you know, is a jagir of Dutya. Then there's Rajjab Khan. He's a subedar in Samthar and is in charge of a fort in Lohagarh. I've heard he's gathering a force of Pathans from Lohagarh. Even in Panna, there's Mukund Singh who's making a lot of noise against the British.'

There was silence for a while. Chandraki heard the bushes behind her rustle. The nalkee bearers were probably returning. She ran back to the babul tree and flattened herself against it. But she didn't see anyone approach.

Suddenly Lord Hamilton's voice rang out, loud and clear. 'But why would Lokpal Singh go against us? Ajaigarh is our ally.'

'Wrong! Ajaigarh is not your ally; only Ranjor Singh is, whom you have chosen to put on the throne now that Mahipat Singh's son is dead. And this, you've done by overruling the claims of Diwan Lokpal Singh. I've heard he's joined hands with Farzand Ali, the advocate at Ajaigarh. As you can see, it is not good to meddle in our internal matters, Lord Hamilton!'

'Do you believe so? Haven't we recognized you as the proxy ruler as well?'

'No, you have nothing to do with it.'

'In that case, what is Orchha's stand? Can we expect you to support us?'

'No!'

There was silence again. Chandraki was now sweating, her palms clammy. Her lips had run dry, and she trembled slightly.

'But Your Highness, we thought Orchha is our ally!'

'By no means, Mr Hamilton! We don't fall under your jurisdiction. Am I clear enough? We will not go against you, but we will not support you either. We don't need to,' the queen of Orchha said firmly.

Chandraki waited behind the tents for some more time. The voices were now lowered and were hardly audible. After a little while, she heard Rani Larai's voice again.

'We have arranged for a cultural programme for your pleasure this evening. I also take this opportunity to invite you to witness the wedding of salagram and the tulsi plant for which we shall proceed to Ladhaura tomorrow morning. I hope you will grant us the pleasure of your company,' she said. Chandraki heard the shuffle of cloth as the queen rose to leave.

Chandraki stepped out from behind the tree and ran the little distance back to where the crowds were milling about. She quickly blended into the group of people who waited outside for the queen and the sahib to emerge.

Inside, Lord Hamilton folded his hands and bowed as he watched Rani Larai leave. His mind was in turmoil. He wouldn't survive the wedding of salagram and the tulsi. He was already forming a series of excuses in his head that he would make when asked to accompany the queen to Ladhaura.

~

Chandraki did not wait for Taravati and started walking back to town. Her steps were quick and light. The town square was not very far, a little less than two miles away. On reaching it, she went straight to the Ram Raja temple. She hoped that the Basors would still be around. She found them huddled in a corner of the huge courtyard under the shade of a lone peepul tree, weaving their beautiful baskets. They looked up when she approached them and smiled at her.

'I see you are still here,' she said as a way of beginning a conversation.

'We are waiting for the rains after which we will move again,' one of them said in rustic Bundeli.

Chandraki's face fell. The rains were a long way off.

'I have seen you sing in Jhansee when the prince was born.' She smiled.

'Yes, we were there. But we were sad to know that the prince died.' One woman, who until now had been intent on weaving a basket, turned to Chandraki. 'Have you been to Jhansee?' she asked. This was the moment Chandraki was waiting for.

'I am from Jhansee. I am married here. I miss my family. Can I send a letter through you to my sister in Jhansee?'

'But we are not going now,' the woman replied. 'You will have to wait for the rains.'

Chandraki was crestfallen. She stood still for a while and then turned to leave. Suddenly, one of the men spoke. 'I may go to Jhansee in the next few days as I need to collect some money from a few customers there. Our business is down at the moment and that money is important.'

'Thank you. That will be very helpful. Just wait, I'll be right back,' said Chandraki as she walked off purposefully.

She needed to write that letter, but how? Should she go back to the palace? If she did so and started looking around for parchment and ink, it would arouse suspicion. She was sure Nathay Khan's men were watching her. Think, think, she told herself as she walked around the temple premises and finally came back to rest against the peepul tree. Its branches, with their heart-shaped leaves, drooped around her, swaying slightly. The tree was sacred, she knew, to the Hindus. Peepul and Ashwathha were demons killed by Lord Shani on a Saturday, hence, the peepul tree was worshipped on Saturdays. It was also the abode of Lakshmi and Vishnu. She knew that Ganesha loved sitting under its canopy. Brahma, Vishnu and Shiva held their councils under this tree. She had also been told that her mother's soul resided in that tree as did those of her ancestors, and she had often sat under the tree next to the temple in Jhansee and wept for her dead mother.

'Please help me, oh Ashwathha,' she prayed. Suddenly a thought struck her. She plucked two large leaves and went over to one of the shops that sold items required for a puja.

'Bhau, I need a little chandanam, some sandalwood paste,' she said to the shopkeeper.

The shopkeeper nodded and took out a slab of sandalwood on which he poured a little water from a pitcher. He then rubbed a small sandalwood bar on it vigorously and within minutes was ready with the fragrant paste. Thanking him, she hurriedly ran across the courtyard and picked up a feather of a crow. She dabbed the calamus with the paste and scribbled a message, forming each tiny letter neatly. Chandraki knew that once the paste dried up, the letters would become brighter and clearer.

'My sister Gauri's house is at the far end of Lakshmi Tal,' Chandraki said as she handed the leaf to her courier. 'Tell her the letter is from the peacock of Jhansee.' She smiled.

The man had a bewildered look on his face as he took the leaf from her and wrapping a piece of cloth around it, gently placed it inside a basket. She knew the Basors could not read so it would be safe with them. Moreover, since they were well known all over Bundelkhand, no one checked them. She sent across a quick prayer to Lord Ram to help her.

Before leaving Jhansee, Chandraki had taken Gauri into confidence and told her she would be communicating with Maharani Lakshmibai through her. The moment Gauri received the letter from the Basor weaver, she ran all the way to the palace and handed it to Maharani Lakshmibai. The queen hurriedly opened the letter.

'Maharani ki jai! I have reached Orchha. All are suspicious of me here, especially Nathay Khan, the diwan. I have not met Jaywant yet.

Lord Hamilton is here. Dutya and Panna are with the firanghees. Tatya Tope and Deshpat are together and fighting the firanghees.

Rani Larai is not supporting the firanghees but is also not against them. There is no plan to attack Jhansee.'

33

To Lord Hamilton's surprise, the evening turned out to be much better than expected. Lala Hardaul's palace, known as the Palki Mahal, was indeed beautiful.

'This is quite a charming place,' he said to his officer as the two of them strolled around Phool Bagh in the evening, amidst the fragrant blossoms and the sweet-smelling fruit trees. Nathay Khan had placed two orderlies at Hamilton's disposal, who doubled up as guides and led the sahib around.

'What are those?' Hamilton asked, pointing at two tall towers that surrounded the garden.

'These are the Badgir Sawan Bhadon towers, Sarkar,' one of the guides supplied. 'They capture the wind that blows to help cool down the palace.'

Hamilton was impressed. 'I say this is some fantastic engineering, Andrew. What do you think? The garden reminds me of the one the Mughals have built in Delhi,' he remarked.

'You are right, sir! This is indeed designed as Charbagh,

the gardens in Faras that inspired the Mughals to build theirs,' the guide said.

In the evening Lord Hamilton was ushered into the tehkhana – an underground chamber specially designed for entertainment purposes during the summer. Silk mattresses wrapped in brocade covers were spread out and exquisite aari and kashida embroidered silk and velvet cushions were strewn around. Low chairs and ottomans had been placed in case anyone preferred to sit on a raised seat.

Lord Hamilton took his seat on one of the ottomans, resting his arm on a velvet bolster, while Rani Larai preferred to sit on one of the low throne chairs, flanked on either side by officials from her immediate coterie including Nathay Khan. Though it was a warm evening, the row of fountains constructed on the eight-pillared pavilion above the tehkhana kept it cool. The lower part of the Sawan Bhadon towers was connected to a reservoir of water which was further connected to a huge bowl called the chandan katora in the pavilion above the retreat. The aquaducts pushed up the water from the reservoir into the chandan katora, from where the water cascaded like a fountain on the roof of the retreat.

For the first time since he had come to India, Lord Hamilton actually relaxed and sat back to savour the evening's entertainment programme that had been especially prepared for him.

Lala Hardaul's tragic story was brought alive through a play that left the British officers much impressed. Everyone in Orchha knew the legend of the twenty-four-year-old Hardaul who though innocent, was poisoned by his own brother Jhujjar who suspected him of having illicit relations with his wife. Hardaul was revered as a god in Orchha.

The play was followed by a comic caper in which a group of comedians acted out scenes depicting the insolence of opportunity-seeking attendants of great men. The audience, which was much amused, did not mind staying up late as the programme continued well into the night.

~

The following day Rani Larai left for Ladhaura to witness the grand event of the union of the stone of salagram with the holy tulsi plant. Lord Hamilton could not manage to excuse himself even though he tried his best to convince the queen that he was somewhat indisposed. His meeting with Maharani Lakshmibai would have to wait, though he didn't know which was more daunting – meeting Lakshmibai or attending the wedding of the stone and the shrub as a state guest of the kingdom of Orchha!

Lord Hamilton, in the fifty-three summers he had spent on this earth, had never seen a spectacle such as the one he beheld now. He was left speechless. The groom salagram, a round fossilized black pebble, revered as a representation of Lord Vishnu across India, was being married to the tulsi shrub, in which resided Goddess Lakshmi, Lord Vishnu's wife. The tulsi plant was dressed in bridal attire, complete with vermilion and garlands, while the 'groom' was wrapped in a dhoti.

The groom arrived, carried by Rani Larai in her lap, swaying on an elephant at the head of a cortege, consisting of six elephants, a thousand camels and three thousand horses all mounted and caparisoned. The queen, who paid for all expenses incurred, supervised the entire wedding ceremony and gave away the bride. This was followed by heavy feasting and merrymaking by thousands of people who had all gathered as friends and family of the bride and groom, after which the newly wed couple were left to relax and bask in each other's company.

Two days later, Rani Larai left for Orchha and Lord Hamilton for Jhansee to meet Maharani Lakshmibai.

'From one queen to another . . . this is what I would call being caught between Scylla and Charybdis.' He sighed as he fortified himself for his meeting with the queen of Jhansee.

~

It was three in the morning and still dark outside. Chandraki sneaked out of her room and emerged into one of the long, narrow corridors. Mostly everyone was away at Palki Mahal and Chandraki knew that the queen was headed for Ladhaura straight from there. And with her would go Nathay Khan and most of his men. The marriage of the stone and the shrub was one of the most important events of the year, Taravati had told her. This was the chance she had been waiting for.

Though most of the mashaals had been snuffed out, the faint light from outside filtered in through the latticed windows that punctuated the length of the corridor. She tiptoed past the rooms and stealthily approached the one in the centre. It used to be the king's room but was now occupied by Nathay Khan during the day. She tried to push open the heavily carved wooden door, but it was shut tight. There was nothing she could do so she decided to climb up the flight of stairs to the first storey where the queen had her quarters.

In the faint glow of the mashaal, she could make out the steep stony steps that led to the upper floor of the palace. She hesitated. Should she go up? Just as she placed her foot on the first step, she thought she saw a shadow flit across the steps. Chandraki froze. She waited for a while, but nothing happened. Was it her imagination? She shrugged and started climbing the first few steps. The shadow reappeared and blocked the light from the torch, plunging the staircase in darkness. This was definitely not her imagination. Without waiting further, she turned around and hurriedly went down the steps. When she reached the bottom of the staircase, she paused. Then gathering her wits about her, she looked up the flight of stairs. The steps showed up clearly in the pale light of the torch. She didn't want to wait now. Hugging the wall, she padded down the corridor that encircled the courtyard. At other times, this place would be filled with people and bustling with activity. But now there was complete silence except for the faint sound of the Betwa river that flowed behind the palace. She knew the guards were on duty outside the main gate of the palace.

As she stepped out into the inner courtyard, she thought she heard a sound right behind her. She looked up at the two storeys above her. Everything was quiet. The stars twinkled in the dark sky. Suddenly a long shadow was cast over her as though covering her with a shroud. She stood completely still. She had broken into a sweat, and small beads of perspiration appeared on her forehead. She didn't dare to look behind. Whatever it was, or whoever it was, stood right behind her, very close. She could feel its presence and knew that if she reached out she could even touch it. It had followed her all the way from the stairs she had left behind.

'What are you doing here at this time?' A deep voice rang out in the stillness of the dark night. Too terrified to look behind, she stood motionless, gaping at the fountain in front of her.

'What are you doing here?' the question was repeated. Caught unawares, at first she didn't recognize the voice. But now she suddenly knew. She drew in her breath and slowly turned around. Her taut nerves eased.

'I'm looking for a place to stay.'

'Where are you staying presently? Surely, not under the open sky?' Riyaz Khan asked, his tone laced with sarcasm.

'The room where I'm staying is hot and dark. There's a musty smell and I can't bear it any more, she replied with all the bravado she could muster. Her heart was fluttering. Would he have guessed her intentions? This was the first time their paths had crossed since that fateful day in Rani Larai's court.

'I don't believe you, but since I do not wish to spend the rest of the night chatting you up, I will let you go. Make sure the next time you are hunting for a room, it's in daylight. No one goes around in the dead of night looking for a place to stay,' he said. Though she couldn't see his face, she could feel the sting in his voice. Without a word, she returned to her room. But she knew it wouldn't be easy to sneak around henceforth. She was sure Riyaz Khan's suspicions had been aroused. She would have to be very careful.

Rani Larai returned two days later and summoned the durbar.

'The Company Sarkar is happy with us, and even though some of our neighbours have had their kingdoms seized, Orchha continues to be independent. I wish to announce the formal anointing of Raja Hamir Singh, so that it becomes clear to Fort William that there is no dispute for the throne of Orchha. I will, meanwhile, continue to rule in his name.'

She paused to let the applause die down.

'I'm leaving for Tikamgarh tomorrow and will return to Orchha only on Janmashtami, two months from now. I have invited some important people for the event, including a few kings from our neighbouring kingdoms. I want a grand cultural evening organized and want our guest from Jhansee to perform at the event, who I'm told is a fine dancer. If she can please us with her skills, she can continue staying here till the time she meets her husband who she claims lives here. Until then she can stay in the zenana.'

'Now that you have a place to stay finally, I do hope you won't be caught loitering around these premises in the middle of the night,' Riyaz Khan said to Chandraki as she walked out of the hall, his words spelling out a clear warning.

Nathay Khan who was passing by saw Riyaz talking to Chandraki. He walked up to them. Riyaz saluted him. He nodded and turned to Chandraki.

'I would have loved to have lodged you in my quarters, my lovely lady, but Riyaz insisted that I find you a place to stay. How could I turn down the request of my officer? But that still doesn't stop you from coming to my house whenever you want. It's just around the corner. Riyaz will show it to you.' He grinned as he walked away.

Riyaz looked from one to the other, his brows knitted in a frown. Then composing himself, he said matter-of-factly, 'I'll send Meher to you. She will guide you around.'

Chandraki looked at his receding figure, too surprised to react. So it was Riyaz Khan who had pushed her cause for a room. Why? She could not fathom his intentions try as she might. What was he up to?

34

Now that she was formally initiated into the zenana, Chandraki had more freedom to move around both within the palace as well as outside in the city. But she was sure that she was being followed. Nathay Khan, she knew, was watching her like a hawk. She was now extremely careful, and every now and then she looked over her shoulder. She imagined shadows where there were none; she heard whispers even when she knew there was no one around. She was sure this was not a part of her overactive imagination. Something told her that she was being tailed. She expected to run straight into someone when she turned corners. Always on edge, Chandraki's mind was forever alert, her senses sharpened.

She started getting out of the palace and roamed the streets of Orchha. She would occasionally see firanghees walking around the town, the sahibs and memsahibs, incongruous in this ancient city. They mostly came as guests of Rani Larai, who actually lived in Tikamgarh, where all the rulers had lived since the capital of Orchha shifted there in 1763. But the queen kept visiting the erstwhile Bundela capital city and stayed in the palace during festivals or when she entertained state guests.

Though Rani Larai sat on the throne, the real ruler, approved by the East India Company, was little Hamir Singh. But who was he?

'When Rani Larai's husband, King Dharampal, died she contested for the throne, but she was denied it as Dharampal's brother Sujan Singh took over the throne. It was only when Sujan Singh died that she managed to usurp the throne and place Hamir Singh on it. He is the son of her distant relative, informed Taravati, who had seen fifty-two summers in the palace.

'Is she on good terms with the British?' Chandraki asked.

'Her Majesty doesn't want to antagonize the firanghees. If she rebels, they will defeat her quite easily. On the other hand, if she toes their line by sending her troops to support their battles, the Company would allow her to continue ruling Orchha. They have not touched Orchha. And she wants to keep it that way,' Taravati said.

~

One of the friends Chandraki had made in the palace was Meher. As promised by Riyaz, she had turned up in her room one day. Meher had been brought up in the palace of Orchha itself. Her mother had been one of the concubines of the previous king. Lacking in intellect, Meher more than made up for her cerebral deprivation with her skills in the craft of lovemaking and seduction. Well equipped in the art of charming men, Meher had no inhibitions when it came to the art of lovemaking. Fed on a diet of erotic techniques straight out of the Kamasutra, she used her exquisite looks and her ample assets to her advantage. However, not all men were impressed with her. One of them was Riyaz Khan. Although he did not hesitate to exploit the sexual favours she lavished upon him, her endless chatter and lack of intelligence irritated him.

She, on the other hand, was completely smitten by him. When Meher told her this, Chandraki was aghast. She tried her best to warn the younger girl.

'He has five wives and ten children,' she exaggerated, hoping to put off the lovelorn girl. But Chandraki's words had no effect on her. As is the wont of amour, Meher continued pursuing him with the kind of passion that defied all logic. Riyaz, on his part, took advantage of the situation and often used her services both in bed as well as in gathering information about the events in the palace, all of which she was happy to provide. He would then convey this information to Nathay Khan. Riyaz's skill at swordsmanship had won Nathay Khan over, and he was already commanding a small regiment in Rani Larai's army.

'Incredible!' Chandraki mumbled. Her mind went back to the day she had first met him in Jhansee. She shivered involuntarily. Much as she tried to shake him out of her mind, he refused to vacate it. 'What is it about him that disturbs me so?'

'Who disturbs you so?' Meher asked. Chandraki jumped. She had no idea when Meher had joined her as she strolled through the orchards and sweet-smelling blossoms that surrounded a charming two-storeyed house that stood between the Raja Mahal and the Jahangir Mahal.

'Riyaz Khan!'

'I thought you didn't like him. Chandraki, you knew him in Jhansee, didn't you? What was he like? Tell me all you know about him.'

'He treats you so badly, yet you keep going back to him.'

'I don't mind it. I love him,' insisted Meher.

'What surprises me is how that man manages to always rise to the top, and so quickly,' Chandraki said, deftly changing the topic. 'He did the same in Jhansee.'

'Have you seen him flourish his sword or ride a horse? He's the best we've got.' Meher, as always, sprung to his defence. 'I'm very happy,' she said all of a sudden.

'Why? Is he going to marry you?' Chandraki taunted.

'No! But I love him and I always will whether he has three wives or thirty,' Meher said, ignoring Chandraki's sarcasm.

'Then why are you so happy?'

'I'm happy for him. When I was with him last night, he said he would soon be a big man, and he would find better women and would no longer want to spend time with stupid girls like me!'

'And you are happy about that?' Chandraki asked angrily.

'I'm happy that he's going to be a big man soon,' Meher repeated.

True love indeed, thought Chandraki resignedly. But she was thinking about the reason why Riyaz Khan had made such a statement. Perhaps he'll be appointed as the next General of the Rani's army. He had managed to win over the trust of not just Nathay Khan, but the queen as well. She shrugged. Tired of discussing Riyaz Khan, she hurried along up the steps to the second storey. The moment she stepped into the balcony, a gust of cool breeze greeted her.

'What a lovely house,' she said aloud as she walked through its spacious rooms. The huge windows let in the cool breeze from the river. Exquisite paintings of dancing girls adorned the walls. Its wide archways gave a splendid view of the hills and the Betwa on one side, and the Jahangir Mahal on the other.

'Who lives here?' Chandraki asked as she flicked the strands of hair that blew into her face. It was quite windy up here, but she was enjoying walking down the balconies.

'No one lives here now. It's used to lodge guests of the state. At times, mehfils are held here,' Meher answered as she waltzed in and out of the rooms, emulating the various poses of the dancers painted on the walls all around.

'But someone must have lived here sometime?' Chandraki insisted.

'Rai Praveen!' Meher said.

'Who was she?' Chandraki asked.

'Raja Indramani, who was one of the kings of Orchha, built this palace for Rai Praveen. She was his chief courtesan and escort. I've heard that she was beautiful, bold and fearless,' Meher prattled. 'Just like you are with Nathay Khan!'

Chandraki turned around sharply. 'What do you mean by that?'

'I've seen how Nathay Khan leers at you and has tried to engage with you. You turn him away each time. I wish I could do that too.' She sighed.

'Then why don't you? Don't let him bully you. The next time Nathay Khan calls for you, refuse to go.'

'Ya Allah, are you crazy? Don't you know that the sword of his wrath will come swiftly on my neck? I'm no Rai Praveen, nor is he as magnanimous as Emperor Akbar. Do you know what Rai Praveen said to the Shahenshah when he summoned her to Agra to dance?' Meher asked. Chandraki shook her head. Every day, she heard a new story about Orchha. 'Vineet Rai Pravin ki, suniye sah sujan, Juthi patar bakhat hain, bari, bayas, swan – the emperor was so touched by her loyalty to her paramour that he sent her back to Orchha with full honours,' said Meher as she narrated the legend. 'Nathay Khan, on the other hand, will kill me. But you wait and watch. One day, I will occupy this palace,' Meher said.

'Who will give you this palace?' Chandraki asked, incredulous at the girl's optimism.

'Riyaz Khan, when he becomes a big man, and I, his chief woman.'

Astounded at her stupidity, Chandraki looked at Meher pitifully and sighed knowing that Meher's dream of becoming Riyaz Khan's 'chief woman' would never be realized. There had been so many Mehers in Riyaz's life. But . . . why did he tell her that he would be a big man soon?

35

For Chandraki, Orchha was like a solitaire pearl, set deep in the heartland of Vindhya Pradesh. It was as though the lime-white buildings of Orchha relieved the stark ochre Bundelkhand landscape of its dreariness. She often spent hours by the river. Each time she saw it trip playfully over the many stones and rocks that lay strewn across its course as it wound its way through the plains of Bundelkhand towards a destination unknown to her, she would think of the course her own life had taken and how she had embarked upon a journey marked with such great uncertainty.

As she passed the river today as part of the royal procession headed towards the Lakshmi Narayan temple, she could barely resist the urge to take a dip in its waters, yet again. It was a hot day, and the river beckoned her enticingly. But she ignored it and walked along with the procession. This was her first visit to the temple. It was situated on the western side of the palace, perched on a hilltop. The queens of successive rulers visited it to worship the goddess of wealth and prosperity.

Rani Larai's entourage was often led by Riyaz Khan, who waited with the soldiers at the foot of the hill while the Rani and her small group of attendants went ahead for the darshan. On this occasion too, it was Riyaz Khan who headed the small procession as it made its way towards the temple. On reaching the small hillock, the palanquin was put down and the Rani stepped out.

'Chandraki!' she called. Chandraki had wandered to the edge of the hillock and stood there looking down the cliff. The town of Orchha spread out before her. Far ahead in the distance, she could see the palace, and to her right, the Betwa sliced its way across the rocky terrain. To her left, towered the spires of the Chaturbhuj temple.

'Would you like to come inside or just wait outside admiring our kingdom?' the queen asked. She was visiting Orchha on the occasion of Janmashtami.

As Chandraki entered the temple, she was welcomed by colourful images representing scenes of courtship that sprang up at her from the walls. The cool interiors shielded her from the fierce glare of the sun. As she made her way further into the temple, she noticed that corridors criss-crossed each other, and at every intersection, she saw splendid paintings portraying scenes from the Ramayana. Wherever she turned, she was greeted by colourful motifs depicting exciting events from the lives of Krishna and Vishnu as well as scenes from the Bhagavad Gita and the Puranas.

'This is beautiful!' she exclaimed.

The walls on either side were lined with exquisite murals, paintings and floral motifs in mostly maroon and white, unlike the prominence of the colour blue used in the fort. Themes from the ragamalas adorned the walls. She looked longingly at the painting of a peacock that had spread out its plume to woo its beloved, or perhaps to celebrate the onset of the monsoon. Ah, Chandraki, she smiled. There were images of swings – metaphoric depiction of the season of amour. She touched one of the paintings gently. A crust of white powder dusted the tip of her finger.

'What is this?'

'It's the paint,' her companion replied, pointing at the paintings. 'It's made from a mixture of lime plaster, marble and seashell powder.'

The queen, meanwhile, had moved towards the sanctum sanctorum which was built in such a way that the first rays of the sun fell on it. While the queen offered her prayers, Chandraki went around the corridors. Iron rings hung from the ceilings. She had seen similar rings in Jhansee where they were used to hang swings during the festival of Teej.

'Do you celebrate Teej here?' she asked. Her friend nodded.

'The swings are suspended from these,' the girl said, looking up at the iron rings above. 'There are flowers, plants, music and dance and we rise high up in the air as we push each other on the swings.' The girl clasped her hands, closed her eyes and jumped with joy. Chandraki smiled and thought of Jhansee where they celebrated all festivals in pretty much the same way.

Tearing herself away from the richly hued walls, she followed the retinue through the long passageways. It was unlike any temple she had seen before. It was octagonal in shape and she had to walk through a narrow passage to reach a corridor that was lined with beautiful paintings as well. The corridor ended in a flight of stairs leading up to the terrace. As Chandraki stepped on to the terrace, she stood there, stunned. The arched doorways that punctuated the entire length of the wall that barricaded the terrace were intricately carved in white stone. She peered through one of the latticed windows and was greeted with a panoramic view of the lush green hills in the wake of the couple of recent showers that the region had just witnessed. From the centre of the terrace, a spiral staircase went further up to the central dome that like everything else had elaborate carvings and panels of vibrant friezes.

After the puja, the queen and her attendants stepped out for a pradakshina around the rectangular building. The magnificent structure had four bastions projecting out of its four corners. She walked up to its entrance from where the building looked like a huge triangle made out of stone with the central spire penetrating the azure sky.

After their tour of the temple, the little group joined the body of guards waiting below. Chandraki stopped to watch Riyaz Khan, who stood a little away from the rest. He looked pensive. What was he thinking? Embarrassed at her own thoughts, she quickly turned away to join Larai Rani's procession. Suddenly she changed her mind and walked up to him. Riyaz, surprised, straightened himself.

'So you are going to be a big man soon?'

Riyaz frowned and looked at her questioningly. He had no idea what she was talking about.

'You are going to be a big man, Riyaz Khan? But you are already so big. A huge, big bear,' Chandraki mocked him and ran away laughing.

Riyaz was stunned at this sudden onslaught. He had no clue where that had come from. What on earth was she talking about? He narrowed his brows, thinking hard. By then the Rani's entourage had reached the bottom of the hillock, and he quickly took up his position to lead the procession back to the palace.

That night Riyaz couldn't sleep. He stood beside the window looking out at the horizon as the sun set. The rays of the descending sun poured into the room through the latticed network, creating an intricate golden pattern on his face. The shadows that were dispelled by a few candles enhanced Riyaz's pensive mood. It was a sinking feeling, something he always felt whenever he saw the sun set. He was trapped in a jumble of emotions that overwhelmed him. Yet it was a beautiful evening that was at once melancholic and ephemeral, and an evening laden with agony. He was consumed with thoughts of Chandraki and of her strange statement. She returned to haunt him again and again. He paced up and down the room, restless and agitated and continued to do so until the break of dawn after which he sprawled on the bed and fell asleep.

Chandraki, though, was unaware of the fact that she had kept Riyaz awake the whole night. She had her own concerns. Meher had told her a few things that had set her thinking.

36

The money that Lakshmibai had given Chandraki had been confiscated at the gates of the palace. As the days passed, and there was no sign of Jaywant, she felt the need for it. Meher asked her to meet the khajanchi. She approached him in his room where he sat sorting out the accounts.

'Can I have my money back?' she asked the chief treasurer.

Farzand Bakshi, engrossed in his huge ledger, looked up from his papers.

'What money?'

'I was carrying some money with me when I came here from Jhansee. That was taken away. I need it now.'

'Aren't you paid for your dances?'

It was true that ever since she had been inducted into the zenana she was being paid a small amount every week. She was also paid each time she performed on stage. But she needed more money. She wanted to buy a dagger, if possible, even a sword. Besides, it was *her* money that they had taken away.

'I do, but I want *my* money back!' she said firmly.

The khajanchi was getting on in years. Impatient at this sudden intrusion, he stroked his beard and sat back in his chair. 'Come to my house in the evening. We'll talk this over and see what can be done. I'm busy now,' he said, dismissing Chandraki.

~

It had been more than four months since Chandraki had left Jhansee. If she did not find Jaywant in the next one month, she would return to Jhansee. Here she had been reduced to a court dancer. She didn't like it one bit. She never got a chance to practise sword fighting or ride Bijli, who had been kept away in the royal stables. What really troubled her, though, was something else. She was getting fed up of Nathay Khan's lecherous advances and it was getting more and more difficult to ward him off.

She was also bewildered by Riyaz Khan's attitude. She had been scared when she first saw him in Orchha. She knew he had known that she had informed the king about his negotiation with the firanghees. She had expected revenge, for his fury to be unleashed on her. But nothing happened. Over the past few months that the two had been here, he had shown little or no interest in her, sometimes even ignored her completely. They rarely saw each other.

Riyaz Khan – she had known him for years. She had disliked him from the very first day she had seen him and wanted him out of Jhansee. Why? It was true he had never been spiteful or mean to her. He had never been nasty, nor had he made any overtures towards her. In all those years, Riyaz had never once humiliated her. Why did she always feel uncomfortable in his presence? Why did her heart always beat so fast when she saw him?

Chandraki stood at her little window and looked out. It was a clear night and the moon was bright in the sky. The same moon was shining above Jhansee too, she thought. She wondered how the Maharani was. She missed Jhansee, her home. And Jaywant. Where was he? She thought it odd that instead of thinking about him, it was thoughts of Riyaz that crept into her mind lately.

His was a name that led to the eruption of a wave of intense emotions in her, a potpourri of hate, fear and apprehension, and . . . something else, a strange warm sensation that she couldn't identify. She tried to wrench herself away from thoughts of him, but it seemed that there was an invisible string that kept them bound together, and their paths crossed again and again. Now years later, it had happened once again. But strangely, she was no longer uneasy in his presence. In fact, she felt almost reassured by his familiar presence amidst unknown and hostile people.

For the first time she smiled as she thought of him and how he had looked when she had called him a bear.

'But I still shouldn't trust him,' she told herself quickly as though ashamed that she no longer felt any hate for him. She suddenly realized that Riyaz Khan was no longer her worst enemy.

The next day, she bumped into him in the palace. Along with Nathay Khan, he was on his way to meet the queen.

'So no news of your Jaywant?' Nathay Khan grinned. Chandraki ignored him and moved on. Nathay Khan caught her arm.

'Why are you wasting yourself on a man who doesn't even exist? You are a beautiful woman. Please me and I will make your life.'

'Leave me alone, Nathay Khan. Have you seen your face in the mirror? Get lost!'

Nathay Khan was taken aback by her sharp retort, and though infuriated, he let it pass. He was determined to get this girl. He could have forced himself upon her long ago. He knew nobody would have pointed a finger at him. He was the Rani's khaas. But somehow the thought of getting Chandraki by force did not appeal to him. He wanted her, and he wanted her with her consent. Sooner or later, she would give in, he knew. It was no fun if he could get her easily. There was no challenge in the game. And Nathay Khan loved challenges.

'All right. Come to my room this evening during the mehfil, and we'll sort out this business of yours. I'll line up a few men and you can check if one of them is your Jaywant.'

Chandraki knew if Nathay Khan wanted to, he could find Jaywant for her. Should she take a chance? She hesitated and Nathay Khan knew he had won this round.

Chandraki did not reply. But her silence conveyed the words that Nathay Khan wanted to hear. He quickly walked away, afraid that his expression would unmask his elation. The timing was perfect. He knew that everyone would be busy at the evening mehfil. If Chandraki resisted, there would be no one to hear her protests and come to her rescue. He rubbed his hands with sheer glee, a wicked smile playing on his lips. The moment had come. He recalled that night, many months ago, when he had seen the woman dance under the open night sky in the frothy waters of the Betwa, naked and delicious. He had known all along that it had been her, and until he felt that luscious body underneath him, he could not rest. 'Tonight! Tonight!' he hissed and ran his tongue over his lips.

Chandraki waited for the evening to arrive with trepidation. Would Nathay Khan really help her? He would definitely ask for something in return. She knew very well what that would be. Yet she must take the chance. She had no alternative, no other way to find Jaywant other than to just wait for him to show up. And how long would that wait be? It could stretch for weeks, months or even a year perhaps? How long would she have to continue staying in Orchha, far away from her queen, her Jhansee?

'Let me take this chance,' she thought, trying to convince herself of his honourable intentions.

Her heart was beating really fast as she walked towards General's room. Would she finally meet Jaywant? What if Nathay Khan had lied?

As she was about to enter his room, someone called out to her. 'Chandraki!' She turned around to see Riyaz Khan walking towards her.

'There's no use going into that room. He's not in there,' he said.

'Who are you to stop me? He's called me to his room himself!'

'How is it that you agreed to warm his bed so easily?'

'It's none of your business, Riyaz Khan.'

Riyaz laughed. 'Anyway, Nathay Khan has been called away by the Rani on some urgent business. You can look for Jaywant Singh on your own.'

'You are lying!'

'No, I'm not. Why should I? It will give me the utmost pleasure to witness a meeting between Nathay Khan and you. I wouldn't want to miss such a chance,' he said with a smirk. 'But he's not in there. He asked me to tell you that he'll call for you later.'

Disappointed and relieved at the same time, Chandraki turned to go when Riyaz Khan's whisper tickled her ear. He was standing very close to her. He brought his head down, close to her face.

'What happened? Lakshmibai threw you out as well?' he asked with an amused look on his face.

'Why should she? I'm not a traitor like you. And, unlike you, I haven't come to seek refuge in an enemy state,' Chandraki replied holding up her head as high as she could.

'Then why have you come here, my little Meera? As an ambassador of peace between two warring neighbours?'

Chandraki was stunned. This was the first time he had addressed her by her real name. It had been years since anyone had called her Meera. Once Maharani Lakshmibai had given her the new name, no one had called her Meera. She felt a strange sensation of warmth flood over her.

'I've come looking for my husband.'

'That is if he exists. As of now, that looks a little improbable. If you need any help, remember me!' Riyaz Khan said, a lazy smile hovering on his lips.

'Wipe that smirk off your face, Riyaz Khan. I'll die before I seek your help!' she said and walked away in a huff.

As usual, Riyaz was uncomfortable in her presence. But he still managed a smile as he thought of the expression on her face when she'd learn he had just helped her preserve her honour from the lecherous Nathay Khan. He took a deep breath. What she didn't know was that she had already sought his help.

The next day Chandraki was summoned by Rani Larai. The orders were to appear immediately. She was scared. Had she done something wrong to have the queen summon her all of a sudden?

'Where is Jaywant?' the queen asked. Her voice was stern.

'I . . . I don't know,' she stammered.

'What made you come to Orchha to look for him?'

She knew Nathay Khan was watching her. She had to think of a convincing answer.

'It had been a long time since I had met him and there was no news from him.'

Rani Larai pursed her lips. 'You've been here pretty long. How long do you propose to wait?'

Chandraki had no answer to that question. She had no idea how long she would have to wait.

Without waiting for her reply, the queen said, 'We will give you two options. If your Jaywant Singh doesn't show up in the next ten days, that is, the day after Vijaya Dashami, we will consider you a liar and a spy who has been sent by Maharani Lakshmibai. In that case, you know the punishment. And unlike Jhansee, we have not yet banned capital punishment. The second option is that you become a resident of our kingdom for good and sever all ties with Jhansee and your Queen Lakshmibai forever.'

Chandraki felt a strange ringing in her ears. The courtroom seemed to spin. She could not see anything clearly. She sat down suddenly. A murmur went down the courtroom. Some courtiers rose from their seats, their hands reaching out for the swords dangling by their sides. Nathay Khan's eyebrows cocked up. He looked at the queen enquiringly. She raised her hand motioning him to remain seated.

'If you choose the second option, let us know earlier. You know we all like your dancing. You are most welcome to become one of my subjects,' Rani Larai told Chandraki.

Chandraki remained seated long after the court was dismissed. Why did the queen suddenly summon her to give her this warning? When everyone else had left the hall, Nathay Khan came and stood beside her. Chandraki cringed.

'What did you think? You can fool me? Fool Nathay Khan, eh?' he growled.

Chandraki stood up and faced the boorish General who stood inches away.

'What . . . what do you mean . . . fooled you?' she stammered, terrified at the thought of him knowing about her secret mission.

'I called you last evening, didn't I? And you had the cheek to keep me waiting all evening and not turn up? How dare you? Do you have the slightest idea what I can do to you?' barked Nathay Khan.

At first, Chandraki was too surprised to offer an explanation. So he was upset about last evening. She was relieved. She remembered Riyaz had stopped her from going in. She was about to open her mouth to say so when she hesitated. Something told her not to tell Nathay Khan the truth. She closed her mouth abruptly and stood silent.

'Thank your stars that the queen has given you ten days. If I had my way, I would not have given you any time at all. So what happened last evening that made you change your mind? Do you not want to know where Jaywant is?'

'I was unwell,' she replied brusquely.

'Unwell, eh? You think I'll buy that? I've already checked. You had left your room to come here. What happened midway?'

'I had a headache,' she said firmly.

Nathay Khan leered at her. Chandraki squirmed.

'I'll let you go this time, but next time don't try your tricks on me,' he said sharply as he grabbed her arm. She winced. Then suddenly, he let go of her arm and stormed out of the hall.

Chandraki returned to her room, her steps heavy with the burden of an imminent doom that awaited her. Riyaz had prevented her from going into Nathay Khan's room. Why? Was he aware of Nathay Khan's intentions? It was difficult for her to accept that Riyaz would care for her honour. 'That man intrigues me.' Chandraki sighed. But there were other matters that needed her immediate attention. The queen had given her time until Dussehra. Ten days was all she had. If she hadn't achieved her mission in four months, how would she be able to accomplish it in just ten days? What should she do? 'Oh Durga Ma, help me please,' she prayed.

That evening, Chandraki decided to go see Farzand Bakshi. She needed money desperately. As she made her way down the cobbled driveway that led from the Jahangir Mahal towards the houses of the noblemen at the far end of the walled area of the fort, she sensed someone following her. She stopped and looked behind. The road was lined on either side by houses surrounded by shrubs and creepers. She stepped to the side of the road and went around the hibiscus shrub to her left. She couldn't see anyone. She stepped back on the road and continued walking towards the last cluster of houses built in a semicircle. The second house was the khajanchi's. She saw his wife laying out gooseberries on a charpoy to dry in the sun. A young man was pulling two bullocks that dragged a grinding stone through a circular depression, making a limestone preparation to be used for building as well as repairing houses.

Chandraki walked up to Bakshi's wife and enquired about her husband. He came out quickly.

'I found out about your money,' he said without further ado. 'It would be returned to you only if you decide to stay in Orchha. Your horse, too, will be returned to you on that condition. If you are found to be a spy, you will, as you know perfectly well, be sentenced to death. Of what use will the horse and the money be to you then?' he asked brusquely.

Chandraki was shocked when she heard this. The queen had actually not given her any other option. There was now only one way out for her – to escape from Orchha.

37

Preparations were on in full swing for Dussehra. This was the most important festival of the kingdom, and the Ram Raja temple in the Rani Mahal was bedecked like a bride. The whole town of Orchha had taken on a festive look. The bazaars were buzzing with laughter and chatter.

Inside the palace, the idol of Ram Raja was being cleaned and adorned for the ten-day-long festival. Musicians started arriving from all the neighbouring regions to participate in Orchha's famous music festival to be held during Dussehra. The dancers were undergoing rigorous practice sessions. Chandraki was one of them, but her heart was heavy. She knew her time was running out. The thought of the choice she would have to make ripped her apart on the inside. But she had no time to ponder over that. She had instructions from the queen that she had to perform in the music festival, although that was the last thing she wanted to do right now. 'It would perhaps be my last dance here,' thought Chandraki. Did she suddenly feel a tug at her heart? She had begun to like Orchha. She liked its people, even the queen herself. The only sore point was Nathay Khan.

The monsoons had come and gone, and the sun was back, shining more fiercely than ever. It scorched the red earth, and even though it was early October, Bundelkhand was hot as smelting coal. The road that connected Orchha to Jhansee was lined with thick forests, but the forests disappeared in the summer months, giving way to a scrubby vegetation and sparse undergrowth. Only the area between the rivers Betwa and Dhasan was really green, and that lent Orchha a cooler climate as compared to its neighbour, Jhansee.

It was late afternoon. On the first day of Navratri the palace had turned into a busy hub of activity. Chandraki, along with Taravati, went to the groves that lined the river to pluck flowers required for her dance later that evening. The groves were resplendent with frangipani, red hibiscus and juhi and their lingering fragrance permeated the afternoon air. Chandraki often came here in the mornings to pick shefali flowers that lay strewn like a white carpet on the green grass that glistened with the morning dew. She loved to offer those at the temple altar.

After plucking as many flowers as her wicker basket could hold, she climbed on top of the wall that stretched along the outer boundary of the fort complex. Taravati stood on the ground facing her, looking out at the river that flowed behind the wall.

'Is Dussehra the most important festival in Orchha?' Chandraki asked Taravati, who reminded Chandraki of her mother in her younger days. Taravati too was fond of her. She was her best dancer, a natural performer. The two often came together to collect flowers and relished each other's company.

'You can say so. Dussehra marks the end of Navratri, which is dedicated to Goddess Durga. It also symbolizes Lord Ram's victory over the demon king Raavan. And Ram is really revered in Orchha.' She paused. 'Do you remember you had once asked me why Lord Ram is worshipped here when the kings of Orchha were worshippers of Lord Krishna?' Chandraki nodded. 'Let's walk by the river while I tell you the story,' Taravati said.

Chandraki jumped off the wall and started walking along with Taravati. It was a pleasant afternoon. The October sun was mellow at this hour, and the perfume from the flowers pervaded all around.

'Our king Madhukar Shah's wife, Queen Ganesh Kunwari, an ardent devotee of Lord Ram gave instructions for the Chaturbhuj temple to be built for her Lord. The king was not too pleased with his wife's devotion to a god other than his family deity. When he was on his way to Brindaban, the abode of Lord Krishna whom he worshipped, his queen expressed the desire to go to Ayodhya, Lord Ram's birthplace. The king, infuriated at her preference of Lord Ram over Lord Krishna, banished her from the kingdom with the order that if she ever thought of returning, it should only be with her Lord Ram.'

'But faith is your own choice. It cannot be forced,' Chandraki remarked.

Taravati nodded as she continued the story. 'The Rani,

after months of penance by the river Sarayu in Ayodhya, decided to end her life by jumping into the river after her God failed to present himself before her. When people rushed in to save her, a baby boy emerged from the water holding her in his arms. He was none other than Lord Ram. On hearing her predicament, he agreed to accompany her to Orchha but laid down three conditions. He told her that the journey should be completed within the auspicious month of Pukh, he should be enshrined where he would be first placed, and lastly, he would be the king of Orchha, and thereafter, there would be no other king living in Orchha,' Taravati narrated.

'Is that why the kings of Orchha don't live here?' asked Chandraki.

The older lady nodded. 'Yes. It is to honour the promise that the queen made to Lord Ram. How can two kings rule over the same place?'

Taravati continued her tale. 'The king was visited by Lord Krishna in his dream who admonished him for his cruelty towards his wife and ordered him to welcome her back. But as she stepped into Orchha, the month of Pukh had ended and the Chaturbhuj temple was also not ready. The queen decided to place her Lord Ram in her palace until the temple was ready, but once she did so, Lord Ram could not be moved from the queen's palace thereafter. The king then built the Ram Raja temple there.'

The birds had struck up their evening orchestra yet again and the sky was turning grey. It would be dusk shortly. The woods around them looked darker with the sun having disappeared over the horizon.

'So, who looks after the fort when . . . when . . .'
Chandraki suddenly trailed off mid-sentence.

'What happened?' Taravati asked.

'Hush! There's someone here,' she whispered.

She had heard a sound. It came from somewhere among
the trees. This was the wooded area that lay behind the
block of houses that belonged to some of the important
noblemen. The woods were usually dry, dotted with
tamarind trees and the occasional acacia. But the monsoons
had given it new life, and there was a dense undergrowth
with some trees reaching up to over six feet. Beyond that,
portions of the Jahangir Mahal loomed up through the
trees. To her left was the five-foot-high boundary wall
of the palace behind which flowed the Betwa. Taravati
stopped walking and turned to look at Chandraki.

'What is it?' she asked.

'Shh!' putting a finger to her lips, Chandraki silenced
the older woman and narrowed her eyes, trying to focus.
There was a movement in the undergrowth ahead, and
she saw some green branches spring back as though just
released from an unknown force. There were two people,
but it was hard to make out who they were in the failing
light. Chandraki crouched, signalling Taravati to do the
same. Then she slowly inched forward and cleared out
some branches by her hand before she stood up. She could
see one of them clearly now. She was not mistaken. It was
Jaywant.

38

After a sleepless night, Chandraki strode out of her room and walked purposefully towards the queen's chambers.

'I want an audience with the queen,' she told the attendant waiting outside.

'I'm afraid Her Majesty cannot be disturbed. There are strict orders.'

Chandraki had no choice but to wait until the court commenced. She paced up and down the room. She knew she could not be wrong. She had recognized Jaywant easily. But what was he doing in those woods? Who was with him? She was about to accost him, but before she could do so, the two men simply vanished. She had searched for them frantically, but there was no one in those woods. Dejected, she had returned to the palace.

The court commenced at four in the afternoon. When it was her turn to speak, the words tumbled out even before the queen permitted her to speak.

'Your Majesty! I saw Jaywant last evening. In the woods

behind the Jahangir Palace,' she said without catching her breath. There was a stunned silence in the courtroom.

Nathay Khan rose from his seat. 'How could you have seen Jaywant when there is no Jaywant? It is obvious to all present that he's a figment of your imagination, a ploy to mislead us,' he said menacingly.

'I saw him yesterday, talking to someone in the woods behind the palace,' Chandraki insisted.

'Really? How strange, isn't it Your Majesty, that he is visible only to Chandraki and not to anyone else. Does he practise black magic?' Nathay Khan mocked her.

The queen, who was quiet all this while, now spoke up. 'If he works here, as you say he does, why should he hide?'

'I do not know if he was hiding or not, but I have clearly seen him. It is him and no one else,' Chandraki said emphatically.

'I think you need to rest, Chandraki, your nerves are frayed. We will meet after a few days,' the queen said.

Chandraki was swiftly dismissed from the court. She had no idea what to do. It was already the fourth day of Navratri and she had to find Jaywant in another six days.

~

It was Dussehra. Devotees thronged the Ram Raja temple and were gearing up to witness the grand spectacle of Raavan's effigy going up in flames. There was much excitement and jubilation all around. But Chandraki was devastated. She couldn't get Jaywant's face out of her mind. Had she really seen him? Perhaps she was mistaken. She played the scene in her mind again and again. Each time, she was more and more convinced that it was Jaywant. She followed the queen's procession that was headed to the temple and stood in a corner to watch the puja that commenced amidst much fanfare after which people herded towards the open ground behind the Chaturbhuj temple where Raavan's effigy would be burnt. There was complete chaos as multitudes of people pushed each other to reach there. Chandraki was nearly crushed in the ensuing madness. Someone pushed her roughly, and she fell on a man in front of her, and for a few seconds both of them lay in a heap. Pushing her away, the man tried to get up, and the blanket covering his face fell off. Chandraki was about to apologize when she saw who he was. At that moment, the fireworks went off, lighting up the night sky as Raavan burst into flames with a deafening roar.

Chandraki tried to grab the man's arm but he pushed her away and fled. She ran after him, and just as she saw him turn around the corner, she crashed into a woman sending her tray of sweets and garlands flying.

'I'm so sorry.' Chandraki panted as she hurriedly picked up the tray and handed it over to her. She stood on tiptoe and tried to locate the man.

'Is there a problem?' asked the woman whose tray Chandraki had dropped. Do you need help?' she asked, steadying Chandraki.

'Yes, I'm looking for my husband.'

The two of them exited the temple premises and headed towards the grounds where Raavan was still burning. Sparks fell in a shower around the demon king's huge frame, and in the light of the glowing embers, Chandraki spotted Jaywant.

'There he is!' she exclaimed.

The woman smiled. 'Now that you have found him, I'll go. *My* husband will be wondering where I've disappeared. By the way, I'm Jhumroo. Let's meet again sometime,' she said.

Chandraki nodded absent-mindedly. She wouldn't let Jaywant out of her sight this time and proceeded towards him. Jaywant watched her approach. This time he did not move away. Chandraki went up to him and for a few seconds they looked at each other. Suddenly she broke down.

'Why are you hiding from me, Jaywant? I came all the way from Orchha and have been waiting for you here for six months. Do you know if I do not produce proof of your existence within the next one week, they'll kill me?' She shook him, sobbing pitifully.

Jaywant stood looking at her blankly. 'Stop crying, Chandraki. Everyone's looking. Can we go somewhere else and talk about this?' he said after a while.

'Let everyone see us. I want everyone to see us. No one believes me here. They don't even believe that you exist. You will come with me right now to see the queen.'

Dragging Jaywant behind her, Chandraki ran up to the palanquin that was making its way back to the queen's chamber.

'Stop, stop!' she told the bearers and held on to the palanquin.

It was put down. The queen, hearing the commotion,

parted the curtains and saw Chandraki bathed in sweat, her mouth open and panting.

Riyaz Khan who was heading the queen's procession as always, stepped forward.

'Please carry on, Your Majesty. I will send them to you shortly.'

In court some time later, Chandraki and Jaywant stood before the queen and her council of ministers. Without further delay, Rani Larai spoke.

'Our guest from Jhansee claims she has found the man she came looking for in Orchha,' she announced, mocking Chandraki's words. Everyone turned to look at the pair.

'Is this your Jaywant?' The queen asked Chandraki. She nodded.

Nathay Khan got up instantly. 'His name is not Jaywant. It is Keshav,' he said.

Rani Larai turned to Nathay Khan and signalled him to keep quiet. Nathay Khan sat down on his seat unwillingly. Turning to Jaywant, she asked him, 'Do you know Chandraki?' Jaywant nodded.

'Then why did you lie to her about your name?'

'Your Majesty, I had to hide my identity since I was in an enemy kingdom,' said Keshav. 'My friend Sankara had invited me to his home where I met Chandraki. I feared that being in an enemy state I would be arrested if I disclosed my real identity. And if anyone came looking for me here, they would find no one by the name of Jaywant.'

'Is she your wife?' Jaywant nodded.

'So what do you plan to do now?'

'As you know, Your Majesty, the situation is not good.

Jhansee has lapsed to the British as have many other kingdoms around us. I travel to all these regions, and I know we are looked upon with suspicion since the Company Sarkar has not annexed our kingdom. Moreover, there is a lot of discontent brewing against the firanghees all around us. The British have left us alone so far, but they may begin to eye us with suspicion soon enough. They may also change their mind about not annexing us. You never know these firanghees. They aren't honest people. On the other hand, Jhansee may misinterpret my intentions.'

'So what do you propose?' the queen asked.

'I think it is better to wait and watch before we take our next step,' Keshav replied.

Rani Larai looked at Chandraki who had been quiet all this while. 'Chandraki, do you have anything more to say?' Chandraki shook her head.

The queen turned to Keshav. 'Will Chandraki then return to Jhansee?'

'No, Your Majesty,' Keshav replied. 'It is not safe there. She will stay back in Orchha for the time being. She will live here like one of us.'

39

Chandraki resigned herself to the fact that it could be a long while before the political situation in Bundelkhand improved, and she would return to Jhansee. The East India Company had annexed many kingdoms in India that had no natural claimant to the throne such as the riyasats of Punjab, Sikkim, Satara, part of Sind, Oudh, Sambalpur, Jaitpur, Udaipur and Nagpur, and Jhansee and Jalaoun in Vindhya Pradesh. This did not go down well with many kingdoms in India, and there was discontent brewing against the British in many places.

Orchha remained untouched, unspoiled, enveloped in a slumberous indulgence. Surrounded by kingdoms whose fate had changed overnight, this once mighty Bundela capital, wrapped in a cover of opulence, sparkled like a gem through the shroud of misery and hopelessness cast over its neighbouring kingdoms, untouched by any internal or external conflict. The queen and her kingdom basked in the knowledge that the throne of Orchha was secure, and she didn't want to do something foolish to upset the apple cart.

On the other hand was Jhansee, caught in a tight grip of intrigues, politics and misfortune. Chandraki felt the sharp contrast that prevailed between the two kingdoms. She did not begrudge Orchha for its peace, security and grandeur, but she did wish that Jhansee's fate too would change for the better.

She often shared her thoughts with Jhumroo, her new friend, whom she had met in the temple on Dussehra. She had bumped into her a few days later in the bazaar.

'Do you remember me? You had sent my tray flying,' Jhumroo reminded her with a laugh. Chandraki, who was most embarrassed, apologized.

'I'm so sorry about that day. I was very disturbed.'

'So is all well now?'

Chandraki nodded.

They got talking. Jhumroo lived in the city outside the fort palace. Chandraki met her often during her visits to the bazaar or the temple. Jhumroo had never seen anyone as brave as Chandraki. Just the thought that a woman could enter an enemy kingdom in search of her husband intrigued her. One day, she invited Chandraki to her house.

When they entered her house, Jhumroo pointed to a young man seated on a charpoy in the spacious courtyard outside. 'This is my husband Haridas Gahoi.' Jhumroo introduced him to Chandraki. On seeing her, he rose and greeted her with folded hands.

'My wife has often spoken about you.' He smiled. 'You have come from Jhansee?'

Chandraki nodded as she sat on one of the four mooras scattered around. The sun-dappled courtyard was lined with marigold flowers and the aroma of spices wafted from within the house.

'It is a beautiful house,' Chandraki remarked as she looked around. The house seemed newly constructed. It had two storeys, with the living quarters below, and an open terrace above it. It reflected affluence and prosperity. Hari's successful business allowed them to afford a few luxuries, of which this house was one. It was a three-bedroom accommodation with a courtyard in front and a small vegetable garden in the backyard. A little further down the main bazaar of the town, it was located next to the road that led to Jhansee. They had only one neighbour, an old lady whose house was about 200 metres away.

'God has provided us with all that we need,' Jhumroo said. 'My husband is a trader who deals in spices and grains. He travels a lot around central India and brings home good money.' She smiled as she offered Chandraki a tumbler of water.

'I also deal in sugar and salt,' Hari said. 'Jhansee's strategic location makes it the centre of major trade. I can trade across Agra, Cawnpore, Nowgong and even up to the Narmada valley.'

'Then why do you live in Orchha and not Jhansee?' Chandraki asked.

'My ancestors are from Orchha. They traded in weapons such as bows, arrows and spears, and Jhansee, famous for the manufacture of all warfare items, was at the time a part of Orchha. So they kept shuttling between the two cities. Of course things have changed now.' He sighed. 'Jhansee is good for business, but now that the firanghees have taken over, this is a more peaceful place to live in,' replied Hari.

Hearing about the firanghees, Chandraki asked the question that sprang to her lips.

'What is happening in Jhansee? Has the Company Sarkar recognized Damodar Rao as ruler? How is Maharani Lakshmibai?' Her questions came in quick succession.

'No, the Company Sarkar is sitting tight in Jhansee, and from what I can see, they are there to stay. Jhansee has been brought under the supervision of Captain W.C. Erskine, who is the commissioner of Saugar and Nerbudda territories. Under Erskine are Captain Alexander Skene, who is the superintendent of Jhansee and Jalaoun, and the deputy superintendent, Captain Gordon.'

Chandraki was crestfallen. 'So the Maharani's appeals didn't work?'

Hari shook his head. 'On the contrary. The British are penetrating more and more into the region and are now poking their nose even in religious and social matters. The ban on cow slaughter has been lifted in Jhansee,' he said, shaking his head as any Hindu would.

'What?' Chandraki was shocked. The slaughter of cattle had been strictly banned in the kingdom.

Hari shrugged. 'Maharani Lakshmibai and her people have vehemently protested, but in vain. I've heard that the British have a deadly motive. They are hoping that lifting the ban would please the Muslims and would create a divide between the two communities. But contrary to their expectations, the Muslims and Hindus remain united. The Company Sarkar is quite disappointed about that.'

Both Chandraki and Jhumroo were silent. Though from different states, they were Hindus, and this was sacrilege as far as their religion was concerned.

As Chandraki sat talking to Haridas, Jhumroo went in and returned with a tray carrying three tumblers that contained a whitish liquid. She offered Chandraki a glass. Chandraki thanked her and took a sip. It was sweet, fragrant and tangy, spiked with a dash of lime. She had never tasted anything like this before. She took a few more quick sips, and before she knew it, she had drained the glass. Within minutes she felt light-headed.

'What is this drink, Jhumroo? It's over,' she said sadly as she inspected the empty glass. Her words were slurred.

'Aren't you feeling refreshed?' Jhumroo asked.

'A bit too much,' Chandraki replied happily.

'It's a drink made from the mohua flower. I have added some lime juice to it. It'll keep you cool in this weather,' Jhumroo replied with a twinkle in her eye.

Hari gave more news of what was happening in Jhansee. 'You know that the revenue from two villages goes to the Mahalakshmi temple, the Newalkar rulers' family temple, right? But the British have put a stop to this too, which has left the people considerably angry,' he told Chandraki.

'How can they do this? Why are they interfering in our religious matters?'

Chandraki became increasingly incensed as Hari related the religious and social transgressions of the British in Jhansee. The sun disappeared behind the gently rising uplands and finally beyond the low faraway ranges. Chandraki rose to take her leave. Somewhat unsteady, she slowly made her way towards the palace. Hari and Jhumroo saw her off till the marketplace after which she insisted she could go on her own.

The moment she entered the palace, she bumped into Riyaz Khan whose eyebrows shot up on seeing her wobble. He walked up to her.

'Where have you been and what have you been up to?' he asked with a frown.

Chandraki, who by now was beginning to feel sleepy, looked up at him. Pulling a straight face, she said, 'It is none of your business.'

'It is my business. Anything that goes on here is my business. It is my job.'

'Your job is limited to the events inside the palace, not outside. What I do outside with my friends is my business. Move on, let me pass,' she said, giving Riyaz a slight push.

'And which friend of yours got you drunk?'

'I told you to ... you, it's none ... none of your business!' she stammered.

Riyaz looked at her. 'Allah knows what this woman has been up to.' He sighed as he shook his head. It was better to let her go inside before anyone saw her in this condition. 'I need to watch her closely,' he told himself. 'But why should I?' he asked himself. Was it because Nathay Khan expected him to? Or was there some other reason that compelled him to be close to her as often as possible?

Riyaz was troubled. Why did his heart beat faster when she was close? Why did he feel uneasy when she was around, and yet he searched for excuses to be next to her? He knew she hated him, he knew she always looked for ways to get him into trouble. Then why did he think of her all the time? Was it because she was attractive? But there were far more beautiful women he had known. Yet it was she who he thought of all the time. He could have taken her whenever he wanted to. He was powerful. No one would have asked any questions. But, strangely enough, he didn't want to. He didn't want her in his bed. He just wanted to spend every waking moment with her. This was sheer madness.

'Why, Allah, why?' he screamed within the confines of his room. 'Why are you torturing me like this? She has ruined me. Then why do I want to be with her, talk to her? Why do I worry about her?' It couldn't be love because there was only one woman he had ever loved, only one woman he could ever love – Heera! He could never love anyone else ever again. He fell on the ground and sobbed piteously. He deliberately pushed away thoughts of her, but he realized he was beginning to think of her more often than of Heera. He felt guilty. 'Forgive me, forgive me, Heera!'

He remembered the time when he had first seen Chandraki. She had looked so frail and forlorn. He wouldn't have noticed her if she hadn't looked up at him briefly with those large dark eyes of hers. They held him spellbound and he had sensed a deep agony that tore through his heart. He had moved away, but he couldn't push away that image. It continued to haunt him throughout his stay in Jhansee. Their paths had rarely crossed, and he was content with his life with Heera. Yet he had felt irresistibly drawn towards her. Even when he knew she had informed the queen of his betrayal, he wasn't angry. If it hadn't been for her, he would still be in Jhansee.

And then he saw her here in Orchha. He could feel her intense dislike for him, and it pained him. And the pain translated into anger – anger towards himself for allowing her to control his thoughts. How could he be so vulnerable? It had all happened slowly. He didn't know when this strange pull that he felt towards her had begun to consume him entirely. She had taken complete possession of him, his mind, his heart, his soul. He wanted to be a good man again.

Suddenly he was scared. What if he lost her too? Just like he had lost Heera. Just like he had lost his children. Just like he had lost his honour. Whatever he cherished had been wrenched away from him. No, he told himself. He couldn't let that happen. He couldn't let her go.

He knew she belonged to another man. He knew there was no place for him in her heart. But at least she was around. He could see her every day. He could ensure that she remained undefiled, unravaged. He would be the ring of fire around her even though the fire may consume him. He had no idea why each time he thought of her there was an acute agony that gnawed at his heart. It was so painful, this swell of emotions that rose within him. Was it possible for him to love another woman?

He must keep away from her. He couldn't let her go. He couldn't lose her. He wouldn't allow his heart to play games with him once again. He must be in control. He wouldn't allow destiny, or even Allah, to control his life. 'This time, I won't allow you, God, to play with my kismet. I will not succumb to your machinations. I will not allow her to come near me because I want to keep her close to me. This time, I will set the rules and won't let you upset them. This time, I will win, not you. I will not let you take her away from me. And for that if I have to keep away from her, I will.'

~

Chandraki brooded over what Hari Bhau had told her. She wondered how Lakshmibai was managing with the British breathing down her neck. She had not communicated with the Maharani ever since she sent that letter through the Basors. Could Hari Bhau carry a message to Jhansee? He often visited the state for business, and no one would suspect or search him. Not many knew the couple in Orchha either.

'Thank God, I did not reveal Jhumroo's name to Riyaz when I was drunk that day,' thought Chandraki. 'I need to be more careful.'

She sat down to write a letter to Lakshmibai and handed it to Haridas the next day.

The note that went across to Queen Lakshmibai carried the following message:

Maharani ki jai! I hope you are well. My heart weeps to think of how devastated you must be.

Although I'm in Orchha, I think of you and my beloved Jhansee all the time. But I know it is my mission that has brought me here.

I met Jaywant only a few days ago. His real name is Keshav and he is the shahi daakiya.

Nathay Khan is also the military general of Larai Sarkar's army. He is not a good man, and I don't trust him.

I see firanghees here too. Orchha is not an enemy of the Company Sarkar, so the Rani is allowed to rule. She is kind, but Nathay Khan manipulates her. She is angry that Jhansee, which once belonged to Orchha, was taken away from it.

Keshav says we can't go to Jhansee right now because the political situation is tense. He doesn't want the Company Sarkar to think that Orchha is friends with Jhansee.

So I may have to stay here for some time more. Please don't worry about me.

I miss riding and the sword fights. I have not told anyone that I know how to wield a sword.

I'm sending this letter through Hari Bhau who is the husband of my friend Jhumroo. You can send me messages through him. I will now take your leave, Your Majesty. May Durga Ma be with you.

Riyaz Khan is in Orchha. He is now a top officer in the Rani's army and reports to Nathay Khan.

Your humble servant forever,
Chandraki

Chandraki sealed the letter well and handed it to Hari, knowing she could trust him.

'And now that you are going to be here for some more time, we can meet more often,' Jhumroo said as Hari took the letter inside. It was a pleasant afternoon and Chandraki, for the first time in months, felt relaxed. She was happy to have made new friends.

'How different is our kingdom from yours? My husband tells me that the Jhansee fort is very imposing, but the weather there is hotter than in Orchha. They don't have a river, you see.' Jhumroo smiled.

Chandraki often marvelled at the opulence of the palaces here, which were embellished with beautiful frescoes and colourful stones, unlike the stark, military facade of the Jhansi fort. The Diwan-e-Aam was splashed with colourful gems and mirrors and plastered in scarlet, gold and blue tiles. Its walls and roof were lined with magnificent friezes depicting gods and goddesses, animals and floral motifs. The palace in Jhansee also had pillars and archways decorated in green, scarlet and gold and sported similar motifs. The rooms too were richly furnished with Persian carpets, ottomans, couches and other exquisite furniture and the upholstery had gold embroidery on satin and silk. But the palaces of Orchha were even more splendid.

'The Jhansee fort was built by Raja Bir Singh Deo as a military fortress to protect Orchha, the capital of the Bundelas. It was not meant to be a palace for kings. This palace, built by King Madhukar Shah, is 300 years old. The royal family lived here for several generations until the capital was shifted to Tikamgarh about seventy years ago. There will be a difference between palaces in the capital city, and a fort built as a defensive structure, isn't it? By the way, do you know what Orchha means?' Hari asked.

Chandraki shook her head.

'It means the hidden one. And do you know how Jhansee got its name?'

Chandraki shook her head again.

'Raja Bir Singh was entertaining the Raja of Jaitpur and pointing to the Jhansee fort from the terrace, asked him if he could see it. The Raja of Jaitpur said he could but "jhainsi", which means indistinct or shadowy. That's how Jhansee got its name,' laughed Hari.

40

Chandraki and Keshav often spent time together, but unlike earlier times, things were not very smooth between them. This troubled Chandraki. Keshav was always restless. She decided to ask him what it was that was bothering him. Was he not happy to see her after so long?

They were sitting by the Betwa, with their backs to the palace. The sun was already behind the horizon and the shadows of dusk coated the surrounding hills. Chandraki perched on one of the rocks, her feet splashing the waters of the river. She was upset with Keshav, who sat beside her looking across towards the horizon.

'The taweez is no longer on your arm. Don't you love me any more?' Chandraki asked.

'It had fallen off one day while I was bathing. So I kept it away safely before it got lost. I do love you. It's just that you belonging to Jhansee puts me under suspicion,' Keshav replied.

'Has anyone said anything to you?' she asked.

'Not exactly. But Nathay Khan looks at me rather

suspiciously these days,' Keshav said, averting Chandraki's gaze. 'Chandraki, you shouldn't have come here. You have put me in a very awkward position.'

'I wouldn't have had to come here if you had come to Jhansee. But you didn't.'

'I didn't get the time. I'm the shahi daakiya, a messenger. They sent me all across Vindhya Pradesh ... Saugar, Dutya, Panna.'

Chandraki nodded. 'It's fine. So I came. Once the situation improves, we'll go back to Jhansee. I will speak to the Maharani to get you a job in her palace which will keep you close to me forever,' she said cheerfully, squeezing his hand.

'I won't leave Orchha. This is my home, I've grown up here,' Keshav replied sharply.

Chandraki looked at him, not sure if she had heard him correctly. Keshav looked away from her, annoyed.

'But Jhansee is my home! I can't live in Orchha.'

'You came here on your own. I didn't ask you. What made you think that I will leave Orchha forever?'

Chandraki suddenly rose and started off towards the palace.

'Chandraki!'

Keshav called after her. She didn't look back. He rose and caught up with her.

'If you don't come to Jhansee, then I will give up my life,' she said as she walked towards the palace.

Keshav walked fast to keep pace with her.

'Don't blackmail me.' Keshav caught her arm and turned her around. 'I won't leave Orchha, all right?'

'Okay. Do what you please. I'll go back to Jhansee tomorrow,' she threatened.

'Fair enough. In any case, Jhansee is part of our kingdom,' Keshav shot back.

Chandraki stopped in her tracks. And then slowly walked back to him.

'Say that again,' she commanded.

'Jhansee is part of Orchha. We gave it to you as a gift.'

Chandraki looked deep into his eyes. 'That's a good joke.'

'This is no joke,' Keshav retorted and pulled her to him. He brought his face close to hers. 'Jhansee was gifted to Peshwa Baji Rao by our Raja Chhatrasal in return for the military support the Peshwa offered against Mohammad Khan Bangash, the Mughal subedar of Allahabad. Our Raja offered not just Jhansee but several regions as well as his daughter Mastani. That's how the Marathas placed their foot on the soil of Bundelkhand and then later took Orchha in 1742 after igniting disputes between the Bundela chiefs. Jhansee belongs to us – *we* built Jhansee.'

Chandraki jerked her arm away and walked off without a word.

Keshav left Orchha once again in less than a week of their fight. Chandraki was somewhat relieved. 'It will give him time to cool off,' she thought. Her anger had dissipated especially when she found the amulet tied on Keshav's arm once again. She had been reassured. She realized that what she was asking of Keshav was not fair. Just like she loved Jhansee, he loved Orchha. It was natural for him to be loyal to his queen, to his motherland.

41

With the appearance of Keshav, Chandraki's plan to escape from Orchha was now on hold. Moreover, she was now pretty sure that Orchha had no plan to attack Jhansee. Even Nathay Khan was beginning to relax as far as she was concerned. No one eyed her suspiciously any more. News had spread that she was Keshav's wife. She had also won over Rani Larai with her charm, and the queen began to summon her frequently.

Chandraki found Rani Larai's society quite pleasant. She knew that most of the affairs of the state were conducted with the counsel of Nathay Khan, who unlike the queen, was plain wicked and ambitious. Rani Larai would often ask her questions about Jhansee and was curious to know of her counterpart in the neighbouring kingdom. Always cautious not to reveal much, Chandraki spoke about her days with Lakshmibai, and how the East India Company had taken over Jhansee. The information she shared was common knowledge, much of what the queen already knew. She liked Rani Larai. She was a good ruler and kept her subjects happy.

'It is wonderful, Your Majesty, that you have abolished the practice of sati in your kingdom.' Chandraki complimented the queen.

'Sati is a grievous crime against any woman. Besides, the Company Sarkar punishes anyone who practises it, even rulers who encourage the practice in their kingdom. I didn't want to play into their hands. You never know what they may do in the name of punishment.'

'I cannot imagine the firanghees doing anything good for our country. They have deceived Queen Lakshmibai. Maharaj was always faithful to them. How can they not recognize Damodar Rao, his adopted son, as his own? Damodar Rao even performed his last rites. Chhal kiya,' she told the queen.

'But the Company Sarkar does not recognize adopted heirs,' the queen of Orchha said matter-of-factly.

Chandraki reminded Rani Larai that she too sat on the throne as a proxy ruler. 'Hamir Singh, the king of Orchha, is also not the direct descendant of your previous king. Moreover, it is you who rule on his behalf because he is a minor. Why has the Company Sarkar not annexed Orchha?' she asked the queen innocently.

'That's because we do not fall under the jurisdiction of the East India Company. We are an independent state,' Rani Larai replied to Chandraki's question. 'The Peshwas handed Jhansee over to the British, who in turn handed it over to your Maharaj Gangadhar Rao. The

Company Sarkar is considered the paramount power
there and has the authority to decide the fate of states like
Jhansee. Therefore, Lord Dalhousie's Doctrine of Lapse is
applicable to Jhansee and not to us.'

Chandraki was silent. The possibility of Jhansee being
returned to Maharani Lakshmibai seemed distant.

'Does your queen sit on the throne like a man or a
woman?' Rani Larai asked, changing the topic. The image
of Lakshmibai astride a horse, wielding a naked sword,
wearing a tunic, pyjamas and a turban flashed before
Chandraki's eyes. She smiled.

'The Maharani mostly wears a sari, but she dresses up
like a man occasionally. She rides horses and fights like a
man, though,' Chandraki said.

Rani Larai would come to Orchha every now and
then. For the most part of the year, she was in Tikamgarh.
Nathay Khan always accompanied the queen, and Riyaz
Khan was now often left behind in the fort of Orchha to
supervise in the absence of the queen and her diwan.

In Orchha, every day was a celebration, especially
during Rani Larai's visits. The evenings were filled with
music and dance. Laughter echoed in the palaces and
orchards. When the Raja Mahal was illuminated in the
evenings, the reflection of its lights was scattered across
the Betwa like little droplets of gold. The strains of a dadra
or a thumri could be heard wafting through the night,
very often. In the summers, a cool light breeze from the
river swept across the city, carrying with it the fragrance
of madhumalati, jasmine and juhi flowers.

The queen was visiting once again, and like always

when she came, the mehfil was in full swing. Inside the
Raja Mahal, the queen sat on the balcony above while
the artistes performed on the raised stone platform in the
open courtyard below. A fountain in the centre of the hall
sprayed scented water, whose fragrance mingled with the
fragrance of the flowers that wafted in from outside. The
muslin drapes with their exquisite embroidery fluttered in
the breeze, casting a shimmering veil over the audience. The
floor was sprinkled with marigold and rose petals. Strings
of tube roses formed a canopy over the stage.

The air was charged with the mellifluous voice of the
beautiful Charuprabha as she crooned 'Main toh piya se
naina laga aayee re' to a mesmerized audience. Her disciple,
the seventeen-year-old Zahara, picked up the strains
whenever her teacher took a break.

Chandraki was standing behind the purdah in one of
the corridors that lined the music hall when she saw Riyaz
Khan. She hadn't seen him in a while. He stood at the
main gate that formed the entrance to the queen's palace.
His commanding presence was overwhelming, dwarfing
all others around him. She gazed at him and instinctively
he looked up. Their eyes locked. The air was redolent with
the perfume of the flowers as Charuprabha's rendition of
'Lai hayat aae qaza le chali chale' penetrated through the
darkness of that magical night, and the strains from Inayat
Khan's sarangi permeated the air with their soulful melody.

Suddenly, as though from nowhere, a draught of wind
drifted into the open hall, and the glow from the lamps
flickered, plunging the mehfil hall into a play of shadow
and light. In that joust of light and darkness, Chandraki

felt Riyaz's presence right beside her. She could smell him. She tried to touch him and his hand caught hers in a warm grip. He moved closer to her, and she felt the heat from his body overwhelm her. She felt him lift her chin with his finger, and in that moment of surrender, she yielded to his lips as they closed in on hers. With their bodies pressed against each other, Riyaz and Chandraki obliterated all that surrounded them and challenged destiny to change the course of their lives.

When the light from the lamps steadied, Chandraki found Riyaz in deep conversation with a guard at the gate. She was perplexed. What was it that she had just felt? She had sensed his hand in hers, she had touched him, smelt him. They had stood wrapped up in each other. Then how did he reach the gate? While talking to the guard, Riyaz looked in her direction once and then strode out of the durbar. Outside, the night wore on, and the stars came out. Behind the palace, the Betwa flowed merrily, oblivious of the flames of passion that had just erupted in the hearts of two unhappy and forlorn human beings. But neither was ready to succumb to it.

42

Riyaz Khan was Nathay Khan's most trusted aide. In the short span of one year, he was made the cavalry commander. The General increasingly depended on him for advice on matters of the court as well. He saw in Riyaz a younger version of his own self, as brutal and clinical in his execution of deadly tasks, and one who wouldn't question an order, no matter how lethal the consequences. Nathay Khan liked men who didn't ask questions. He loved the streak of brutality in men that made it easier for them to perform tasks that were not humane. 'I will personally train this man in my image,' Nathay Khan told himself. 'Just the kind of man I need for my purpose,' he gloated.

Nathay Khan took Riyaz under his wing and within months got him rigorously trained in warfare. Riyaz had always proved to be a good student, and this time was no exception. He had honed his military skills in the last one year in Maharaj Jayaji Rao Scindia's army. But he was now restless. He wanted his revenge. The news that the British had annexed Jhansee had made his day. But he didn't trust the British. He had just used them to settle his score with the Maharani.

Nathay Khan was a hard taskmaster. His rough disposition bordered on brutality, and his punishments were always severe. His subordinates were mortally terrified of him and took great pains to ensure that he was not offended. But for Riyaz, Nathay Khan was nothing except a means to destroy Lakshmibai. Riyaz had a single purpose – use Nathay Khan's force to overthrow the queen of Jhansee. He considered himself lucky to be trained under the General. His swordsmanship sharpened with each passing day, and his intent became more resolute. Nathay Khan's ruthlessness stoked any dormant bestial streak in a human being. And Riyaz Khan was no exception. Under the General's command, he emerged with the kind of cold-bloodedness that few had seen. This suited Nathay Khan. Somewhere he saw in the younger man the viciousness that was beginning to erode in him over the last few years. It could be due to his advancing age – Nathay Khan was past forty – or simply a life that had reached a saturation of violence and bloodshed.

43

It had been a long and languorous year. Chandraki hardly saw Keshav. He was mostly away on some errand or the other, and it would be weeks, sometimes months before she saw him. They had frequent fights but would be seen back together soon, walking through the streets of the city, sitting by the chhatris or going for long walks across the Betwa.

But it was from Rani Larai one morning that Chandraki heard the next bit of news about Lakshmibai. She was filling up her hookah when Rani Larai, in a pleasant and chatty mood, told her that Maharani Lakshmibai had not yet accepted the pension. 'She keeps threatening the British that she will leave for Benares,' Rani Larai said as she drew on her Bidri hookah.

'Why would she want to do so?' Chandraki asked with an air of pretence. She knew it was Lakshmibai's favourite ploy, one she had used earlier to get the Company to agree to some of her terms, one of which was to forbid the police from entering her palace.

Rani Larai shrugged. 'I don't know. But my sources tell me that given the treatment that the East India Company has meted out to her, including denying her and her son their royal inheritance, she does not wish to be treated like one of the masses, but like a raees. She wants to be exempt from the jurisdiction of the magistrate and put directly under the supervision of the Governor General's agent, which in this case is Robert Hamilton, as you know. She also wants the state's debts to be delinked from the pension which until now she has still not drawn.'

Chandraki was distressed. Were things really as bad? She must get in touch with Lakshmibai.

Later that afternoon, she took out her quill and inkpot and sat down to write a letter to the queen of Jhansee. Jhumroo had told her just yesterday that Hari would soon be leaving for Gwalior and would pass through Jhansee. Dipping her quill into the inkpot, she wrote,

Maharani ki jai ho! I hope you are well. How is our prince Damodar Rao . . .

She stopped. Wasn't that the bugle blowing? She looked out of her window. Dusk was still a few hours away when the next change of shift would take place and the bugle would sound. Then why was it going off now? This was unusual. She put down her quill and parted the curtains of her room. She saw women rush past. There was an uproar in the zenana. Chandraki stepped out of her room and looked around. She spotted one of the girls who had recently entered the harem on Nathay Khan's special recommendation.

'What's the commotion all about?' she asked the girl.

'Nathay Khan has ordered a check of the armoury. I heard him telling Riyaz Khan that they have got some new rifles that may be greased with the fat of cows and pigs. The soldiers have to tear them with their mouths. Ya Allah, that would be sacrilege, isn't it?'

Chandraki was shocked. 'Oh Durga Ma. That is terrible. Now what?'

The girl shrugged. 'Someone called Mangal Pandey refused to use the rifle, so he has been hanged. But he and some other soldiers killed a few sahibs too.'

'Who is Mangal Pandey?' Chandraki asked.

'All I know is that Mangal Pandey is a sepoy somewhere far away. I was with Nathay Khan in his room when Riyaz Khan came to meet him. He dismissed me, but I stood outside his room and overheard what I just told you. Both looked very worried,' the girl said.

Fortunately, the greased cartridges turned out to be a false alarm for Orchha. With the panic over, everyone heaved a sigh of relief. Even Nathay Khan relaxed, and Chandraki found him less aggressive, though he never missed an opportunity to leer at her and pass some lewd comment each time she passed by him. Peace returned after the few days of mass hysteria, following the news that Sepoy Mangal Pandey of the 34th Bengal Native Infantry, a regiment of the East India Company, stationed in Barrackpore, had mutinied and was hanged. The reason was that the new Enfield rifles recently introduced in the Bengal army used cartridges greased with the fat of cows and pigs, and since they had to be torn off by the mouth, both Muslim and Hindu sepoys refused to use them. When forced, Pandey opened fire on his British officer and killed him. Many sepoys from the regiment had refused to carry out the orders of their officers, and the battalion was subsequently disbanded.

Rani Larai's army had ordered a new lot of rifles a few weeks earlier, and the news of the greased cartridges spread like wildfire. Though these were not the Enfield, a check was warranted. There was a lot of apprehension about these cartridges too; it was suspected that they may be greased with animal fat. If so, then all hell would break loose. Nathay Khan personally carried out the supervision. When it was found that the cartridges were not greased with animal fat, everyone relaxed. Rani Larai decided to celebrate it with the Ram Navami festival.

44

Ram Navami brought with it joy and festivities and traders. Women and children frequented the marketplace. Stalls had already come up days before the festival. The celebrations were somewhat subdued though. Mangal Pandey's execution had dampened everyone's feelings, and there was a foreboding of disaster.

Chandraki was worried about Jhansee, Lakshmibai, her own future with Keshav, and her time in Orchha. But, at this moment, she didn't have much of a choice, and since she couldn't steer the course of her life in the direction she wanted to, she decided to go ahead and enjoy the festivities.

She was in the market to select a few bangles for her dance in the evening. She went to a shop that stood a little away from the rest. As she looked through the colourful spread of the bangles lined up before her, someone tapped her from behind. She turned around but before she could blink, a chapatti was thrust into her hand. Perplexed, she took it, and was about to stop the person, but he was gone.

She looked at the rolled chapatti. Why would anyone give her a chapatti? Mystified, she unrolled it and found a note in it. She quickly hid the note in her fist and stepped to the side. Then slowly, she uncurled her fist, and casting furtive glances, took out the note and read it.

'Khalq Khuda ka, Mulk Badshah ka, Raj Maharani Lakshmibai ka! We are ready for the attack. Expect to see you soon,' the note read. It was from Khuda Baksh, a rissaldar in Jhansee fort.

Chandraki's hands trembled. Her palms were clammy. What attack was Khuda Baksh talking about? She rushed back to the palace, and on reaching her room, bolted the door. She read the note once again, but still couldn't make anything of it. She thought of showing it to Jhumroo but decided against it. There was only one option. She had to go to Jhansee.

The next day, Chandraki called Meher to her room.

'Why the sudden summons for me?' Meher asked.

'I was thinking we should learn how to use a sword.'

'Why would I need to use a shamsheer? I'm not a soldier. I'm a dancer.'

'I knw. But these are dangerous times. What if tomorrow, we are attacked suddenly, and we don't know how to defend ourselves?' This gave the other girl something to think about. She paused.

'I guess you are right. But where do we get a sword from? They are all in the armoury.'

'Yes, I know. And the keys are with . . . with . . .' she trailed off as she looked at Meher from the corner of her eye.

'Riyaz Khan. One set of keys is with him, I know. I also know where he keeps them.' She giggled. Chandraki giggled too, playing along. 'It would be fun to take it from him, wouldn't it?' Chandraki hinted.

'Oh, he'll never part with it. Not a chance. And if he gets to know that you and I want to take out a sword from the armoury, he'll tell Nathay Khan, who will send us straight to the gallows.' Meher shuddered.

'We can always steal it,' Chandraki said with the utmost caution.

'Are you crazy? Do you know the punishment for stealing a weapon? And that too from the armoury?'

Chandraki looked at Meher. '*You* don't steal the sword,' she said.

'Are you going to request someone to steal the sword, and someone will actually do it for you?'

'No,' Chandraki replied.

'Will the sword then come flying into our hands?'

Chandraki smiled. 'I will steal it,' she whispered.

Meher stared at her hard. 'Have you lost your mind?'

Chandraki shook her head. 'Here's the plan,' she said. As Meher heard Chandraki out, a smile played on her lips.

'Allah!'

'So, it's done. Simple!'

'This is madness,' Meher exclaimed. She giggled. 'But this should be fun.'

Chandraki nodded. 'I know. When are you meeting him next?'

'Tonight.'

'Then it has to be done tonight. And not a word of this

to anyone! You know the consequences!' Meher nodded, smiling as she trotted out of the room.

The day wore on slower than usual. Chandraki survived it, but she was on edge throughout the day. Meher moved about in an excited state. This girl will ruin everything, thought Chandraki. But she knew it was only Meher who could carry this out without raising suspicion.

Meher waited for Riyaz impatiently. She was nervous. She had never done anything of the sort earlier. But it sounded like fun. She heard the bugle call for the change of guard. She knew Riyaz was with his troops after which he would come into his room. She waited nervously for him to conclude his duties for the day. He never allowed anyone in his room in his absence – no one was allowed to either wait for him in his room or linger after he had left.

He arrived finally and saw her waiting for him. She followed him into the room and drew the curtains.

'You look tired,' she said as she helped him undress.

'Yes, I am. It's been a long day. We have to keep checking our rifles when a new lot comes. The Enfield rifles have created a mess. Thank God, we don't use them.'

'But are our rifles greased with the fat of cows and pigs, too?'

'No. It is Allah's mercy. Otherwise, we too would have been in the middle of a mutiny.'

'Do you agree with what Mangal Pandey and the other soldiers did?'

'Yes. It's a matter of religion. We can't tinker with that.'

Meher was not much concerned with the intricacies of any political or military events, so she didn't ask any more questions. She pushed Riyaz gently on the bed and bent over him, bringing her lips on to his. Riyaz pushed her away.

'I'm tired. I think you better leave,' he told Meher who was slowly undressing him.

'Just relax. Enjoy the moment, huzoor,' she crooned and unbuttoned his shirt, running her hands over his broad tawny chest, her fingers curling around the dark growth. She traced her finger slowly, very slowly up his throat, and chin, then allowing it to linger on his lips, she tickled his moustache.

'Meher . . . I really . . . don't,' Riyaz Khan mumbled, but Meher placed her finger on his lips.

'Hush, my darling!' she murmured in his ear as she slowly brought forward her braid, entwined in strings of the fragrant tagar flowers, and ran it all over his stomach, chest and face. She knew he loved its fragrance, and she often wore it in her hair and lulled him to sleep. There was just one solitary shrub on the banks of the river that somehow sustained the heat of central India, perhaps due to the cool and wet soil near the Betwa.

Riyaz was too tired to move or indulge in lovemaking. He inhaled the perfume of the flowers that came on stronger than usual. His eyes slowly closed. Within minutes, he had drifted into sleep.

Meher sprang up and jumped off the bed. Bending down, she looked under it. There it was. She dragged out the wooden chest from under the bed, trying her best not to make any noise, and took out the iron box that lay inside. On opening it she found a pair of keys. She took the keys and stuffed it into her bosom and casting a quick glance at the prostrate body of Riyaz, ran out of his room and made her way towards the rear of the palace. There would be guards there, she had forgotten. So she went back to the zenana and rummaging through her belongings found a blanket. She wrapped it around herself and slowly made her exit through the huge gates. The guard stopped her.

'Who are you?' he asked.

Meher spoke through the thick layer of the blanket that covered her face. 'I'm ill. I'm going to meet the hakeem.'

'Isn't there one in the zenana?'

'She's gone out. Please let me go, can't you see I'm shivering?'

The guard eyed her suspiciously and then reluctantly let her pass. The moment she was out of his sight, she started running towards Jahangir Mahal. Skirting Rai Praveen's Mahal, she emerged from the back gate of the palace into the woods outside. Under the cover of the night and trees, she made her way to the armoury. She was about to reach it when someone pulled her roughly behind a bush.

'What . . . Chandraki!'

'Shh! Don't make a sound,' she warned.

'I got the keys,' she said as she took them out and handed them to Chandraki. 'Won't we go in?'

'There is a problem that we didn't think about. The guards!'

Meher looked at her wide-eyed. 'Now what?'

Chandraki thought hard. 'There are two here and two behind. They have guns, by the way.' The two women stood behind the bush. Meher's mind went blank. Chandraki was thinking hard.

'Can you divert their attention? Seduce them or lure them away? You are pretty good at it. You have practised it often enough with Riyaz Khan,' she said. Meher sighed.

After a few minutes, she emerged from behind the bushes. Pulling the blanket over her face and wrapping it tightly around herself, she rushed past the guards, her anklets tingling. Instantly alerted, one of the guards called out, 'Who is it? Stop! Stop!'

But Meher was gone. One of the guards decided to give chase. 'If I don't return within ten minutes, you follow in the same direction,' he told the other guard.

Hiding in the bushes, Chandraki heard every word. She prayed that Meher would lead the man far away. Each minute seemed to pass like an hour. Finally, the second guard cast a furtive look all around and ran after the first. A shot rang out.

Chandraki came out from behind the bushes and took out the keys that Meher had given her. She wondered why there were two keys. She inserted one into the padlock that hung from the door of the armoury and turned it around. The lock snapped open. She took the key out and stuffed it inside her blouse. Hoping it wouldn't creak, she slowly pushed open the medium-sized door. It made no noise. The moment she stepped in she was greeted by an overpoweringly rusty smell that lay thick in the air. Besides, it was pitch dark. She needed to find the swords quickly. The guards may return soon, and on finding the door open would raise an alarm instantly.

She walked carefully. Now that her eyes had adjusted to the dark, she could see the vague outlines of huge chests and boxes on either side. Something sharp pierced her palm.

'Ouch!' she cried out and bent closer to find out what had injured her. The swords! They were there, some lying unsheathed on the box beside her. She reached out for one of them, and almost instantly there was a huge commotion, and she could hear angry voices. Within minutes, the room was lit up with the light of several mashaals, and she heard dozens of men rush into the armoury.

'Catch them. Don't let them go!' It was the unmistakable voice of Riyaz Khan!

Chandraki stumbled, then regaining her balance quickly, crawled behind one of the boxes. The wound in her palm was bleeding. She wrapped her veil around it tightly. The swords lay a little ahead in front of her. It was now too late to pick one up.

'Where are the scoundrels? Don't let them go!' Riyaz Khan bellowed. The lights streamed into the huge room, casting long shadows. There was a scramble and suddenly the whole room was filled with men. Two men rushed past the box behind which she was hiding. Chandraki pressed herself against the wall behind her and held her breath.

Suddenly the clamour came to a halt. 'Can you see anyone?' Riyaz Khan asked.

'No, huzoor, there is no one here.'

'Check the inner room,' Riyaz's voice boomed. Chandraki crouched further down. Then slowly she extended one hand to reach out for the sword kept nearest to her. Just at that moment, one of the men came up close to where she was hiding. She could hear his footsteps right in front of her. She withdrew her hand instantly and shut her eyes. She would be discovered any minute now. Waiting with bated breath, she prayed hard. The footsteps came closer and stopped inches away from where she crouched. She could see the man's shoes. Her heart was beating too loudly, she felt. She could hear the other men search around the room, moving chests and banging things. Once in a while, something would hit metal and set off a huge clanging noise that would echo around the room. The effect was deafening. The man who stood next to her had the tip of his sword pointing towards her, almost touching her chin. Chandraki flattened herself even more against the wall.

'I don't think they are here, huzoor,' one of the men said. Most of them had moved into the inner room where the ammunition was stocked. They now returned without success.

'Check if any of the weapons or ammunition is missing. Damn these rebels!'

Rebels? What was Riyaz Khan talking about?

'Nothing seems to be missing,' one of them said.

'Fine. I'll get an inventory taken tomorrow. Let's get out now. There's enough happening outside as well,' said Riyaz Khan.

Finally, the footsteps receded. The voices died down, and the lights went out. The room plunged into darkness once again. She heard the door close.

Chandraki let out her breath. She needed to get out of

here as quickly as possible. Emerging from her hideout, she took tentative steps towards the huge iron door and tried to pull it open. It was heavy, and it had been easier to push it than pull it back. The door did not budge. They had locked it!

She retraced her steps back into the room. There had to be some other way to get out. And she had to get out in the night. There would be a thorough search of the armoury surely in the morning. She looked all around the room. There was no skylight, not even a crack anywhere. It was too well secured. She took out the keys from inside her blouse. They were of no use to her right now.

'I must give them to Meher to put back in Riyaz's room. That is, if Riyaz hasn't yet discovered that they have gone missing,' she said. As she toyed with the keys, they fell from her hand. As she bent to pick them up she noticed a sliver of light peeping out from the floor.

Getting down on her knees, Chandraki looked closely. To her surprise, she found a crack between two flagstones. She tapped on one of them and was greeted with a hollow sound. She tugged at it and pulled it. It moved a little. Using more force, she slid one of the stones. The crack widened. A dim shaft of light emanated from it. She slid it a little more, and the gap widened just enough for her to slip through. She pushed her legs through the gap and slowly slid underneath. She was of slight frame, thus it was not much of an ordeal, and she cleared the gap easily. Letting go of the edge of the stone above, she dropped on the ground below with a thud. A narrow flight of stairs went down from there.

'It's a secret passage!' Chandraki exclaimed. Overjoyed, she climbed down the uneven stairs and before long reached a narrow corridor. She went along it, feeling the cold damp walls on either side, and at the end of it, she came up against yet another wall. It was a dead end. But she was sure there was a way to get out. She tapped on the walls around her and suddenly winced. Her wound that had stopped bleeding opened up again and she could feel the blood trickling. What had pierced it? There was nothing she could see that could have pricked her wound. She felt the wall again with her other hand and came up against something sharp that was protruding from the wall. She scratched it and a bit of plaster came off revealing a nail head. She pulled at it and suddenly a small portion of the wall gave way to reveal a concealed iron grille. It was locked.

'Now what?' she asked herself. Of course! The other key! She inserted it into the lock and it clicked open. She pushed the grille a few inches to check if it would creak. It didn't. The Orchha army kept its gates well oiled. The small iron grille opened into the night outside. Chandraki knew there would be guards here too. She crouched once again and slowly made her way out of the tunnel. This wasn't too difficult to achieve. There were two guards, but fortunately both were sitting with their backs towards her, smoking and chatting.

Chandraki stepped out to find herself in the middle of a scrubby wasteland. She shut the iron gate behind her and still crouching, made her way through the clumps of acacia shrubs. After about half a mile, she straightened up and started walking. She had no idea where she was.

The faint glow of dawn was lightening up the eastern sky to her right, and she heard the first stirrings of a new day.

A woman headed towards her with a pitcher. She went up to her. 'Didi, what is this place? I am a visitor to this kingdom and have lost my way.'

The woman looked at her doubtfully. Then pointing in front of her, she said, 'The great kings rest there.'

Chandraki was puzzled. The woman looked at her expression and pointed far ahead to their right.

Chandraki saw the line of cenotaphs set again the crimson horizon, standing majestically in a row, mute witnesses to a glorious era gone by. So, she was on the other side of the city. Beyond the tombs, she could see the rippling Betwa that was gradually kissing the first rays of the sun, its silver waters turning to gold. The gurgle of the river reached her ears in the silence of the morning hour. Though she was a long way away from the palace, she was relieved that she had survived the deadly night.

When she met Meher later in the day, she handed over the keys and asked, 'Where did you disappear last night?'

Meher grinned. 'I'll tell you later. Did you get the sword?'

Chandraki shook her head. Meher's face fell. 'So, after all that, it was a wasted effort?'

'I don't think so. Look what I got!' Chandraki said as she held out a dagger with a curved tip and a carved wooden handle. 'I didn't come out empty-handed.' She grinned.

45

An unusual atmosphere prevailed in Orchha these days. A sense of fear hung in the air, and the consequent lull that followed the events of the last few days was eerie. Less people lingered in the streets. The mood of the kingdom was subdued. Chandraki was desperate to find out what was happening, but she got no clear information. All the discussions took place behind closed doors between the queen, Nathay Khan and the council of ministers. Riyaz Khan too was a part of the meetings sometimes.

A few days later, Keshav had to leave on yet another trip.

'I am taking Bijli with me,' he informed Chandraki.

'I can't give you Bijli, she belongs to Maharani Lakshmibai!' Chandraki retorted.

When Keshav insisted, Chandraki asked, 'What happened to your horse?'

'He's not well. And I need a swift-footed horse. Besides, Bijli now belongs to our royal stables.'

Chandraki ignored what Keshav had said. 'How long will you be away?' she asked.

'I can't tell you,' he answered impatiently. 'I will be gone for a few days. Don't go anywhere.'

Chandraki wasn't happy about Keshav taking Bijli with him. The mare was much beloved of Maharani Lakshmibai, who had entrusted her in Chandraki's care. What if something happened to Bijli? What would she tell the Maharani? But it wasn't as though Keshav was taking her permission. She had no choice anyway. She was herself more or less a prisoner here and had no control over anything. Besides, she didn't want any more fights.

Keshav rode away on Bijli early next morning. Chandraki went up to the palace gates to see him off. As she turned around to go back into the Raja Mahal, she looked up at the sky instinctively. Although it was early morning, the sun was well up in the sky and the parched earth of Bundelkhand would simmer through the day. 10 May 1857 was going to be a hot day, a very hot and cruel day.

Chandraki was restless for most of the day. Something was not right. The events of the last few weeks had cast a shroud of gloom all around. In court, everyone seemed to be in low spirits. Streets were mostly deserted by early evening, and everyone was on edge. First, the news of the hanging of Mangal Pandey and Jemadar Ishwar Prasad in faraway Barrackpore, followed by reports of fires and unrest in Ambala, Agra and Allahabad had trickled in. This had caused quite a bit of concern. From the news gathered in bits and pieces, it was heard that there were several groups of plunderers who were rapidly moving across northern and central India, and were now headed towards Bundelkhand, ransacking and destroying whatever came in their way. They were looting houses, shops and travellers. No one knew where they were from, and where they were headed. It was this news that had prompted the check of the armoury at precisely the moment Chandraki had been inside it.

She had been quite amused when Meher told her how she had lured the two guards deep into the woods behind the armoury and left them there and returned to Riyaz's room just as he received news that there were intruders in the palace premises. He was even told that there was a woman among them.

'That woman was me.' Meher giggled. 'The guards had set off the alarm. They even shot at me! Missed me by a few inches! I reached Riyaz's room seconds before he was pulled out of his slumber and spirited away by Nathay Khan. When he returned, I was still waiting for him outside his room like a devoted lover.' She chuckled.

'Didn't Riyaz miss the keys?' Chandraki asked.

'No, he didn't. There was so much happening that I think it didn't strike him to check for his own set of keys. They thought the plunderers had simply broken into the armoury. We were lucky. Once you returned the keys, I put them back immediately, explained Meher.

Chandraki's mind was spinning. So much was happening all of a sudden. And now Keshav had suddenly disappeared with Bijli just when she needed her the most. As she mulled over these events, the call went out that the queen had summoned court immediately. Chandraki hastened to appear in the durbar.

In the next one hour, Rani Larai addressed a huge gathering in the Diwan-e-Aam.

'The Indian sepoys from the 3rd Bengal Light Cavalry that is stationed in Meerut have mutinied and killed British officers, along with British civilians including women and children. Meerut is up in flames, and from what I hear the rebels are already on their way to Dilli. They are slaying firanghees left, right and centre. Many other native troops across provinces have mutinied. Among them are also robbers and thugs who are making the most of the situation and indulging in loot and arson. Huge bands of these rebels are now marching south towards Bundelkhand. We are hoping that they will not cause any damage to Orchha as we have no British forces stationed here. But all our neighbours are now vulnerable,' she said in a matter-of-fact way.

Pausing briefly to catch her breath, she continued, 'I warn everyone that no one is to offer any refuge or help to either the firanghees or the mutineers. If anyone is found guilty of the same, the punishment will be severe. I do not want unnecessary carnage and bloodshed on the soil of Orchha,' the queen announced.

There was complete silence in the courtroom. Her words pierced through the gathered crowd like an arrow.

Rani Larai further continued, 'In the event of any disturbance caused by either of the warring factions or even by our hostile neighbours, I assure all my subjects that they will be given full protection. My General and Prime Minister Nathay Khan will personally supervise all operations. I leave the gates to the palace open for anyone from our kingdom to take refuge.'

The fort was now crawling with soldiers, with men in uniform marching up and down. Several more regiments were formed. Rani Larai's army had spilled over in the streets and all over town. Even the temples were not spared.

Chandraki was thinking hard. She needed to get to Jhansee before anything happened there. She remembered the message she had received a few weeks ago from Khuda Baksh. She now understood what it meant. When Chandraki had left Jhansee two years ago, there was a small British force stationed in the fort after Maharani Lakshmibai vacated it, a small contingent of Native Infantry and Cavalry. 'I don't think there would be more than a hundred Britishers in the city,' Chandraki thought. 'I have to reach Jhansee and help out.' But Keshav had taken Bijli, and she had no other means to get to Jhansee under the present circumstances.

The following day Rani Larai announced, 'The first call to freedom is out all over the country. Kanpur, Lucknow, Bareilly in Rohilkhand, Shahbad and Gwalior in central India are all in the grip of this bloody tornado that is sweeping across the country, leaving behind a trail of doom and destruction. All around, the East India Company's troops have broken out in mutiny. The whole country is burning. Dilli has been wiped out and the rebels have put the Mughal Shahenshah back on the throne.'

46

The month of June in central India is a cruel one. The sun beats down so fiercely that even the birds are terrified and reduce their chatter. The skies are usually very clear, thus allowing the heat to penetrate into the very bosom of the earth. The wind hushes up, though once in a while it blows with a vengeance menacingly, raising clouds of dust and forcing men and beasts not to challenge its course. The stillness that pervades all around is threatening and fearsome.

On one such afternoon in June 1857, the 5th of June to be precise, about a month after several native troops of the East India Company broke out in mutiny and let loose a drama of horror and bloodshed across most of northern and central India, Rani Larai in Orchha called for durbar immediately. Everyone had to be present.

'What's happened?' everyone asked one another as they made a scramble to reach the durbar hall. It was an emergency meeting.

Rani Larai's council of ministers took their seats in the

Diwan-e-Aam while the rest of the people thronged the area just outside the hall. Seated on her throne, Rani Larai looked troubled. Her fierce gaze had dimmed, and her lips were dry. People waited anxiously. Chandraki was nervous. It had been weeks since Keshav had left, and there was no news from him. She knew the nature of his job, and it was unlikely that anybody would know of his whereabouts, especially in times like these. 'Durga Ma, please protect my Keshav wherever he is,' she prayed silently as the people waited for the Rani to speak.

No one moved. Not a rustle, nor a whisper. A stunned audience greeted Rani Larai's news with stoic silence. Outside, it seemed that even the birds had stopped chirping, and the stillness of the summer afternoon hung oppressively.

~

As the Rani addressed her durbar in Orchha, twenty miles away in the British cantonment of the principality of Jhansee, Superintendent Alexander Skene was ordering all the British officers and their families to get inside the Jhansee fort. Collecting his wife and two children he left for the fort himself on foot without even waiting for his carriage to arrive.

'Some of our sepoys have mutinied and seized the Star Fort. As you all know the Star Fort contains all our ammunition and about four and a half lakh rupees in our treasury. There are thirty-two of our sepoys missing though the rest are loyal to us. Captain Gordon has written to Captain Erskine and Major Western for help, and I have

already sent letters to Cawnpore and Gwalior and have
appealed to the Rajas of neighbouring kingdoms for help. I
think we all are safe here. Well, at least for the time being.'
Skene's voice rang out firm and clear as he addressed his
men gathered inside the fort of Jhansee.

There were sixty-six of them – sahibs, memsahibs and
children. They looked at each other not knowing what
to make of Skene's words. The artillery had been seized.
As Skene spoke, he heard a shout below the fort walls.
Looking down from its ramparts he saw two sowars who
had broken away from the Star Fort shouting and riding
towards them.

When they came up to the wall of the fort they asked,
'Why are you hiding in this fort?'

'You have mutinied,' Skene shouted from the fort's
ramparts.

'Only thirty-two sepoys have. The rest haven't,' assured
the sowars. Skene refused to believe them. He had been
fired at as well as the garrison commander Captain Dunlop
and Lieutenant Taylor, but luckily, they escaped, he told
them. The sowars shrugged and went away. Skene stood
there for some time, then turned around and gave orders
for dinner to be prepared.

Around eight in the evening, Skene saw two riders
approaching the Jhansee fort again, but to his relief they
were Captain Dunlop's messengers.

'Dunlop sahib has called a meeting and wishes you to
be present,' they conveyed. Skene nodded.

~

In Orchha, Rani Larai was narrating the morning's events
to her spellbound audience.

'The Indian platoon of the British cantonment stationed
in Jhansee, led by Havildar Gurbaksh Rao, has stormed
into the Star Fort, the armoury, and seized the treasures
and the ammunition. Pulled away from their morning cup
of tea, Skene and Gordon were shot at, but have survived.
The British in Jhansee have panicked and taken refuge in
the old fort, though Superintendent Skene believes that
his small contingent would continue to be loyal to the
Company Sarkar.'

Within minutes of receiving the news, pandemonium
broke out in the palace. Nathay Khan and Riyaz Khan
spurred into action.

'If anyone is seen creating panic, he will be shot
immediately. Get back to your quarters, right now! It's an
order!' bellowed Nathay Khan.

~

In the Jhansee fort, Captain Dunlop said to the subedars
of his platoon, 'Ask your men if they wish to serve in the
army, they must do so properly. If not, they may return to
their homes. But there should be no mutiny.'

'There is no mutiny, sahib. Only thirty-two soldiers
have rebelled,' one of them assured.

But the officers were not reassured. 'We can't give in
like this, Skene. I'm going to sleep in the barracks tonight,'
Dunlop said.

'That would be highly dangerous, sir!'

'Do you expect me to show the rebels that we are scared and have given in to them?'

The next day, on the morning of 6 June, in a show of defiance, some British officers came out of the fort and walked outside. One of them was Captain Gordon, who after his walk around the fort, returned to his bungalow for breakfast.

After breakfast, he called one of his men and said, 'I'm going back to the fort, but I will return to my bungalow shortly.'

Meanwhile, the sepoys who had stormed into the Star Fort returned to the lines. This prompted an emergency meeting of the British officers and the native commissioned and non-commissioned officers.

'Since those rebels haven't left, no one will go near the Star Fort. Captain Dunlop will make the necessary arrangements. I've asked Maharani Lakshmibai to send across four elephants which given our friendly relations, I'm sure she will,' Skene told his men.

Captain Dunlop set up a picket a little distance from the Star Fort. 'No one is to communicate, nor send any food to the mutineers, is that understood?' he told his men.

No further activity followed these orders. There was an eerie lull that prevailed. No one knew what would happen next. The morning dragged into afternoon without further incident. But the apparent quiet was the calm before the storm as they say. A few hours later a hysterical mob surrounded Maharani Lakshmibai's palace.

'We want your support, Your Majesty!' the mob screamed. 'We want you to announce publicly that you support us, and together we will throw out the firanghees! Come out, come out!' Lakshmibai locked herself inside the palace and refused to rise to the bait.

Soon, a few men broke away from there and headed towards the military barracks. Mullah Ahsan Ali called for the evening prayer. Almost simultaneously, the prison warden Bakshish Ali opened the gates to the prison and freed its inmates. Kaale Khan stormed into the fort and led the attack. The sepoys seized their weapons and fired at the British officers. All hell broke loose as the rebels ransacked the British quarters screaming 'Deen ka jai!' The first three officers who resisted were killed. Among them was Captain Dunlop.

~

Orchha received the news of the three British officers killed with much consternation.

'Who were they?' Chandraki asked Riyaz.

'Captain Dunlop, Lieutenant Turnbull and Lieutenant Campbell,' Riyaz replied matter-of-factly. 'Rani Larai will call for a session in a few minutes. You'll know everything then,' he replied and walked off.

In less than an hour, the Orchha court gathered again.

'We have some bad news. As you must have heard, three British officers were killed this morning by the rebel forces. The fort of Jhansee is under siege, and there are around sixty-three of them including women and children hiding in the fort. From what I hear, it was Rani Lakshmibai's men who killed the officers!'

This was not possible, thought Chandraki. Much as she disliked the firanghees, Maharani Lakshmibai would have not complied with the rebels, she was sure of that.

~

In the fort of Jhansee, Skene had by now lost all hope of any survival either for himself or his people. Nevertheless, he sent three of Gordon's men to Lakshmibai for help. The message didn't reach the queen, and all three were killed. Madar Baksh, who was in charge of ordnance and who was a captive too, was sent off with a message from the rissaldar to be handed to the British officers. The message said that if the British surrendered and left the fort, they would be given safe passage. But he was denied admission to the fort.

'The Rani has ordered that no one is to be allowed into the fort,' one of the sepoys told him. 'If you want to deliver the message, you will have to take permission from Her Majesty.' Madar Baksh left for the Rani's palace.

Addressing Lakshmibai, he pleaded. 'I have to deliver a message from the rissaldar to the sahibs, but the sepoys tell me I can't enter without your orders. I want a purwanah from you, Your Majesty!'

~

Nathay Khan sat with Rani Larai with a map of Bundelkhand spread out before them. Pointing to the areas surrounding Orchha, he said, 'The Rajas of Dutya,

Charkari and Panna are helping the British forces while
Banpur and Chhatarpur, under its commandar Deshpat,
have revolted openly.' He looked up at the queen. 'There
is also the possibility that some plans are taking flight in
the lines of the 12th Native Infantry and 14th Irregular
Cavalry stationed at Nowgong. The regent Rani is
supporting the rebel forces,' he said, tapping his fingers
on the maps. 'The Bundela Rajput chiefs have been upset
with the British for their actions in their states as well, and
have set their sights on each other too. So trouble can be
expected from those quarters as well. Raja Mardan Singh
of Banpur hopes to regain the whole kingdom of Chanderi,
which belonged to his ancestors.' He paused. 'Rani Sahiba,
our neighbours are up in arms!'

Having listened to Nathay Khan, Rani Larai took
a deep breath. 'I heard that the thakur landowners of
Karhra intend to attack. I do not wish to embroil our
kingdom in this mess, and I repeat, anyone seen or heard
supporting either the rebels or the firanghees will face
dire consequences,' she reiterated. 'By the way, what news
of Jhansee?'

He was quiet for a while. 'Frankly, at this point I don't
envy Jhansee's situation. The mutineers have brought
Sadashiv Rao, Gangadhar Rao's distant relative, and
intend to put him on the throne. Lakshmibai is helpless.
If she helps the firanghees, with whom she is currently at
loggerheads, then she will antagonize her own people who
may then support Sadashiv Rao,' Nathay Khan informed
Rani Larai. 'In any case, I don't think she is in much of a
position to help them. Her own life, property and home

are under threat. She's being squeezed of huge amounts of money by sheer force. I can just visualize her condition,' he smirked.

~

The British in Jhansee lived under the shadow of death for the next few days. The fort of Jhansee lay under siege for forty-eight hours. As the rations and ammunition dwindled, one of Skene's servants, Shahbuddin, was sent out to procure some food. On returning, he found Skene and Gordon walking on the ramparts of the fort. They lowered a rope to which Shahbuddin tied the food basket. As he was tying the basket, some sepoys saw him doing so. They rushed towards him and arrested Shahbuddin.

~

A day later Nathay Khan sought an audience with the queen. On being ushered in, Rani Larai asked, 'What news? Any new development?'

Nathay Khan nodded. 'Bad news for the British, Your Majesty. Several of them who were inside the fort have been killed. This includes Captain Gordon.'

'Oh, that's a pity,' the queen replied, not really meaning it. 'Have the rebels finally entered the fort?'

'Yes. They started shelling the fort with the one cannon that they captured when they attacked the fort, but the British returned the fire. So they withdrew the cannon a little further away from the walls of the fort. But this created panic among those inside. According to an eyewitness, Sheikh Hingan, who has managed to escape and is now here in our palace, two servants of Captain Burgess opened one of the gates from the inside and tried to flee despite orders that they shouldn't. He was shot dead, of course, by one of the officers, but the other turned around and killed the officer. Then Captain Burgess killed him and twenty more sepoys but was finally shot dead himself. The mutineers gained entry into the fort, and they killed whoever came in their way. One of them was Captain Gordon.'

'That is a heavy blow to the British. It will bring down their morale. When did this happen?'

'Yesterday, in the morning, around eight. There is more,' Nathay Khan said. Rani Larai nodded, signalling him to continue.

'Sheikh Hingan tells me that Rani Lakshmibai sent around 150 of her own men probably from the same bodyguard that Skene had earlier provided at her request. He tells me that Gordon, on seeing this earlier in the day, sent her a message that she could take command of the state, and they would move to a place that she could choose. But her reply was that she had no control over anything, and that her own safety, her very life, was in jeopardy. He sent more messages to which she didn't reply.'

'So, now what?'

'Let's wait and watch how the events unfold. We have nothing to gain or lose either way,' declared Nathay Khan.

The conversation was taking place in a room on one side of the central courtyard where the mehfils usually took place. The queen often held small urgent meetings here which were attended by her immediate coterie of minsters. Many of her meetings with Nathay Khan would also commence in the small room. The room lay right next to the green room where the performers waited before or after cultural shows. The girls would gather here, giggling and chatting as they dressed for their roles. The room was always strewn with clothes, flowers and jewellery, and the fragrance of ittar would linger permanently.

Chandraki entered this room to look for her anklet that she had left behind a few days ago. Though the two rooms had a thick wooden door separating them, there was a skylight that had been left open. Nathay Khan's deep voice filtered through this gap, and Chandraki clearly heard him in conversation with the queen. She pushed one of the couches to the wall and stood up on tiptoe. She couldn't reach the gap, but she could now hear every word clearly.

'How did this man from Jhansee reach Orchha?' Rani Larai asked.

'When all the mayhem ensued in Jhansee yesterday, he fled. He had no idea in what direction to go. He ran like a madman and took the first road he saw near the cantonment, and only on reaching here did he realize that he had jumped from the frying pan into the fire!' Nathay Khan's face lit up with glee as he narrated the events to the queen. 'Jhansee's in a complete state of anarchy. No one knows what's happening there.'

'So what should we do with this Sheikh Hingan?' the queen asked.

'He has already given me more information than I

require.' A sly smile spread across Nathay Khan's face. 'But I would like to keep him with me for some time, Your Majesty. It gives me great pleasure to see one of Lakshmibai's subjects at my mercy!' He smiled lazily.

'You are a rogue, Nathay! Merciless!' said the queen and rose. 'Where have you lodged him?'

'In the camel stables, there is a small space that is usually used for storing fodder. I've dumped him there. Let him rot there for a few days, and then I'll set him free. Maybe we'll send him back as a return gift to the Maharani of Jhansee two days before Janmashtami. With our compliments, of course.' Nathay Khan grinned.

47

Chandraki hadn't slept for many days now. Feeling totally helpless, she ran from person to person every day for news from Jhansee.

'We don't know,' was the answer she received. Other than the soldiers and their officers, there was no one she could ask. People were mostly indoors, the queen had retired to her chamber, Keshav had not returned, and the gates to the palace were locked. People only spoke in hushed whispers. She was completely cut off from the world. 'I'll go mad if this situation continues,' she thought.

Desperate, Chandraki ran after Riyaz Khan one day and caught hold of his hand as he descended the staircase to inspect one of the passages that ran down from the central courtyard of the Raja Mahal.

'Riyaz!' she called out. Riyaz Khan turned around and was surprised to see her following him. The staircase was very narrow and steep, and there was just one lantern at the top that threw its light on the stairs, barely illuminating the last few steps. Chandraki climbed down the few steps to where Riyaz was standing and stood facing him. She was pressed hard against him as he turned around, almost squeezing the air out of her.

Riyaz Khan's breath came up short as he felt her body against his. She aroused in him a sharp feeling of thrill that he had never experienced before. He tried to ignore it and move away but couldn't. There was just no space. The two of them stood there, pressed against each other.

'I . . . I . . .' stammered Chandraki. 'I'm scared. Stay with me,' she blurted out before she could stop herself.

For a moment, Riyaz Khan stopped breathing. Did he hear right?

At a complete loss for words, he stood pushed to the wall with Chandraki's body pinning him against it. He could feel every part of her body so clearly that it was almost as if she stood naked before him. He closed his eyes. 'Allah, please help me, I can't bear this,' he prayed. 'Don't do this to me,' he implored silently. But there was no mercy. Chandraki put her arms around him and rested her head on his shoulder. 'Don't leave me, Riyaz,' she whispered.

Riyaz tried to push her away and in doing so his hands swept across her body. It was so warm, so relenting. She was his in this moment. His Meera. She was all his. Yet she wasn't. It hurt so much, this pain of feeling her right next to his heart. It tore him apart. He wanted to bury his head in her bosom and cry. Cry his heart out. But he couldn't have her in his arms. He couldn't touch her. He didn't want to lose her. He suddenly stiffened and regained his composure.

'Why?' he asked simply.

'I . . . I don't know. I feel safe when I'm with you,' she replied.

Riyaz Khan drew in his breath sharply.

'Move out of the way, Chandraki! Let me go,' he said, pushing her away.

Chandraki held his arm tightly. 'Please. Don't leave me. I'm alone. I'll do whatever you want me to, but don't leave me here alone.'

He looked into those deep, dark eyes. There was no malice in them. For some time, he stood spellbound. Then suddenly, before she could say another word, he wrenched his arm away from her and climbed down the rest of the stairs and was gone.

Chandraki stood alone on the staircase, her body casting a long shadow in the light of the lamp. She was stunned. He had pushed her away. He had rejected her. Why?

And then she thought, why not? What was she expecting? That the moment she would offer herself, he would lunge at her and take her? Why did she assume that he would be interested in her? It suddenly dawned upon her that in all the years she had known him, he had never made any advances towards her, he hadn't touched her. It never occurred to her that if given a chance, Riyaz wouldn't want her.

For the first time, she felt respect for the man.

Riyaz was tormented by Chandraki's behaviour. Why, he asked himself? Why would she want to be with him? However tempting the idea may be, Riyaz Khan was no fool to imagine even for a moment that Chandraki would want him. He knew her well enough. There was something up her sleeve. She was not as helpless as she pretended to be. Scared? Chandraki? That was impossible. There was something else . . . what was it?

He paced up and down in his room. He poured himself some wine. His mind was a complete mess, his heart aflutter. Ever since the day Heera had left him, Riyaz Khan had not allowed his emotions to control him. But, for the first time since that day, he was in a fluster. He ran his hand across his forehead. Beads of perspiration dotted it. Not as much from the heat as from the emotions that Chandraki had evoked. From the day he had set his eyes upon her, a strange sensation had enveloped him that always left him feeling exposed in her presence. It was bearable when they were mean to each other. He could mask his emotions, but how could he resist her when she appeared this vulnerable? He knew she was playing games with him, with his mind, his senses, his very soul and he could do nothing to prevent it. He was completely at her mercy. Yet, when he had looked into her eyes, they had been bereft of any guile or deceit.

'Ya Khuda! Help me! What do I do?' he cried aloud. 'Don't test me like this. I just can't bear it any more,' he howled as he fell to his knees, his hands clasped, begging for mercy. 'Oh Meera, Meera, leave me alone! Please!'

48

No further news came from Jhansee over the next two days.

'The firanghees are huddled inside the fort. They are running out of food and water,' Chandraki heard one of Nathay Khan's men telling another.

'Serves them right, doesn't it?'

'Shh! We are not to say anything.'

Rani Larai called upon her council of ministers. 'Alexander Skene has asked for help against the mutineers. I'm not in favour of sending our troops or ammunition. What do you have to say?'

Nathay Khan smiled. 'I'm simply loving this. I would love to go there personally and watch the drama.'

'Nathay Khan! This is serious business. Do you have any suggestions?' Rani Larai admonished her General.

Nathay Khan straightened himself. 'I agree with you, Your Majesty. There is no need for us to get involved in this. We follow the policy of non-alignment. I wouldn't send my forces to save those wretched firanghees. Have they ever helped us? They could have got back Jhansee for us.'

It was thus agreed that Orchha would not respond to any plea of help from any quarter. The queen dismissed court.

The afternoon of 8 June dragged on. The sun beat down mercilessly, but a strange calm prevailed on the streets of Orchha. The gates of the palace, which were now mostly shut, opened every day for an hour to allow the queen's retinue to pass through on its way to the temple. Only the queen and just a handful of her trusted aides comprised the small procession. Chandraki was not one of them. Desperate to go to Jhansee, she thought of joining this group somehow and get out of the palace. 'Once I'm out of the palace, I'll find a way to reach Jhansee,' she thought. She knew that a headcount took place each time the procession left the palace and then returned. She requested one of the girls who usually went with the queen to allow her to go in her place since she wanted to pray for her dead mother.

'I'm not allowed to go out, so let me go in your place,' Chandraki begged. The poor girl was terrified.

'If you are caught, Nathay Khan will have me executed. No, I can't do so,' she refused.

Taking her hand and placing it on her own head, Chandraki said, 'I promise you, nothing will happen.' The poor girl gave in to Chandraki's request, against her own will.

Chandraki covered her face with the girl's veil and quietly walked out with the rest of the procession, her head bowed. Once the counting was over, she heaved a sigh of relief. It was a short puja these days. On the way back, once the group reached the road that connected the Rani Mahal to the fort, Chandraki broke away and hid behind a clump of bushes. The group moved on, and she was about to turn around to walk the other way when a blood-curdling shriek pierced the frightening stillness of the morning. The air was suddenly rented with pathetic cries. Chandraki almost jumped with fright, but quickly regained her composure and peeped out from behind the bush.

She saw a group of firanghees – men, women and children, advancing on horseback from the Jhansee gate towards the fort of Orchha. Curious, she waited, and as they came closer, cries of 'Help! Help!' shattered the air.

The firanghees rushed past her and turned towards the main fort gate. Once they had passed her, everything was completely still for a few minutes. Then suddenly, she felt the ground under her feet tremble. At first, she thought it was an earthquake. The ground shook, and then she heard a murmur rolling into town, the air throbbed with a deadly fanaticism, and then suddenly, from nowhere a huge company of horse riders crashed on to the roads, their eyes bloodshot, their teeth bared, and their weapons naked. It seemed as though the whole of creation was on a rampage.

She saw huge clouds of dust being raised as scores of men on horseback thundered through the city of Orchha in hot pursuit of the firanghees who ran in front of them. Flourishing swords and daggers, loading rifles and screaming, they slashed their way through the groups of firanghees, killing anything that came in their path with a blood-curdling vengeance. The sahibs fell like flies. These were the Devil's men who had unleashed a whirlwind of terror and bloodshed. Shots rang out and Chandraki saw two Englishmen fall right in front of her. She cowered behind the bush, numb with terror. The men on horseback thundered through the cobbled gateway of the fort, following the firanghees who had by now almost reached the palace gates.

Suddenly there was a spray of bullets from the ramparts of the fort. The bullets caught some of the men on horseback off guard, and they fell off their horses, dead. The rest continued pushing through the group of firanghees, while simultaneously returning the fire from the fort. The gates that had been opened minutes before to let the queen's retinue pass were immediately shut, and the sahibs could not enter. The riders pounced on them, chopping them into pieces, while shooting with their rifles at the guards positioned on the ramparts of the fort. Heavy firing continued, and after about ten minutes, the fighting ceased.

Chandraki looked around her. Bodies lay in heaps. Those of horses, and men and women. All the riders lay dead at the gates of the Orchha palace. Several firanghees lay dead or mutilated, and some headless. There was blood all around, and limbs torn asunder strewn across the road that led up from the palace to the temple. The fort was once more engulfed in silence. Chandraki shuddered.

Suddenly, she heard someone weeping. She cautiously stepped out from behind the bush on to the road. She found a young British woman and two children standing in the middle of the road, turned to stone.

'Who are you?' Chandraki asked feebly, still reeling from the shock of what she had just witnessed. The woman did not reply. She walked up to them, and just as she was about to talk to her she heard the sound of hooves advancing towards them. She looked up and found a lone rider riding towards her. He crossed the road and came up to her and got off his horse.

'What are you doing here?' Riyaz Khan asked Chandraki quietly. Then he looked at the three Britishers who stood terrified beside her. He turned to Chandraki again.

'Get on to my horse.' Chandraki did so, without a word. Motioning to the memsahib, he asked her to follow him. The small group then proceeded towards the palace. He spoke at the gate, and it opened up to let the group enter the palace.

~

'We owe no allegiance to anyone.' Rani Larai's voice rang out in the confines of the durbar hall. 'Neither to Jhansee, nor to the British. We are on no one's side, nor are we to help anyone, you understand?'

Those present in the durbar nodded. Chandraki saw a party of six Britishers standing huddled in one corner, petrified. The woman and her two children were among them.

'The Raja of Banpur forced Captain Gordon to hand over the state of Lalitpur to him. Three of these firanghees come from there. They have been saved by Prem Narain, our prince's tutor. This woman, with her two children, was saved by Riyaz Khan,' Rani Larai said, pointing at the woman Chandraki had found on the road. She stood in one corner, trembling in terror. 'They have come to us seeking refuge. Though my diwan Nathay Khan advises me to turn them away and has refused them shelter, I have decided to allow them to stay here until things improve in both Jhansee and Banpur. But the gates of Orchha will be closed to any fugitive hereafter. No one is to venture out of the fort premises,' the Rani thundered.

'But what about Jhansee, Your Majesty? Do we help Rani Lakshmibai?' one of her ministers asked.

Rani Larai turned to look at Chandraki. 'Should we?' she asked in a menacingly sweet voice. 'What do you say, Chandraki? Should we send our forces to assist your Rani?'

Chandraki returned her gaze with a blank stare. She was stunned by Rani Larai's question thrown at her suddenly.

'Why are you quiet? Tell me, what should we do?'

'I . . . I don't . . . don't know, Rani Sahiba,' Chandraki stammered. 'As you wish!'

'As you wish, she says.' The queen now addressed all present. 'As you wish, she says,' she repeated. Then turning to Chandraki once again, she asked, 'Do you know what Jhansee did to us? Do you know?' she thundered, her voice reverberating around the courtroom. Chandraki had not seen Rani Larai so incensed before.

'Jhansee was ours. It belonged to us. We created it. That fort of yours in which your Maharani lives, or rather lived, was constructed by *our* Raja Bir Singh Deo. What was Jhansee? Nothing – it was just a fort to protect us. We were the rulers. The Marathas returned our Raja Chhatrasal's noble gesture with betrayal. One of Jhansee's subedars killed one of our kings and burnt Orchha. They handed over Jhansee to the firanghees. And those firanghees, the scourge of this earth, put puppet kings on the throne. One of them was your Gangadhar Rao. We just ceased to exist for it.' Her face had taken on a dark hue, her eyes flashed as she rattled on.

Chandraki's face had gone white and her limbs numb. Riyaz Khan stood a little away, his face not betraying even a flicker of emotion.

Once the court was dismissed, Nathay Khan charged out. Soldiers and refugees, both Indian and white, and the palace folk cramped the huge central courtyard of the Raja Mahal, many spilling beyond to the gardens and the Jahangir Mahal.

'Flush out the damn refugees!' boomed Nathay Khan's voice, piercing through the uproar. 'Riyaz, scatter your men to the Jahangir Mahal. And don't forget to check the camel and elephant stables. Close the main gate!'

The heavy iron doors that marked the entrance to the grand fort of Orchha slowly closed, shutting out the world outside, a world laden with cries and blood, death and destruction. Orchha was now secure . . . the gem that still sparkled in the blackness of doom . . . was now truly hidden.

49

Shaken by Rani Larai's lethal words, Chandraki made her way through the prevailing chaos inside the palace towards the quieter Jahangir Mahal. The three-storeyed structure stood tall, and if she were to stand at the highest point, she could even see up to Jhansee. The palace had been built by Raja Bir Singh Deo, almost two hundred years ago to welcome the Mughal prince Jahangir, who later spent one night in the palace when he fled Agra following his fallout with his father, Jalaluddin Muhammad Akbar, the emperor of Hindustan.

Chandraki wandered through the huge rooms of the palace that were lined with precious stones, mirrors and exquisite paintings. She had noticed that turquoise tiles were prominently used here. There was a huge fountain in the central courtyard, and the row of balconies with the lattice jharokhas that went around the palace seemed as though they were hanging from the facade of the fort. Though a Hindu kingdom, the Islamic influence in its construction was quite evident in its architecture, characterized by both Mughal and Hindu styles.

She climbed up the palace steps to the uppermost floor and stepped out on to one of the narrow balconies that overlooked the forests and the river beyond. Everything was silent here, and she could not imagine that there was so much carnage and destruction happening all around just a few miles away.

'I wish I was beside Maharani Lakshmibai right now,' Chandraki said to herself as she looked over the ramparts.

'Thank your stars that you are not.'

Startled, Chandraki turned around. Riyaz stood before her. 'What do you mean?'

'You wouldn't be able to bear to see the condition she's in,' said Riyaz, a flicker of a smile hovering on his lips. Chandraki looked away nervously. A flush of embarrassment swept through her. Ever since the day she had stood with Riyaz on the staircase, Chandraki couldn't look into his eyes. She had no idea what had come over her. She asked herself again and again why she had behaved that way. Much as she tried to arouse feelings of hatred towards Riyaz, she couldn't. On the contrary, strangely, she felt secure when he was around.

Riyaz stepped forward. 'Give up the idea of returning to Jhansee. There's nothing left there,' he whispered in her ear.

It was from Riyaz Khan that Chandraki heard about the fury that had been unleashed on Jhansee.

Sixty-five Englishmen, women and children, including Captain Skene and his family, had been massacred in Jokhan Bagh, an area behind the walled city of Jhansee, where they were led by the rebels with their hands tied, in a procession. No one was spared. Bakshish Ali himself killed Superintendent Skene.

'They fled from the carnage in Jhansee, some of them escaped to Orchha, the ones who have been allowed refuge here,' Riyaz said quietly.

'So, what does Maharani Lakshmibai have to do with it?'

Riyaz Khan burst into laughter.

'What does Maharani Lakshmibai have to do with it?' he repeated her question mockingly. 'Why, it is on her orders that this massacre was carried out. She promised the British shelter and a safe passage to leave Jhansee if they vacated the fort. And they were supposedly being led to safety when the rebels pounced on them.'

'Impossible!' Chandraki said defiantly. 'The Maharani would never do such a thing.'

'Oh yes? You know how pleased she is with the British, don't you?' Riyaz said sarcastically. 'They've usurped her kingdom, lifted the ban on cow slaughter, used the funds for her son's sacred thread ceremony, and usurped the villages that supported the temple. And threw her out of her own home. Do you really think she wants to see them alive? They have denied her even the king's personal fortune which is rightfully her inheritance,' he said.

'She hates the British, I know, but she's not so inhuman. She will never order the massacre of women and children,' Chandraki insisted.

'Hah!' Riyaz Khan scoffed. 'My dear Meera and her unwavering loyalty towards her vile queen. Wake up!' Riyaz

Khan lifted her chin with his forefinger, looked into her eyes and smiled. Chandraki was always rattled whenever he called her Meera. She actually liked it. She was about to say something when he put his finger on her lips. Then suddenly, he turned around and walked away.

She was stunned. That man! He had the audacity to touch her! And what was worse, she didn't stop him.

50

The sun singed the earth of Bundelkhand while Jhansee burned. Chandraki needed a horse. Keshav turned up five days later. It had been over a week since the massacre at Jokhan Bagh took place.

'Where had you gone?' Chandraki asked him.

'Palera. I had to dispatch a message to Raja Ramdhir Singh. I'm off again tomorrow morning to Dutya.'

'Is your horse better?' Chandraki asked him.

Keshav hesitated for a second before replying. 'No, not yet. Why?'

'I need Bijli,' she said simply.

'Why? Are you thinking of riding off somewhere despite knowing what the situation is like?' he asked angrily.

Chandraki was silent. Then she said, 'I want to go to Jhansee. The Maharani needs me there.'

Keshav took her hand in his. 'Jhansee is in bad shape, Chandraki. After the Jokhan Bagh massacre, the city has been taken over by the rebels who have forced your Rani to help them with ammunition and money. She has not just given them what they need but also her diamond necklace.'

Chandraki couldn't believe her ears. 'That's not possible. The Maharani will never help the rebels for such a cause.'

'But she has. They threatened her that they would blow up her palace. It is not safe for you to go there. Jhansee has been cleared of all the Britishers, and all officers stationed there have been killed along with their families. Not one has been spared. The rebels attacked the queen's palace, captured her and put her relative Sadashiv Rao on the throne.'

Chandraki herself felt like a captured bird inside a cage. Neither could she continue to live inside it nor could she get out.

~

The chapatti came to her inside her flower basket that Taravati brought in for the evening puja. Chandraki was making the usual garland of the jasmine flowers when she noticed the rolled piece of bread tucked under the flowers. She quickly took it out and stuffed it into her bosom.

'Jiji, where did you pick up the flowers from?' she asked.

'From our usual place by the river,' the old lady replied as she strung the flowers into a beautiful garland. She looked up at Chandraki and smiled. 'You are the daughter that I always wanted. Go home.'

Chandraki clasped the old woman's hands. 'Thank you!' With tears in her eyes, she hastened to her room and after shutting both the door and the window, unrolled the chapatti. As expected, there was a note inside. It read:

'Maharani Lakshmibai ki jai! She now rules over Jhansee.'

She looked for the sender's name, but there was none.

Chandraki was so overjoyed on reading this that she almost shouted 'Maharani Lakshmibai ki jai', but quickly controlled her emotions.

'Maharani Lakshmibai is back on the throne, Keshav!' she told him when they met next on his return.

'Yes, I know! But for all practical purposes, it is Erskine who, on orders from Fort William, has asked her to manage the kingdom until the Company Sarkar decides on its next move. The British haven't left. They are very much around and they will be back.' Then suddenly he looked at her.

'How do you know that Maharani Lakshmibai is back on the throne?' he asked.

Chandraki thought it was time she took Keshav into confidence. She was tired of playing hide-and-seek with him. She told him about the chapattis, and how she had been asked to join the forces in Jhansee a few days before the mutiny broke out in Meerut.

'And what did you do?'

'Nothing. I wanted to go, but you know I couldn't have managed without Bijli. Moreover, you were travelling a lot that time, so I couldn't tell you anything.'

Keshav nodded. 'Yes, I know. I've hardly been around. But I'm glad you didn't make it. It would have been terribly dangerous for you to go to Jhansee at the time. And who knows, maybe you would have never returned. I could have lost you,' he said, his eyes moist.

Chandraki was surprised. It had been a while since she had seen Keshav like this. It was reassuring to know that he still cared for her.

'Now that Maharani Lakshmibai is back on the throne and both the British and the mutineers have left Jhansee, could we perhaps go back there? I don't think Rani Larai would have a problem with it. I'm sure the hostilities have somewhat waned with the exit of the firanghees in the neighbouring regions. Could we take her permission and go seek Maharani Lakshmibai's blessings?' Chandraki asked.

Keshav pondered over this for a while. 'Yes, I think so. Since the region is somewhat peaceful now that the mutineers have left, we could perhaps make a visit to Jhansee with the Rani's permission. Let me think about it, Chandraki.' He smiled as he took her in his arms.

They were sitting in front of the chhatris, on the riverbank. The forests of Tikamgarh spread out in front of them across the gently flowing Betwa that sparkled in the sunshine as though sprayed with gold dust.

Finally! Chandraki felt a surge of joy welling up within her, but more than that she felt relief. The past couple of years of uncertainty, ever since she stepped into Orchha, had been agonizing. And, to go back to Jhansee, her mission unaccomplished, was not something that she wanted. She loved Keshav and wanted to take her home with him. And now that she was almost sure that Rani Larai, though she nursed her grudges, did not plan to spring an assault on Jhansee, she felt that there was no reason for her to stay in Orchha any more. That night she wrote a hurried letter to Rani Lakshmibai that she planned to send through Haridas who she hadn't met for some time due to all the mayhem of the last few days.

She reached Jhumroo's house in the early hours of the evening the next day. If Hari was not there, she would hand it over to Jhumroo as she had no idea when she would be able to get out of the palace next. But, on reaching Jhumroo's house, she found it locked. Surprised, she went around it, but there seemed to be no one. She went to the neighbouring house and knocked. She knew the old lady who lived there.

'Mousi, where is Jhumroo?'

'Ah Chandraki. You come after a long time. Don't you know about them?'

Chandraki had no idea what the woman was talking about. 'What happened?'

'Jhumroo's husband Haridas died a few weeks ago. Murdered. He was found lying on the road to Jhansee. Jhumroo has gone away from here. She is scared to live here alone now,' the old lady said.

Chandraki was shocked. Hari Bhau had been murdered?

51

Chandraki was heartbroken. She thought of Jhumroo, who she would probably never see again. She recalled the lovely times they had spent together. They hadn't done anyone any harm. Then why did God punish them so? Unable to stay inside her room, she went downstairs and out into the garden, trying to shake off her gloomy thoughts.

Meher joined her there. In the wake of the recent series of incidents, it had been a while since the two had cosied up for a chat.

'Chandraki! It's been so long since we've spoken,' Meher said.

Chandraki smiled and the two embraced.

'You look happy. What's the matter? Has Riyaz Khan agreed to marry you finally?' she teased, trying to shake off the feeling of gloom that enveloped her presently.

Meher shook her head. 'No, not yet, but one day he will. And I don't care whether we are married or not as long as he comes to me. Last night, too, he was with me.'

'Oh I see!' Chandraki said stiffly. Why did she feel

uneasy thinking about Riyaz and Meher being together? It had never bothered her earlier. 'I admire your passion for him, and I honestly wish for your sake that he feels the same for you. So, how was it?'

'What?'

'His lovemaking. Brute force or the gentle lover?' Meher had often provided Chandraki with graphic details of Riyaz's lovemaking. She would sometimes describe him as ruthless in bed, mauling her like a wild animal, and at other times, he would caress her and gently make love to her like a passionate lover. For Meher, it made no difference, as long as he would spend his night with her.

'He was restless, and unlike other days, didn't come straight to bed. When I asked him what the matter was, he evaded the issue,' Meher replied to Chandraki's question. 'Something was bothering him. He's not a man to waste any time. Rarely have I seen him so agitated,' she said thoughtfully.

Chandraki thought of the time when both had stood pressed against each other on the staircase, their bodies fitting perfectly into the contours of each other. A warm sensation engulfed her as she remembered his hardness against her soft belly. She gulped. Chandraki tried to push away the disturbing thoughts.

'Perhaps he's been anointed the new General of Rani Larai's army.' She laughed, trying to lighten the atmosphere, but more to distract herself from thoughts of Riyaz Khan.

'When I prodded, he told me what was bothering him. Orchha plans to attack Jhansee, Chandraki,' Meher mentioned casually, ignoring Chandraki's statement. 'And he will lead the attack.'

The numerous trees had shed their flowers, and the garden lay strewn with frangipani and jasmine. Their sweet fragrance filled the evening air. There was a slight breeze blowing. The region had witnessed its first few showers in the past week, heralding the onset of the monsoons. The bare ochre hills of Bundelkhand had turned green almost overnight. It was the perfect setting for a girl who was about to be united with her lover.

But for Chandraki, everything came crashing down. She dropped the frangipani flower that she was twirling in her hand and stood rooted to the ground, as if she had turned to stone. Had she heard right?

'Wh—what did you say?' she stammered as she asked Meher who was loading her wicker basket with flowers.

'Orchha is planning to invade Jhansee, and Riyaz Khan will lead the attack.'

'Are you sure you heard right?' Chandraki asked again, hoping that this stupid girl had misinterpreted Riyaz's words. 'What did Riyaz say exactly?' she asked.

Meher turned to look at her. Speaking each word deliberately, she said, 'Riyaz said now that the British were no longer in Jhansee, it would be a good idea to claim the kingdom back.' She turned towards Chandraki. 'You know what happened at Jokhan Bagh. The firanghees think that Lakshmibai instigated the mutineers and even paid them. The Rani there is in a vulnerable situation as she is trying to cover up for the excesses that the mutineers have heaped on the firanghees and is too busy explaining to the sahibs that she had no role to play in the attack. It has made her case rather weak. Riyaz feels that this is the right time to attack Jhansee as the queen is defenceless from all sides. The British are furious with her, and the mutineers are at her door demanding all sorts of things. At this time, she would neither expect an attack from Orchha, nor be prepared for it. She doesn't stand a chance against Orchha's army.'

Chandraki prodded further. 'What else did he say?'

'He said that since Vindhya Pradesh was caught in the throes of violence, she would get no help from any Raja. He also said something about revenge, that it was just a matter of days before he would get his revenge.'

'What revenge?'

Meher shrugged. 'When I asked, he didn't answer. But he said Nathay Khan has promised to make him the commander of the army for the attack on Jhansee. And then he would like to see Lakshmibai's face, that is, if she is alive till then. The Rani and the people of Orchha hated the British too. He thanked the mutineers for paving the way for Orchha to attack Jhansee by killing those firanghees who had captured what was rightfully its territory.'

There was no hint of doubt in what Meher had just said.

'Did he say when they are planning to do it?' Chandraki asked cautiously.

'It would be soon.'

Chandraki's mind was racing. Suddenly, she turned and walked out of the garden.

'Chandraki!' Meher called out after her. 'What happened?'

Chandraki hurried towards the palace. She had to find

Keshav. Right now. She went to his room, but he wasn't there. Perhaps he was in the shahi dak ghar. On her way there, she spotted Keshav coming out of the armoury, in deep conversation with Nathay Khan. Without a thought, Chandraki yelled, 'Keshav!'

Startled, Keshav turned around to find Chandraki running towards him. Immediately he turned to look at Nathay Khan who stood beside him, his legs apart, his hands behind his back, his eyes narrowed as he watched Chandraki approach them. Keshav fumbled briefly but steadying himself, walked up to her.

'What do you want, Chandraki?' His annoyance at this sudden intrusion was clearly visible.

'I need to talk to you. Right now,' she said as she caught her breath.

'Not now! I'm busy.'

'No business of yours can be more important than what I have to tell you,' she said angrily.

Keshav knew her well by now. There was no evading her.

'Tell me,' he said with an air of resignation. She looked over his shoulder to see Nathay Khan standing a little distance away, watching them.

'Not here,' she said, lowering her voice as she pulled him away behind some bushes, and out of Nathay Khan's line of vision. 'Orchha plans to attack Jhansee. I don't know when, but it's going to be soon. I have to warn Maharani Lakshmibai.' The words tumbled out of her mouth before she could stop herself.

Keshav stared at Chandraki. There was a look of disbelief clearly written on his face.

'What? Who told you?' he asked, shocked.

'How does that matter? I need to inform Maharani Lakshmibai. Please take me to Jhansee as soon as possible.'

'Not a word of this to anyone, you understand?' he said as he took her hands in his own. 'Let me find out if this is true, and then we'll work out the details, okay?'

'There is nothing to work out. I have to escape from here at the earliest.'

'I know that, but there is chaos everywhere. The mutineers are still all over the place, and even though the British in Jhansee have been killed or have fled, they are many still lurking in the region. Besides, I have to be careful, too. Nathay Khan is very clever. We can't do anything in haste. Just leave it to me, and I'll do something.'

Chandraki heard him out quietly and then covered his hands with her own.

'Whatever you do, be quick. The attack may occur any time. You know the Rani is helpless at the moment. She has to gather her forces, whatever is left of them, and seek help from wherever possible. I want to be there beside her at the earliest. Just get me out of here, that's all I'm asking,' she pleaded. Keshav nodded and reassured her that he would try and do something.

Chandraki returned to the palace, crestfallen. Would Keshav be able to organize anything in such limited time, and without raising any suspicion? He would need to worry about his own safety, too. She didn't like dragging Keshav into all of this. He had no obligation either to Jhansee or to Maharani Lakshmibai, and especially since his own state was a sworn enemy of Jhansee, there was no reason why he should help her. It could jeopardize his own security. But she was just asking him to help her flee Orchha. After all, she was not a prisoner here.

Chandraki brushed aside her feelings of guilt and proceeded to prepare for her journey. At last! But before that, she needed to do one more thing.

52

Rani Larai declared that since things around them had quietened down, the festival of Janmashtami would be celebrated with the usual pomp. The kingdom greeted this news with much joy, and at once set about prepapring for it, though there were reservations from some of her ministers.

'In light of the recent events in Vindhya Pradesh, with most of our neighbours having suffered huge losses, do you think it would be proper and, more importantly, safe to celebrate Janmashtami?'

'Why not?' asked Rani Larai. 'If Lakshmibai can celebrate all festivals despite what happened to Jhansee, why can't we? She's thwarted the attempts of Sadashiv Rao to usurp the throne, and with the exit of the British from the cantonment, as well as the fort, she has reclaimed the throne and reinstated herself on it,' Rani Larai argued.

'It may be a stopgap measure. Everyone knows her current position is precarious,' one of them said.

'Yes, but the Rani has conducted the haldi kumkum rasam for Goddess Mahalakshmi in the family temple within the palace and prepared for the festival of Teej, in sheer defiance of what others perceive her situation to be. If she's trying to prove a point, then why can't we?' She turned towards Nathay Khan and whispered, 'Send that man Sheikh Hingan back to Jhansee before Janmashtami. It will look as though we want peace with Jhansee. They will never expect an attack from us.'

~

Janmashtami was three days away. It would be a grand cultural evening, and Chandraki was to participate in it. Hers was to be the first dance followed by the raas leela which would be performed by Meher and her troupe. There were some quick rehearsals. Since there was not much time left, the rehearsals would go on until late in the evening. During one such rehearsal Chandraki quietly slipped away under the cover of darkness and cautiously made her way towards the Ounth Khana. It was a double-storeyed structure with the lower portion under the ground. This housed the royal camels, and in order to reach it Chandraki, evading the numerous guards, slithered down the path that hugged the elephant shelter and wound its way below to where the camels were kept. The elephants that were kept chained outside swayed lazily, flapping their huge ears and stomping their feet. The area gave her a lot of cover because of the thick vegetation around and she found no difficulty in giving the guards the slip to enter the camel stables. 'I hope I can find what I'm looking for,' she thought.

53

Nathay Khan had convinced the Rani of Orchha that they would attack Jhansee a few days after the festival of Janmashtami. The army was already prepared and on the move. It would look as though all was normal, and no one would suspect that under the cover of Janmashtami celebrations, a military offensive was being planned. It was perfect timing as far as Nathay Khan was concerned.

The mutineers had given Orchha the opportunity to get back what had been taken from them, and what had rightfully belonged to Orchha. In another seventy-two hours, Jhansee would be theirs. Riyaz Khan was chosen to lead the attack. Nathay Khan knew he was the best choice for this operation.

Although Riyaz Khan's loyalty to Nathay Khan was unquestionable, Nathay Khan knew that Riyaz had a personal stake to settle with the Rani of Jhansee. He knew that Riyaz's allegiance to him was not out of any sense of overwhelming loyalty, but simply because if there was anyone who could help him avenge his humiliation

at the hands of Lakshmibai, it was Nathay Khan. Riyaz
had never forgotten the disgrace he had undergone. He
vowed vengeance, and now was his chance to avenge his
insult. He had offered Nathay Khan his services for this
very special mission and had personally trained the soldiers.
He knew Lakshmibai's weaknesses as well as strengths
and had meticulously drawn up the plan to lay siege to
the fort which he knew like the back of his hand. Jhansee
would fall. There was no doubt about that. Lakshmibai was
doomed as was her Jhansee. That would be his moment
of redemption. And he would do anything, just anything
to ensure that. And for Nathay Khan, there could be no
better motive for his officer to lead an attack.

~

Chandraki and Keshav carefully worked out the plan to
get out of Orchha. Keshav told her that it was true that
Orchha planned to capture Jhansee in a few days. So it
was decided that on Janmashtami, Chandraki would get
out of the palace once her performance was over. Keshav
would ensure that the guards would look away, and as for
the others, they would be busy watching Meher's dance.
Once out of the palace, Chandraki would take to the path
that ran along the fort's outer boundary walls, hugging the
river, to avoid confrontation with anyone. She would go
around the houses of the officers and make her way to the
armoury where Keshav would be waiting with Bijli. They
had decided upon riding one horse to avoid curious eyes.

From there, the two would skirt the Jahangir Mahal and exit the fort from behind. The Jahangir Mahal was not so heavily guarded. Keshav knew the way that passed through the elephant stable. It joined the main path from the gate up to the palace gate. They would cross the hamam and ride across the slightly wooded area that led to the back gate which would then meet the outer wall of the kingdom. He knew of a spot where the kingdom's boundary wall was slightly broken, and they could easily jump over it. In fact, it was to be repaired right after the monsoons. But before that, they would use it to get out of the kingdom of Orchha.

Once over the wall, they would go across the rough terrain of the region, to the main road that would take them to Jhansee. After four miles down the road, at the fork where the road turned towards Jhansee, Keshav would leave her and return to Orchha. Chandraki was confident of covering the distance from there to Lakshmibai's palace alone. She had come the same way with Bijli.

The Tale of the Stone

(August 1857)

54

Chandraki looked out from the latticed windows. The sun finally dipped over the horizon. In the grey twilight, she saw the countryside drenched in the rain that had hit Orchha an hour ago. The room plunged into darkness. She knew the dasis were on their way to light the lamps. As she turned away from the window, lightning flashed, bathing the land in its silvery light. How could any place be so beautiful? She felt a tug at her heart. 'Don't go,' she told herself. But she knew she had to. It was her offering. What she didn't know was that it was her destiny. She hadn't made the choice. It was already made for her.

She tore herself away from the window. The palace was now lighting up and even through the downpour she saw the river throw back the iridescent reflection of the palace lights. The sound of the rain drowned out all other sounds. She could only hear the river now.

The scene inside the palace was quite different though. It was abuzz with activity. People had started gathering. In a while, the dancers would come whirling in. It was no ordinary day. It was the eighth day in the month of Shravan, and the eighth avatar of Lord Vishnu was to appear on the earth at midnight.

The kingdom of Orchha wore a festive look. Normally, devotees spent weeks adorning the town with strings of festoons criss-crossed across the streets, lined with stalls selling wares, clothes, bangles and utensils. Special delicacies were prepared in every home for the occasion. Women and children stayed up late nights to shop for clothes and toys. But this time, it was different, and the preparations had been hurried, as the queen had suddenly announced the celebrations. A lot many things had changed in the last few months.

Midnight was hours away, and the palace was swarming with people. It had been a while since people had been in such a jolly mood. The events of the past few months had plunged the city in gloom, and there was much apprehension among its people. The queen wanted to change that and give them an occasion to forget their worries and overcome their fear. The bad times were over, and Orchha was secure. It was time to indulge in some celebrations.

The Raja Mahal was bedecked with flowers and garlands. The musicians had started arriving. Laughter and giggles echoed through the corridors of the palace. People were running, jostling and pushing each other as they made their way up and down the narrow staircases. Everyone seemed busy. And, to add to that was the rain that poured incessantly creating even more confusion.

The programme would go on till midnight, the hour of Krishna's birth when devotees would storm the Ram Raja mandir to witness the special puja. As Chandraki dressed for the dance, she heard the rumble of thunder. The rain would surely increase, and she prayed fervently that it would give her enough cover as she made her way through the garden towards the exit. And before anyone would realize, she would have escaped through the gate.

Someone came to call for her, and she turned to take one last look at herself in the mirror. She had chosen her mother's turquoise chanderi sari for the dance and hoped that the colour would merge with the blackness of the night as she rode with Keshav later. Also, the choice of the sari was symbolic, a vestige of happier times. She wore it in the khashta style to make it easier for her to ride a horse. Chandraki folded her hands before the little stone idol of Durga, the embodiment of Shakti, before her descent down the steps to the mehfil room. Drawing her veil over her face, she climbed down the narrow staircase that led to the inner courtyard below. Her dance would begin soon, but she thought of the long journey that lay ahead. She was going to ride Bijli, who was as swift as the wind and would respond to her commands spontaneously.

The dances were usually held in the central courtyard, the mandapa, with the singers and musicians lined up in the surrounding corridors. The Rani watched from the covered terrace on the first floor that overlooked the central platform below. But the rain had forced everyone indoors.

There was a covered hall on the way to the entrance of the main palace. The dancers would perform there today, and in an innovative bid, they would go around the corridors. It would now be easier to get out.

~

Chandraki was usually the lead dancer, and this time too, she would be the first to perform. Today's mehfil was dedicated to Krishna, heralding the occasion of Krishna Janmashtami. The prelude to the raas leela would be the depiction of Mirabai's bhakti towards Krishna, performed by Chandraki in the tradition of bhakti ras. Mirabai – the Rajput princess, who having shunned her lawful husband Raja Bhojraj of Chittor, had offered herself to Krishna, her divine love. Chandraki loved dancing to Mirabai's compositions. Her body yielded to Mirabai's passion, and her face easily revealed the latter's ecstacy and pain as she yearned for her Lord.

'Main to giridhar aage nachung' filled the air as Chandraki danced as though possessed. She flung her arms up with the ektara in one hand, her long dark hair covering parts of her face. She knew that time was running out. The palace was filled to its full capacity, and her audience including the queen, watched her mesmerised. Her heart was beating fast. She knew that after this was the last dance she had to perform, and then Meher and her companions would take her place to perform the raas leela. Slowly, very slowly, as she danced, she made her way down the corridor. The audience, too, joined in the adoration of her Lord. As the dance picked up tempo and the octave peaked, Chandraki glided towards a flight of stairs that she knew led out of the palace and was gone. No one noticed her exit for Meher, along with the rest of the dancers, had replaced her on stage to the strains of Jayadeva's Priya Charusheele.

Chandraki ran down the dimly lit staircase. It was the same one where Riyaz Khan and she had stood together once, not very long ago. The music from the mehfil followed her all the way down the stairs. Just before she began to descend, she looked in the direction of Riyaz Khan fleetingly, who was posted at the main gate to the palace. Facing away from her, he was talking to someone. She could visualize the rough, battle-scarred face. He could have been attractive, Chandraki thought, if he had had less venom and a little more kindness in him. He was once a good man. Thankfully, she was going away, and hopefully their paths would now never cross. Yet, she felt a peculiar emptiness in her heart when she realized it. He had become a part of her life , and the thought of not seeing that face again troubled her.

The stairs, rarely used, led to a narrow opening into a courtyard that eventually led to the Jahangir Mahal. As she emerged out into the open, she looked around. There was no one there as everyone was away to enjoy the festivities. She followed the route as planned. She would soon meet Keshav, but would they reach Jhansee by the break of dawn? Some rebels were still around to loot, plunder and seize whatever they could lay their hands on. Besides, on Nathay Khan's insistence, Rani Larai had placed her

soldiers on the road that led to Jhansee to thwart any sort
of assault on Orchha.

Chandraki scrambled through the small stretch of
woods, making her way through the clumps of bushes
and bramble, and after a distance of some 300 metres,
she finally emerged out in the open, bruised and cut, and
took to a path that ran along the outer wall of the palace.

She heard the sound of the river rush past on the other
side of the fort wall. Not wanting to alert anyone loitering
around, she stopped briefly to take off her anklets and her
bangles. Her footfalls were light, and made no sound on
the uneven path, but she winced as some jagged piece
of stone pierced her foot. She was already drenched, her
sari clinging to her slight frame. She kept going until she
reached the daroga's house at the far end of the palace
premises, stopping just once to catch her breath. From here,
she would have to turn around back towards the palace
to continue on her way. It was a long detour to reach the
outer wall of the fort. But, it was safer, and the chances of
encountering anyone on this path were less.

Yet she hesitated. Something told her not to proceed
on the path that Keshav and she had carefully mapped.
She knew Keshav was waiting for her ahead with Bijli,
behind the khajanchi's house near the armoury. She
looked to her left. If she continued straight ahead without
turning, she would reach the river, which at this point
would have overflowed, their raging waters carrying away
everything that came in their way. She would be tossed
against the rocks strewn all across the river. She knew the
Betwa's current was swift, and she would be swept away

immediately, and there would be no trace of her. She had thought of doing so earlier to evade the palace guards. But Keshav was right. It was risky. Moreover, it would take her further away from her destination.

So she turned around as planned. She made her way cautiously through the barracks towards the quarters of the royal staff. It was completely dark with most of the lanterns snuffed out in the rain. The lights from the palace dimly illuminated her way, throwing long shadows. She turned towards the khajanchi's house and headed towards the armoury. The houses were all empty today with the noblemen at the palace. The rest were at the Ram Raja temple absorbed in the celebrations. Lamps flickered in a few houses, but the neighbourhood was almost entirely desolate except for a few stray dogs. It was just a matter of a few minutes before she caught up with Keshav.

Soon she saw in the faint glow of the lights from the palace, the silhouette of the armoury loom up a little ahead. As she approached it, her hand went down to her waist to feel the dagger she had picked up from the armoury a few months ago, and which she had secured tightly with a waistband around her sari. Just in case she needed it. Chandraki continued along the side of the path, parting the clumps of the acacia bushes that surrounded the armoury. She coughed once, twice, giving the signal that was to alert Keshav. Almost immediately, the night air was pierced with the jangle of the temple bells heralding the birth of Lord Krishna. Chandraki jumped. She had almost forgotten that celebrations were still on and had lost track of time. But before she could regain her composure someone clamped her mouth from behind, lifted her and threw her on a horse.

Stunned by the sudden onslaught, Chandraki at first didn't react. Her mouth had been strapped with a piece of cloth. She was placed in front of the rider as he galloped away into the darkness of the night, away from the town lights. She struggled to look into the face of her abductor. But it was completely covered except for his eyes, which were focused ahead. The rider held on to Chandraki tightly with one hand and with the other, held the reins of the horse. Where was he taking her? They tore past the palace walls. The sound of bells clanging rented the air as the midnight puja commenced in the temple outside the fort. She could hear the music flow out of the palace. The mehfil inside was in full swing. The town was caught up in the frenzied fervour of the celebrations, having reached its crescendo with the arrival of the midnight hour.

Suddenly, as though from nowhere, a group of men on horseback accosted them. They had crossed the palace that now lay behind them. The rider jumped off the horse and dragged Chandraki down with him. The moment she was off the horse, Chandraki sprinted, pushing her way through the group of men.

'Catch her!' one of them screamed.

She turned around just in time to see the men in hot pursuit of her. There were five of them. She was thinking fast. She knew she could not outrun them. Moreover, they were armed and had horses. The Ram Raja temple lay before her to the left, a short distance from the palace gates. But how would she get past the sentries posted at the gateway?

Chandraki knew she had to take her chance and simply run past the guards. If she could get to the temple, she would be safe. Without further ado, Chandraki raced down the cobbled path that led from the armoury to the main gate and dashed past the guards before they even realized that she had passed. Once outside, she joined the hordes of people who were on their way to the temple and was lost to her pursuers.

The streets were crowded. She was right in the centre of the brightly lit town. She pushed her way through the jostling crowd of devotees and slid between the women who were queued up for the darshan of the Lord. She saw two of her pursuers make their way into the temple premises on foot. Chandraki drew out the dagger from her waistband and holding it naked in her hand, close to her, slithered her way through the rows of devotees, out into the streets. She knew the narrow roads and the hidden alleys of the kingdom, she knew all the dark corners and the dangers that lurked there. As she turned around a corner to get on the street that would lead her to Jhumroo's house, she came face to face with one of her pursuers. Without a moment's hesitation, Chandraki plunged her dagger right through his abdomen. The man lunged forward on her. She shoved him aside and started running. After covering a few metres, she stopped to look back and found the man lying in a pool of blood. A shiver coursed through her. She had just killed a man. Unable to move, Chandraki just stood there breathing heavily, her hand trembling as she clutched the blood-smeared weapon.

This part of the town was dimly lit with most of the

mashaals snuffed out. Wiping the sweat and blood off her face she tried to take stock of the situation. Who were the people who were chasing her? They were not the guards from the palace obviously. But before she could think further, she heard a faint murmur which gradually became louder as it came closer and closer, and it was no longer a murmur, but a rumble, and then as the sound got even closer, screams pierced the air, and it seemed as though the firmament was set on fire, and the rumble turned into a roar. As though from nowhere, swarms of people descended on the town. She suddenly realized who they were.

'The rebels!' she exclaimed.

Chandraki stood still as she heard screams pierce the night air. She could hear the bells from the temple clang behind her. The shouts were getting closer, and she stood huddled against the fence of Jhumroo's deserted house, unable to move. She felt the ground shudder under her and the road blown up in a cloud of dust. And tearing through the haze was a horseman who broke away from the rest and came towards her. She held out the dagger and bracing herself for certain death, she looked straight into the rider's eyes as he reached for her.

'Chandraki, it's me,' the man said as he pulled up beside her.

'Keshav!' Chandraki cried out, her voice hoarse with terror, and all the dust sprayed around her. She removed the scarf that covered the man's face. Reassured, she heaved a sigh of relief and shoved the dagger back under her cummerbund.

'Thank God it's you. I thought the mutineers had got

me. But why were you not at the place where we had arranged to meet?' she asked him as she looked over his shoulder. There were large groups of people on horseback on the streets, some going from house to house, and several advancing towards the temple.

'Hush. Keep quiet. There are enemies all around. We have no time to lose. Get on to Bijli,' Keshav whispered as he brought the mare forward.

She nodded and mounted Bijli. Just as they were about to set off, she pulled the reins.

'Now what?' Keshav asked impatiently.

'Who are these people?'

'Oh, just some bandits who are out to loot and plunder whatever they can get their hands on. But the city is heavily guarded. They can't do much damage.'

'Are they not the sepoys?'

'Oh no, no. The sepoys departed for Dilli weeks ago.'

'But how do we avoid them? They are all over and are closing in on us.'

'Don't worry. I know some of them. They'll let us pass,' Keshav said as he urged Bijli to move on.

Chandraki hesitated, but just for a moment. 'Okay, let's go. Whatever it takes!'

And they rode away into the dust, and into the darkness, away from the lights of the kingdom of Orchha.

~

The mobs had broken up in groups and scattered themselves across the town. Some headed for the Ram

Raja temple where the Janmashtami celebrations were in full swing. Another lot proceeded towards the Kanchana ghat. Small groups of men hung around deserted streets waiting to pounce on whoever passed by. A huge band of about twenty riders dashed across the old stone bridge to take the road towards Tikamgarh.

'They are all over, Keshav! How will we escape from them?' Chandraki asked, her heart thumping hard each time she heard the terrifying sounds of death. Keshav did not reply and kept to narrow, very dark lanes, dodging the riders through the shadows. They had gone for about a mile and were finally on the road that would take them to Jhansee, and it seemed that they had finally shaken off the raiders when a group of men on horseback emerged from the woodlands on either side and blocked their way. Bijli stiffened and came to a halt. Chandraki's heart sank.

'Where are you going?' one of them asked as the rest circled them.

'We had been to the Ram mandir,' Chandraki said.

The men looked them over. In the dark, Chandraki could not make out who they were or what clothes they were wearing. One of them came closer and leered at her. She pulled her veil over her face.

Suddenly, there was a flash of lightning that lit up the dark night. And, in that instant, Chandraki noticed that the men were neither mutineers nor plunderers. These were familiar faces – Rani Larai's soldiers. She froze. Riyaz Khan sat on his horse as it encircled Bijli, his sword out and glistening in the rain, his rifle slung over his shoulder.

Immobile, Chandraki stared at the men through the

rain. She knew that there was no way they could pass through this group. She clutched Keshav tightly and whispered, 'It's Nathay Khan's men. They've caught us. What do we do now?'

Keshav did not reply. There was complete silence for a few minutes. Only the sound of the rain echoed all around the hills and forests of Orchha. Suddenly, Chandraki heard the dreadful words crack like a whip through the stormy night.

'As decided, I've brought her to you to hand over to Nathay Khan,' Keshav's voice rang out as he got off the horse and stood facing Riyaz Khan.

'Well done, Keshav,' shouted one of the men as Chandraki reeled under the shock of what Keshav had just said. She turned to look at him in total disbelief. He looked back at her with a smirk on his face as he stood beside Bijli, holding the reins.

'We had nearly got her in the palace itself, but she managed to escape,' Keshav said. So that was him who had accosted her in front of the armoury, seized her and bound her. He was there all right, not to help her but to capture her. Tears welled up in Chandraki's eyes.

'Take her to Nathay Khan. He will teach her a lesson,' one of the soldiers shouted over the sound of the rain.

'And we know how well Nathay Khan teaches his lessons,' another man yelled. Everyone laughed.

Chandraki sat on Bijli, motionless. Keshav's words sliced through her heart. What did he say to Riyaz Khan? 'I've brought her to you to hand over to Nathay Khan!' She turned around slowly and singled him out among the horsemen. He was laughing, and the men patted each other.

A lone figure stood a little distance away. It was Riyaz Khan. She blinked through the rain, and then suddenly broke down.

'How could you do this to me, Keshav?'

Three more men were riding towards the group that stood circling Chandraki. One of them broke away and came forward. It was Nathay Khan. He rode up to Chandraki, who was too stunned to move. Grabbing her hand, he turned to Keshav and said to him, 'This woman was too smart for you, Keshav. I knew it the moment I met her. How many women do you think come looking for a truant lover in an enemy state? I said so on the first day when you told me she was the one in Jhansee giving you all the news.'

'But I outwitted her, didn't I, Huzoor?'

'That was all because of me,' replied Nathay Khan, pointing to himself. 'You were nearly caught, you fool, the day she saw you behind the bushes in the woods talking to me. I had already spotted her. It was then that I thought of our plan. And I asked you to continue playing the loving husband, and asked you to pretend that you were a shahi dakiya, not the hurkurus that you actually are. If I hadn't done that, we would surely have lost her. And if she would have escaped, there is no knowing what she would have done. It took me some time to convince Her Highness to clamp that condition of ten days on this woman.'

'Oh yes, Huzoor. I was so shocked to see her in Orchha. Back in Jhansee, I had even faked getting married to her to try and get access into the palace. It drained me at times to keep up the pretence of being in love with her, to look into her eyes, and behave like a desperate lover,' he spat.

'And now what should we do with her, Keshav? After all, she's your wife!' Nathay Khan laughed wickedly.

'My woman is your woman, Huzoor. She's all yours.'

When Chandraki took him into confidence and after promising to help her reach Jhansee, Keshav had informed Nathay Khan of Chandraki's intentions. It was then that they made a plan to capture her.

Riyaz Khan was to lead the attack on Jhansee. He was to join the troops, just short of their entry into Jhansee. But he had now been ordered by Nathay Khan to first bring Chandraki back.

'That wench was a spy, after all. I never did quite trust her,' said Nathay Khan, seething in anger.

Riyaz Khan, who stood a little away from the rest, said quietly, 'I don't think so. I don't think she came here with that intention,' he said, defending Chandraki.

'Oh no, Riyaz, she's as cunning as a fox, trust me. Wasn't she sending letters through that merchant Haridas? When my man reported that he had seen her visit him several times, my suspicions were aroused. Caught that mole on his way to Gwalior and slit his throat. Left the body for the wolves.'

Riyaz Khan looked at Nathay Khan in disbelief. '*You* got Haridas murdered?'

Nathay Khan nodded. 'Nothing escapes me, Riyaz miyan. This woman thought she could outsmart me.

Sending those letters to her queen, giving her news about us. But I have to admit her body makes me slurp. Just couldn't get my hands on her out of fear of Her Highness. If only I could.'

Riyaz Khan drew in his breath sharply. His hands reached for his sword. Checking himself in time, he quickly changed the topic.

'Anyway, what do you want me to do?'

'Take her back to the palace. The rest you leave to me. I'll have some fun with her, and then toss her over to my men, who, too, can have their bit of fun once they return. They deserve their desserts after all that fighting.' He grinned. 'And then, I'll kill her,' he said as he turned around his horse to return to Orchha. 'After that, get going to Jhansee, Riyaz, we don't have much time.'

Lightning flashed across the Tartarean night as Chandraki listened on, her tears flowing freely, mingling with the rain that washed her face. The men laughed loudly, jeering at her. One of them came up to her and pulled her arm. Another reached for her waist. Chandraki punched him hard on his face.

Suddenly, Keshav caught her arm. 'Stop fighting, Chandraki! It's no use. You don't stand a chance against us,' he said. Then bringing his face close to hers, he said with the utmost contempt, 'Finally, I have gotten rid of your painful presence.'

Chandraki looked at him through the rain. Then, slowly she reached out for her waistband and with a jerk, pulled out the dagger and shoved it deep into Keshav's stomach while with her other hand she tore off her mother's amulet from his arm.

'That's for betraying me, Keshav! I loved you! I trusted you!' she said, crying as the reins fell from his hands, and he slowly slumped on to the ground. Bijli started and let out a neigh of terror before she suddenly sprinted. Chandraki snapped up the reins and kicking Bijli, dashed right through the circle of men and made for the road, splashing water and mud into their faces.

'Nathay Khan!' she yelled as she charged ahead. 'Sheikh Hingan has already carried my message to Maharani Lakshmibai warning her of your attack on Jhansee. She's well prepared. Do what you can.'

At first, Nathay Khan did not comprehend Chandraki's words and when he did, he staggered under their impact. Taken aback by her sudden flight, the rest of the men stood motionless for what may have been almost a minute, looking at each other, too shocked to even realize that she had just given them the slip. They had been out on the battlefield for the past fortnight and had already captured Burwa Sagar, Mau, Pandwaha and Garautha on their way to Jhansee. They were to break camp for a few days before launching the attack on Jhansee. But Chandraki's decision to flee to Jhansee to inform Queen Lakshmibai upset their plans, and now they had been ordered to launch the attack without any delay. They were too exhausted to think with a clear mind and stood rooted to the ground.

Suddenly, Nathay Khan's voice boomed through the sound of the angry rain as it lashed across the countryside.

'Catch her, you fools! Don't let her get away. Once I get my hands on her, I will lynch her!'

'Chalo Bijli.' Chandraki spurred the mare and pulled at the reins, urging her to go faster. She turned around once and looked over her shoulder to find the horsemen mounting their horses. Within minutes, they were hot on her heels, and were covering the short distance between them at great speed. Suddenly a bullet whizzed past. Chandraki shrieked as the next bullet came right after. She ducked, but it caught Bijli in her neck. The mare buckled, and before she realized it, Chandraki was thrown off her back and lay on the ground.

'Bijli!' she cried, but she already knew that Maharani Lakshmibai's favourite horse was dead. Sobbing, she caressed the mare. She could hear her pursuers closing in, their horses tearing down the dark, slushy road. There was not much distance between the riders and her, and she knew it wouldn't take them long to close the gap. Hugging Bijli one last time, Chandraki got up and started running. Her sari, wet with the rain, clung to her body, making it even more difficult for her to run. The thought of Keshav and his betrayal brought forth a fresh torrent of tears down her cheeks. She had played right into his hands and Nathay Khan's. She did not plan her escape. He made it for her so that she could be captured easily by Nathay Khan's men.

But she had no time to think about it now. She was unarmed and without a horse. She looked over her shoulder and could see the blurred images of the men a few metres away.

'Chandraki!' Riyaz Khan called out after her. 'Stop! Don't run,' he yelled over the sound of the pounding rain.

For Riyaz Khan, it was easy to catch up with Chandraki.

She was already tired and bruised. But it wasn't the events of the night that had worn her out. Keshav's betrayal had broken her.

Riyaz overtook her easily and blocked her way. Chandraki came to a halt and stood facing him, small and forlorn, her sari torn, her choli unlaced, her hair plastered to her scalp. Only her eyes stood out bright and clear, unblinking even though the rain lashed her face.

She offered no resistance as Riyaz Khan got off his horse and picked her up. He placed her in front of him on his horse and within minutes, was riding off with her, back in the direction from where they had come – towards Orchha.

Chandraki was quiet for a while, too exhausted to fight back. But she knew she had to fight if she wanted to get to Jhansee. She struggled against Riyaz's huge frame and tried to jump off the horse.

'Stop struggling, Chandraki. You don't stand a chance against them. I don't want Nathay Khan to get his hands on you. Or, for that matter, anyone else. They'll tear you to pieces,' Riyaz shouted over the sound of the rain.

Chandraki couldn't believe what she was hearing. Riyaz Khan wanted to protect her from Nathay Khan? He had done so in the past. She had begun to trust him. Yet, it may be just a ruse to take her back to Orchha. So much had passed this evening that her brain could no longer comprehend anything. She didn't know who to believe and who not to believe. She closed her eyes. She had to do something. She wouldn't let him take her back to the palace and throw her before that hungry Nathay Khan.

'Why are you helping me?' she asked.

'I don't want any of those dogs to lay their hands on you. I know what they will do,' Riyaz replied as he urged his horse on.

'But how should that matter to you? You hate me. Won't you be happy to see me being mauled?'

'No!' he replied simply.

'Why not? You've hated me from the day you set your eyes on me in Jhansee. But, look at your misfortune. I never did let you go but followed you all the way.'

'It was you who hated me, Chandraki. You always complained against me to the queen. I was angry with you for sneaking on me.'

'You betrayed Jhansee.'

'I betrayed the Maharani. She never lost a chance to humiliate me. I lost everything because of her. I had a personal score to settle with her.'

They were riding into the night. The rain had increased over the last few hours and visibility was poor.

'I know, once you take me to Orchha, you'll throw me in front of Nathay Khan. That'll be your victory.'

'No, I won't. I'm not taking you back to the palace, but to a place where they'll never find you. You'll be safe.'

Chandraki didn't believe him.

'I want to reach Jhansee. I want to be with Maharani Lakshmibai.'

'There's no point. Jhansee will be attacked tomorrow morning. Everything is in place, and things are going as planned. You will not be able to reach Jhansee before that. The sun will rise in a couple of hours. You'll be caught before that anyway.'

'Let me go, Riyaz.'

'No.'

'But why do you want to save me? What is in it for you?'

'Nothing.'

'Then why do you want to save me, Riyaz?' she asked again.

'I don't know. I just know that I want you to be safe. I don't want those men to get their hands on you.'

The rain whipped the countryside. Nothing was visible for miles as they headed towards the fort. But after going through the first gate, Riyaz suddenly took a sharp turn towards the right. He was taking her away from the fort and the palace. This was her chance. She tumbled off the horse.

'Wh–what the hell!' Riyaz Khan cursed. Chandraki got up immediately and started running towards the river, which lay ahead, some distance away.

'Stop! Stop, I say, Chandraki, for heaven's sake, stop!' Riyaz roared. But she ran. She ran like never before. She could now see the river. She was almost there. She stepped on its slushy bank, tripped over a boulder and fell.

'Chandraki, stop, please trust me. I am taking you to a safe place. We are almost there.' But she paid him no heed. She got up once more and continued running.

'Chandraki, the soldiers will lynch you. They are not far behind. They will get here in a few minutes. They'll never find you if you let me take you to that place. Please allow me to help you. Please!' Riyaz Khan pleaded. He knew if she was left on her own, Nathay Khan and his men would get her within minutes. And then, there was no knowing of the extent they would go to in order to punish her. No, he couldn't let that happen. She had to trust him. He remembered the time she had got him banished from Jhansee. He had lost everything because of her. Yet, he wanted to save her. But nothing that he said could stop her. He rode his horse faster, but the soft mud was slowing him down. He pulled the reins, got off the horse and started running.

'Chandraki, stop, for heaven's sake, stop!' But she kept on, slipping and stumbling on the swampy riverbank.

'Chandraki stop! Stop, or I'll shoot you,' he said as he swerved his rifle and pointed it at her.

Chandraki turned briefly to look at him and saw him with his rifle ready to shoot even as he pleaded for her to stop.

'Riyaz, neither you nor your Diwan Nathay Khan will ever get me,' she shouted, her voice carrying above the sound of the furious river rushing past. 'And, don't take a single step forward or I'll drown myself, I promise you,' she threatened. Riyaz knew if he tried to pull her out of the water, she would definitely carry out her threat. Damn this woman!

'You won't be able to make it far. They are right behind us. Wait for me. Trust me, Chandraki, for once!'

'No, never,' Chandraki yelled as she dragged herself along the wet slushy bank of the river. Although Riyaz pleaded for her to stop, she stepped into the waters of the Betwa.

Riyaz Khan looked behind. The riders were almost upon

them. He looked ahead towards Chandraki. She was well into the waters, but he knew she couldn't get very far as the current would prove to be a hindrance. Moreover, there were too many boulders and stones. She could never get away from Nathay Khan's men. He shuddered to think of what they would do to her. They would get her even before the current swept her. Unless she allowed him to protect her, unless . . .

He took two steps forward. 'Stop Chandraki, believe me, I'll take you away from these dogs. Why are you not believing me, Meera?'

But Chandraki continued wading through the water that was now up to her knees. Riyaz looked behind once more. The men were just a few paces away and could cover the distance between them and Chandraki in a few gallops. He knew he couldn't single-handedly fight all of them, and they would easily overtake him and grab her.

He turned back to look where she was and shouted one last time as he took a couple of steps forward.

'Chandraki! One last time, I'm asking you to stop. They are almost here and will tear you up.' Two men got off their horses and plunged into the river, just an arm's length behind Chandraki. In a few strokes, she would be at their mercy.

Riyaz screamed one last time, his voice carrying across to her through the early morning air.

'Chandraki, stop, or I'll shoot.'

All of a sudden, it stopped raining. He could see the rays of the sun streak the firmament a shade of orange, ushering in a new day. Chandraki was still struggling in the water, forcing her way against the fierce current. Riyaz turned to look at the men who were in the water, advancing towards them. The others waited on the bank, and several riders were closing in and were heavily armed. He didn't stand a chance against them alone. They would get to Chandraki before he could. It was too late.

Riyaz Khan closed his eyes and pulled the trigger. There was no mistake. The bullet caught Chandraki squarely on her back. She fell down heavily, splashing the frothy waters of the Betwa around. Riyaz Khan threw his rifle away and started running towards her. She turned around weakly and saw him coming towards her. She forced herself to rise but before he could reach her, she fell back into the tempestuous river, streaking it red with her blood that flowed out copiously from the fatal wound, her mother's chanderi sari trailing behind her like a blue shroud.

'Damn you, Meera!' Riyaz cursed once again as he picked up the amulet that had fallen on the grassy bank. He kissed it and touched it to his eyes, then stuffing it into his belt, tried to locate her but there was no sign of her. It seemed as though the river had simply swallowed her up.

Riyaz Khan stood by the Betwa for one whole minute. Then slowly, he turned and walked back to his horse. Emptiness engulfed his whole being.

Epilogue

(August 2010, Raja Mahal, Orchha)

The setting sun streaked the sky a bright orange. The palace walls flared up in its glow as though set on fire. Meera stood transfixed in the courtyard, looking up at the three-storeyed magnificent structure that surrounded her. As she looked up, the sun disappeared behind the far horizon, and the evening shadows slowly enveloped the fortress. As the day drew to a close, and the hour of darkness set in, it was time for the tourists to leave. She wound up her last story of the Mutiny of 1857 and with that the passing of an era for Jhansee and Orchha. She spoke about Maharani Lakshmibai of Jhansee, of Rani Larai of Orchha, of Nathay Khan's siege of the Jhansee fort, she spoke of the firanghees, of Keshav and Chandraki. And of Riyaz Khan.

Inside the fort, the guard stood where the scented fountain had once flowed and had enveloped the hall in its sweet fragrance. He looked up to the balcony above and saluted. Then softly, he said, 'It's time for you to sleep now. The kings and queens are gone.'

She climbed up the narrow stone staircase that led to the queen's living quarters and stepped out into the open terrace. She looked beyond the ramparts of the fort. Far ahead across the gurgling Betwa, to her left, she could see the silhouette of the chhatris. She stood there for a while, watching the sky turn into a rose-pink and then a faint lilac. The descending sun cast its fading light over the forests and hills of Bundelkhand. It was time to return. She started making her way out of the palace slowly.

But suddenly, as though from nowhere, dark clouds rushed in to cast a coverlet on the psychedelic sky, and within minutes plunged this bastion of a glorious era into sudden darkness. She walked out of the fort, and as she started walking towards the river, thunder rumbled in the far horizon, and lightning flashed across the dark evening sky. Just as it had on that fateful day, a hundred and fifty years ago.

And, in that moment, a lone figure could be seen walking along the river, slowly descending down the rocks into the bosom of the Betwa. As Meera disappeared into its depths, she cast one last look towards the new bridge that had come up some years ago that led to the road to Jhansee. She turned back and was once again swallowed by the river.

～

Orchha laid siege to the fort of Jhansee in August 1857. The siege lasted for over two months, but Jhansee was prepared and eventually managed to break through the siege. On the insistence of the Queen of Orchha, an open battle was fought in the Rajput tradition between the two queens following which Orchha handed over portions of its kingdom to Jhansee, and for a while there seemed to be peace between the neighbours. A few months later, despite continued resistance from Maharani Lakshmibai, the East India Company took over Jhansee. Lakshmibai was killed in battle by Sir Hugh Rose in June 1958. Following the defeat of the rebel forces of the Mutiny of 1857, India passed from the East India Company, which was subsequently dissolved, to the British Crown. Rani Larai died in 1868 and Hamir Singh continued to rule Orchha till his death in 1874.

Glossary

Miyan ki Malhar: Malhar is an old raga associated with the rains in Indian classical music.

Vineet Rai Pravin ki, suniye sah sujan, Juthi patar bakhat hain, bari, bayas, swan: O good and intelligent! Please listen to the prayer of Rai Praveen. Only bari (a member belonging to the low caste among the Hindus), a barber or a scavenger who would eat from a plate, food from which has been partaken by someone else.

Main toh piya se naina laga aayee re: A well-known composition of Amir Khusrow Dehlavi, a fourteenth-century South Asian Sufi musician, poet and scholar.

Lai hayat aae qaza le chali chale: A famous ghazal by the nineteenth-century Urdu poet Sheikh Muhammad Ibrahim Zauq.

Khalq khuda ka, mulk badshah ka, raj Maharani Lakshmibai ka: The world belongs to God, the country to the emperor. The last part of the sentence was originally, 'Hukm subahdar sipahi bahadur ka', which the rebel sepoys who joined hands with some of Rani Lakshmibai's soldiers replaced with 'Raj Maharani Lakshmibai ka'.

Deen ka jai: When the rebels in Bundelkhand threw open the Orchha Gate, they did so to the cry of 'deen ka jai' which translates to 'victory to religion'.

Main to giridhar aage nachungi: A bhajan written and composed by Saint Mirabai.

Priya Charusheele: A composition from Jayadev's Geet Govindam in which Krishna addresses his beloved Radha in this song with the words 'Oh my love! O my virtuous one!'

Author's Note

Twenty kilometres from Jhansi lies the sleepy town of Orchha. When I lived in Jhansi for a year, I often visited this erstwhile capital of the mighty Bundela rulers who reigned over central India for nearly 400 years.

Over the years since then, Orchha has kept calling me back. I have often wondered why. What makes this little place tucked away in the bosom of central India so endearing? Could it be the beautiful landscape, cleaved by the spirited Betwa River, its mood transformed with every season or the magnificent fortresses and monuments that stand testimony to a tumultuous past? Or the numerous temples that define the region's religious and cultural heritage? These are alluring, no doubt. But for me the strongest draw were the stories that lurked in the dark passageways and wall niches of the palaces. These haunting sagas whispered by the stones spoke of valour, intrigue, loyalty, betrayal and, above all, faith.

This is one such tale that I have woven into the rich tapestry of this politically significant region in the mid-nineteenth century – a period that boasts some of the most lion-hearted personalities India has ever nurtured. Among them is Maharani Lakshmibai, the Queen of Jhansi. Although Lakshmibai is one of the central figures in this book and is, perhaps, crucial to the events that unfold through the pages, the true protagonists are the fictional Chandraki, Lakshmibai's companion, and Riyaz Khan, her bête noire. The third major fictional character is Jaywant.

While the remaining key players are actual historical figures – including the East India Company officials – in some cases, I have taken creative licence to enhance their personality traits and heighten the dramatic effect of the narrative. Furthermore, in the absence of definitive documentation of Rani Larai's character or rule, I have used my imagination to flesh out her personality.

This is a work of fiction set against the backdrop of true events and political affiliations as documented by historians. Of course the authenticity of some aspects may be open to debate because there are contradictory records of that period. For instance, there is some ambiguity as to whether Rani Lakshmibai helped the rebels with resources from the very beginning and on the actual role she played in the Jhansi Mutiny, the involvement of her own soldiers and the extent of her involvement in the massacre of sixty-five Britons at Jokhan Bagh.

The mention of certain customs, rituals and beliefs followed by both the rulers and their subjects as well as Company officials and certain aspects of the lifestyle of the people of the region are based on the written accounts of historians. Descriptions of Orchha, the landscape, its geography and vegetation are based on my own visits to the region.

Acknowledgements

I lived in Jhansi and visited Orchha several times over the last two decades. As I absorbed the flavours and smelt the air, I drew my own impressions that were further enriched by the stories and folklore narrated to me by the local people. But I was up against a political and military timeline of one of the most eventful periods in Indian history, the Sepoy Mutiny, for which I consulted the following books to help me bring alive the period:

The Rani of Jhansi: Rebel Against Will by Rainier Jerosch (Aakar Books, 2007)

The Rani of Jhansi: Study in Female Heroism in India by Joyce Lebra Chapman (University of Hawaii Press, 1986)

Indian Freedom Movement in Princely States of Vindhya Pradesh by A.U. Siddiqui (Northern Book Centre, 2004)

Rambles and Recollections of an Indian Official: Volume 1 by William Henry Sleeman (Cambridge University Press, 2011)

Notes on Indian Affairs by Frederick John Shore (J.W. Parker, 1837)

The Indian Mutiny: 1857 by Saul David (Penguin, 2003)

Other than the above, there were those without whose support and encouragement the book couldn't have been written.

For this I would like to thank Lieutenant General Alok Singh Kler, the then Division Commander of the White Tiger Division, Jhansi Cantonment, for hosting me during my visit to Jhansi and Orchha.

Colonel Raja Ashwani, Commanding Officer of an artillery unit stationed in Jhansi at the time, for providing me during my visit to Jhansi and Orchha, both logistical and moral support.

I would also like to thank Devidayal, my unofficial local guide, whose family members have been residents of Orchha for the past three generations. He regaled me with the most astonishing tales of Orchha handed down by his forefathers. He took me to such places that no 'what-to-see' tourist list would have provided. This helped me immensely in understanding the layout of the different locations mentioned in the book as well as the general topography of the region.

A big thank you to my literary agent Kanishka Gupta of Writers Side (and his team) for believing in the book and offering invaluable suggestions for its improvement.

I would also like to thank my friend Jasmine Sheikh, who sat through the night to read that crucial first draft and was ready with her encouraging feedback in one day.

Above all, I would like to thank my wonderful editor Sasha Mahuli and the vibrant and spirited team at Juggernaut Books, whose constant support and dogged perseverance in polishing up the manuscript went a long way in making it a crisp and engaging read.

A Note on the Author

Moupia Basu grew up in the Delhi of the 1970s and 1980s. She did her master's in English literature from St. Stephen's College, Delhi University, and worked as a journalist with a number of publications including the *Times of India*, *Economic Times*, *Indian Express* and *Business Today*. She has travelled extensively across the country, which has helped her gain insight into the rapidly changing Indian milieu. Her first book, *Khoka*, was published by the National Book Trust of India in 2015. She lives in Pune.

A Note on the Author

1

CRAFTED FOR MOBILE READING

Thought you would never read a book on mobile? Let us prove you wrong.

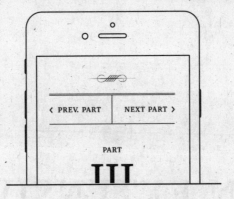

Beautiful Typography

The quality of print transferred
to your mobile. Forget ugly PDFs.

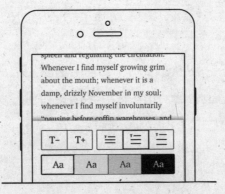

Customizable Reading

Read in the font size, spacing
and background of your liking.

AN EXTENSIVE LIBRARY

Including fresh, new, original Juggernaut books from the likes of Sunny Leone, Praveen Swami, Husain Haqqani, Umera Ahmed, Rujuta Diwekar and lots more. Plus, books from partner publishers and loads of free classics. Whichever genre you like, there's a book waiting for you.

3

DON'T JUST READ; INTERACT

We're changing the reading experience from passive to active.